ELF PRINCESS WARRIOR
QUEENMAKERS SAGA VIII

BY
BERNADETTE ROWLEY

Acknowledgements

To Louise Cusack for her inspiration and advice over the years.

To Duncan Carling-Rodgers for his assistance during the most recent edits of Elf Princess Warrior and for the formatting.

To Dar Albert for her stunning cover.

Titles by
Bernadette Rowley

DEDICATION

Dedicated to my husband and three sons who lift me up, so I can fly free in my fantasy world of Thorius.

TABLE OF CONTENTS

CHAPTER ONE

Gwaethe cursed as her cousin Isiloe helped her through the door and onto the kitchen chair. Pain, from the arrow head in her thigh, made her suck in a deep breath, and she sat battling waves of darkness that tried to drag her into oblivion. The deserted hunting lodge had been a gift from her elven Gods. Her insides curled with shame that she should need this refuge at all; a hunting lodge built by humans in their quest for game and glory.

The mission had started so promisingly. She had led the party of a dozen elves south from Selinore, her home in the northern mountains, to discover traitor High Prince Faenwelar's hideout. It was meant only to be a scouting mission but, at dawn this morning, they had been ambushed by elves from Faenwelar's faction, the *Sis Lenweri*. Six of her party had been killed, leaving her, Isiloe and five others who barely escaped with their lives. Isiloe was the only one not injured.

"Bite on this," Isiloe said, handing her a hunting knife.

Gwaethe bit down on the wooden handle as Isiloe dug the arrow head from her thigh. Pain shot straight to her stomach. She leaned to the side and hurled until her belly ached.

"Hold still!" Isiloe hissed, shoving a moistened cloth at her. It felt cool on her forehead, and she panted away the agony washing over her in waves.

"There, it is out. I will flush the wound and bind it. You will live." Isiloe placed her hand on Gwaethe's shoulder and squeezed. Despite the abrupt tone, her cousin loved her and was her staunchest supporter.

Gwaethe didn't like to think what she would have done without her this last year.

Leaving Gwaethe with a mixture of *hovard* leaf for the pain, Isiloe went in search of the rest of the band who had spread out through the other rooms of the lodge. Gwaethe breathed deeply, sipping the medicine and distracting herself with her surroundings. There was a large fireplace with wood stacked ready for a blaze and four hooks for hanging pans. The walls were carved oak and quite beautiful, the table and chairs made from the same timber. Cooking utensils hung from the wall beside the fireplace, the glow of their copper drawing her eye. If this was the style of the kitchen, the rest of the lodge must be magnificent.

Gwaethe tried to stand, but the tiniest movement sent pain spiraling down her leg and sweat broke out on her brow. Much good she would be to the others now! How could she have been so stupid as to walk straight into the *Sis Lenweri* trap? She chewed on a strand of her long, dark hair as her thoughts flew to the skirmish they had just survived.

Isiloe returned, standing in the doorway of the kitchen, her face grey with exhaustion. "They will all live. Your wound is the most serious. We will return home and heal, and next time Faenwelar will not catch us unawares."

"I must mobilize the others," Gwaethe said. "You take Lomari and rouse our people. Tell them to meet me here in a week. I need a party of at least fifty, perhaps more."

Isiloe snorted. "I am not leaving your side. If I had not been with you today, you would now lie dead."

Anger swept through Gwaethe. "I think you overstate the situation, cousin, and underestimate my talent for survival."

Isiloe raised her pale brows. She was small compared to most of the elven race but could never be called delicate. Her fair hair and blue eyes set her apart from other elves, where dark hair and eyes dominated. "I won't leave without you. That wound needs weeks to heal, not a patch and back on the road. And you cannot make good plans without consultation. We must return home."

"*I* am battle leader, so *I* will decide strategy, with or without consultation. I can do that just as well here as anywhere." Gwaethe frowned as she thought about the one person she *would* give anything to speak to; her half-brother Kain. He had been the human army general until six months ago, but now he was a free agent. Well, not free *exactly*. He would inherit her elven kingdom if he ever acknowledged his heritage. Instead, he was making his nest with his wife, Alique, wasting his time while Gwaethe fought to bring about the fall of Faenwelar and unite the elven people. Perhaps she should try again to contact him through the ring and bracelet. Tonight.

"You are thinking of *him* again," Isiloe said. "You get that look every time. When are you going to admit Kain cares nothing for us?"

"He cares," Gwaethe replied, "but it is hard for him. He must come to terms with the fact he and I share a father who was an elven king. I lived that reality, but to Kain it is just a story. One day he will feel it, and then he will step into his role."

Isiloe snorted. "We don't need him. We don't need any human; any man. You and I are more than capable of leading the *Lenweri*."

"Tell that to those who follow Faenwelar, to the traditionalists amongst our own society. Even Mother would vote against me."

Isiloe frowned. "One day, perhaps, it will not be the case. If that day is to come, you and I must make it so, cousin."

Gwaethe smiled. "There is nothing I would like better, Isiloe, but it will not happen overnight. Kain is the first step. We need him. I need him." The last was whispered as Gwaethe's determination was replaced by doubt. The sounds of horses outside caught her attention.

Isiloe was already at the window, peeking through a crack in the shutters. "Kingdom soldiers," she said. "Thirty of them; armed." She turned to Gwaethe. "Do we fight?"

Gwaethe drew a deep breath, her thoughts chaotic, unwilling to believe they should face more danger so soon. She shook her head. "We must talk first. Find out who they are. Tell the others to hide. At least some may escape to raise the alarm if we are taken."

Isiloe slipped through the door. Gwaethe gripped the edge of the table and tried to rise. Her head spun and pain shot from the wound. She froze and took a shuddering breath. She could not even defend herself in this condition! What if the wound was even more serious than Isiloe had said? She had no more time to ponder as the door slammed open. A dark figure appeared. A man in the spotless uniform of a Kingdom captain.

Her heart beat faster, and it wasn't from fear this time. She knew him! As her gaze swept over the smooth lines of his face - the muscular ridges of his form barely hidden by his uniform - her body heated as it had done only once in the past. Once, six months ago, this man had been on her side, had fought beside her against Faenwelar. But would it be the case this time?

"Gwaethe Arenil," he said, sweeping a graceful bow, "well met."

She took another shuddering breath before she could speak. "Captain Vorasava. I would rise but I fear I am unable to."

Concern chased the arrogant light from his eyes as he took in the blood-soaked bandage around her left thigh. He snapped his fingers, and a stocky young soldier, with brown hair and eyes, appeared. "Corporal Exmund, fetch the medical bag and see to Princess Gwaethe's injury."

Exmund left but returned moments later with a bulging leather satchel. He fixed his eyes on Gwaethe but made no move toward her. The young man cleared his throat and straightened his tunic with his spare hand. "Captain?" he said, licking his lips, "Are you sure?"

Vorasava tore his eyes from Gwaethe and turned to Exmund. "What do you mean, lad? I asked you to tend this lady's wound. Is there something unclear in my request?"

Exmund snapped up straight, eyes directly ahead. "No sir," he said. "Right away, sir."

The young medic knelt beside Gwaethe. "If I may?"

Gwaethe nodded, and Exmund began to gently unwrap the wound.

"I need to cut away these leggings." Exmund produced a knife, ready to strip the clothing from her leg, but Gwaethe grasped his wrist.

"No. Tend the wound as it is." She helped widen the hole made by the arrow head, exposing the jagged puncture without revealing any more of the brown skin of her thigh than was necessary. Exmund packed the hole with a poultice and gently bound it. All the while, she burned under Vorasava's gaze. What was he thinking? That she was a stinking elf? That he would like to be on his way?

Perhaps not. Vorasava was one of the few humans who had treated her as an equal, but was it just inherent politeness disguising his true feelings? Humans thought they were above elves when, really, they were interlopers in these lands. *Her* people had been here since time began; since the trees were young. But Gwaethe believed in peace, and she would live that way, as would her *Lenweri*. There was plenty of land for all.

"What are you doing here, Princess?" Vorasava asked.

Gwaethe raised her head. "I could ask you the same."

"Ah, but I am not trespassing in your hunting lodge."

"*Your* lodge?" She looked around the kitchen, trying to come to terms with Vorasava in this room.

"*My* lodge. I occasionally have to coax a grumpy bear from the woodshed, but I hardly expected an elven princess to have taken up residence."

"Believe me, Captain, I am only passing through. But for this injury, I would not have had to use your home."

He shrugged. "Be my guest."

He stuck his head out the door and shouted orders to his men then turned back to Gwaethe. "My sergeant and I and young Exmund will bunk in here while the others can use the stable. Where are the rest of your band?"

She shook her head. What could she say? The others would be found soon enough. It seemed she must trust him for now. "We are only seven. We lost six in a skirmish with Faenwelar's elves."

Isiloe appeared at the inside door. "I knew you couldn't resist telling this human everything, cousin." She glared at Vorasava. "Gwaethe is always too trusting."

Gwaethe closed her eyes, drawing a deep breath. She didn't want to cope with Isiloe's belligerence right now.

"Lady Isiloe," Vorasava said, inclining his head, "I will take Princess Gwaethe where she can be more comfortable, then perhaps you could show me to the rest of your people."

"If you must address me, human," Isiloe said, "you will call me *Ramar*, or Captain. Anything else is highly inappropriate on a mission."

Vorasava raised an eyebrow at Isiloe then scooped Gwaethe up from the chair. Pain smashed through her body at the sudden movement. She bit her lip to stop from crying out as he strode with her through to the bedrooms. Somehow, he managed to open a door with her in his arms, and she was soon laid gently on a huge bed covered with bearskin.

"My bedroom," he said. "I killed that bear myself." He turned to a wardrobe and pulled a thick blanket from the top shelves, placing it over her.

Isiloe growled from the doorway. "Always the killing," she said. "Are you not able to live in harmony with nature? *Lenweri* only kill creatures when needed for food or hides."

Gwaethe couldn't have cared less at that moment, battling as she was with pain and nausea, and just a little fear if she was being honest; fear of her wound and of the powerful man who stood gazing down upon her.

He treated Isiloe as he would a buzzing fly. "Fetch my man, *Ramar*," he snapped, still not looking at her. "Tell him to attend me here."

Gwaethe held her breath, waiting for Isiloe's angry response to being ordered about.

Isiloe drew herself up. "Fetch him yourself, human," she said. "I was not born to run after you." She left the room, the door closing after her with a sharp click.

Vorasava appeared to barely notice. He took Gwaethe's wrist, frowning. "You've lost a lot of blood, Princess. Your heart is racing, your hands cold."

She couldn't look away from his strong fingers on her skin. She tingled all over and wanton thoughts came unbidden; thoughts of bare skin, sweat and his mouth on her breasts. She shook her head and might have fainted if she were not already lying down. *I must be delirious! Yes, that is the reason for these thoughts.* Indeed, when she tried to focus on his face, it was fuzzy, indistinct.

Trying to push all contemplation of his lips aside, she gathered her wits and met his eyes. "I will be fine with some rest, Captain." Yes, that was much more appropriate for her standing as battle leader and princess.

"Nonsense," he said. "You need careful nursing. I wish now I had brought my doctor with me, but he is getting a little too old for these outings."

"Why do you even care?" she asked without thinking.

"How can you ask that? We are bound by our past, our shared status as warriors on the same side. Of course I will do all I can to help you."

"And that is all?"

Vorasava's gaze fell from hers, his jaw tightening. "That's a lot, Princess. Rest, and I will ensure Exmund gets you something for the pain."

* * *

Jacques Vorasava strode from the bedroom and went in search of Exmund, all the while trying to dampen his reaction to Gwaethe's predicament and her challenging words. She was extraordinarily beautiful and exotic with her dark skin and hair, and deep brown eyes. It was an ethereal, alien beauty that the women of his world didn't have. He was overwhelmed by it. Over the past six months, he had relived the few moments he had spent with Gwaethe when they had battled Faenwelar's forces, and, afterward, when they traveled back to Wildecoast, the King's seat.

The Princess was athletic and fierce, the leader of the *Lenweri* forces, and passionate about bringing her people and Faenwelar's together. Jacques cared not a jot for Faenwelar's elves. They were a direct threat to the Kingdom of Thorius, determined to drive the humans from the land and return it to the forests of ancient times. In Jacques's opinion, there was no going back. The line had been drawn. The war would end with the elimination of the *Sis Lenweri*. Gwaethe and her elves were welcome to stay if they lived in peace.

His interest in Gwaethe was something he had taken out from time to time, examined, then put away. He couldn't afford to get caught up in his feelings for her. They were from different worlds, and his determination to lead the Kingdom armed forces would never come to fruition if he involved himself with an elven woman. Still, it might be fun to explore a relationship with her if they both understood the boundaries.

He walked through his lodge, checking each of the rooms and finding injured elves in several of them. They appeared to be doing well, even though they had little time for his enquiries. Eventually he found Exmund, stitching the shoulder wound of a young elf.

"Exmund, Princess Gwaethe needs a pain draught. Can you attend to her when you are finished here?"

He wiped over the wound and stood. "Right now, Captain," he said, hurrying from the room.

Vorasava caught up to him outside. "What do you think of the Princess's wound? I'm fearful of complications."

Exmund stared at his feet. "Why do you care?" he muttered.

Vorasava couldn't believe his ears. "What do you mean, Corporal?"

Exmund slowly raised his eyes to Jacques. "She's an elf; they all are. We're at war with her people and here you treat them as though we're on the same side."

Jacques slowly straightened himself to his full height. *Impertinent pup!* "I'll have you know Princess Gwaethe fought on the same side as us in the recent battles. That's why I care. Before you speak so again, I would appreciate it if you checked your facts."

The young aide had turned a pleasing shade of pink. "Sorry, Captain. I didn't realize. If I may be excused, I'll attend the Princess right away."

Exmund scuttled away, and Jacques took a deep breath to compose himself. He knew how the lad felt. Elves were mysterious, foreign creatures, not human and rarely seen by the citizens of Thorius. Human youngsters were raised on stories of elves raiding farmhouses and stealing children, for it was known they were slow to have offspring of their own. Perhaps that was what had happened with Gwaethe's half-brother, Kain Jazara. Once commander of the King's army, he was now a disgraced half-human and half-elf. Jacques had been shocked to discover the truth after the last battle against Faenwelar's *Sis Lenweri*. Kain had soon lost his position.

Jacques had never learned how the son of an elven king had come to lead the Kingdom army. The man had seemed honest and was a good leader before his fall from grace. Perhaps he had been one of the stolen children and not half elven at all?

He shook his head. None of this speculation would get him where he needed to be. These elves were a distraction, but they need not stop him from seeing his plan through. He must extract from them what information he could and continue into the northern mountains to seek out the rebel Prince Faenwelar. He returned to the kitchen, hoping to make himself a mug of tea.

He found Isiloe standing before the fireplace, stirring a kettle of stew and muttering to herself.

"Lady...*Ramar* Isiloe, I didn't wish to disturb you."

She glanced at him and returned to her task. "As if you could ever disturb me," she said. "At most you would be like a mosquito buzzing in my ear."

He studied the diminutive elven woman. She was the shortest dark elf he had seen. Her race was generally tall, elegant, dark-skinned and dark-haired. Isiloe barely came to his shoulder, and she had white hair and the palest blue eyes he had seen on anyone. Her pointed ears were pierced from top to bottom with all manner of rings and studs. Despite her prickly nature, Isiloe was beautiful, with a curvaceous figure well displayed by the forest green tunic and breeches which were the habitual garments of the elves. He shouldn't be noticing, but he wasn't the only one. Jacques had observed more than one admiring glance from his men toward Isiloe.

"What do you want?" she asked, still not looking at him.

"I came to make a pot of tea."

"The water is boiled, Kingdom man," she said, pointing to the large kettle hanging over the fire.

Jacques went about making the tea and poured it into two cups. "I'll take the Princess a mug of tea. Would you like one?"

"What are you trying to do?"

"I'm just being a good host."

Isiloe almost snarled. "I know what you think of us, so do not bother." She turned back to her stew, furiously stirring the mixture.

Instead of trying to make more conversation, Jacques placed the mugs of tea on a tray and took them to the bedroom where Gwaethe dozed in his bed. He placed the tray on the breakfast table and sat beside it, sipping his tea and watching the light of the fire play over Gwaethe's features. It made her look even more foreign, like a wild animal. His thoughts wandered to the battle of six months ago when he met her. It had been a fierce confrontation with Faenwelar, with many Kingdom and elven dead, but, in the end, they had won.

Faenwelar and his closest supporters had escaped, but the *Sis Lenweri* had taken a hit and run away like mangy curs. Or so the King and his general had thought at the time. Now, it seemed the *Sis Lenweri* were pushing back into the south; but what was their immediate aim?

There was a rustle on the bed. He looked up to find Gwaethe's gaze upon him.

"How are you, Princess?" he asked.

She appeared so weak she could scarcely lift her head from the pillow. "I am feeling much better thank you." Her voice was stilted, too polite.

He found himself wishing she would look at him with something other than wariness in her eyes.

"I brought you tea," he said, stirring in honey. "It should still be warm enough." He helped her sit up and placed pillows for support, then handed her the tea. She brought the mug to her lips, her eyes fluttering closed as she swallowed.

"That's heavenly," she said, "the perfect temperature."

He watched as she finished the mug, searching and discarding several topics of conversation. "You know your wound is a serious one," he said, finally.

Her eyes snapped to his, and he was speared through his soul.

"I am beginning to realize that," she said, handing him the mug. She looked brighter, but her hand trembled. "I've seldom been this weak. With the energy of battle in me I did not realize how close I was to…"

"You should return to your home, wherever that is. Regroup, recover."

She straightened her spine, looking more regal than Queen Adriana. "I will decide what we should do, Captain. It is not up to you to advise me."

He stood and paced back and forth across his room. "Don't you see how vulnerable you are? He has killed half your force. You cannot go back up there without reinforcements, without more preparation."

"Then you will help us," she announced, her gaze challenging him to accept.

"Oh no, no, no, Princess. I have a mission from the King. I do not intend to jeopardize my reputation by making a unilateral decision to fight with your people. Look how it worked out for General Jazara; or should I say, *former* General Jazara."

As much as he might like to have Gwaethe alongside him, he would learn from the past, not repeat it. No, unless he had a letter signed by the King himself, he would not be working with the *Lenweri* any time soon.

"You would not be fighting," she said, a sly smile lighting her eyes. "You would be gathering intelligence."

"Just as you were trying to do when you were set upon?"

Her fingers gripped the blanket, nails digging through the thick material. "I cannot afford the time it will take to return to Selinore. There is no telling where Faenwelar will show up next, or what he has in mind. We must act now. You are my one hope of continuing this mission."

"Then your mission is at an end." Jacques stood to gather the tea things.

"Captain Vorasava —"

"Call me Jacques."

That gave her pause.

"Jacques, please reconsider. Stopping Faenwelar might hinge on this decision."

There was desperation in her eyes, but she held herself just a hair's width from begging. *Impressive.*

"Oh, my men and I intend to continue north and discover Faenwelar's scheme, but you, my dear Princess, are going home. I won't have your death on my conscience. And I won't work with you, not without royal approval." He continued to the door. "Rest well. Tomorrow you head for home if you are well enough to travel."

CHAPTER TWO

Gwaethe awoke the following morning not knowing at first where she was. She was unused to a mattress beneath her, and the room was warmer than her mountain home. Coals glowed in the fireplace. *Jacques's hunting lodge.* Gwaethe had experienced human residences before, once at the palace of the King and before when on state visits with her father. They made her long for the trees of her forest home.

Isiloe slipped through the door, her gaze going straight to Gwaethe. "Good morning, cousin, how do you fare?"

Gwaethe smiled. "As if you haven't checked on me before this." She tried to pull herself up to sit against the pillows but failed. "I am well, if still weak."

"You scared me yesterday. I think you were closer to death than you realize."

"I scared myself, but that is behind us."

"When do we leave for home?" Isiloe asked.

Gwaethe shook her head. "We cannot give up on this mission, Isiloe. Going home would cost us too much time." She frowned. "However, Captain Vorasava has refused to work with us."

"Why do you wish for *his* help?"

"We need his force, and I *will* have my way. He doesn't know it yet, but I am not so easily thwarted."

Her cousin nodded. "What is your plan?"

"We appear to leave for home, then shadow the Kingdom force. That way, we can ensure the continuation of our mission."

"You are foolish, cousin. The humans will see us eventually. What will you do when Vorasava finds out?"

"His anger doesn't cow me, Isiloe. In the meantime, I will try to reach Kain and let him know Faenwelar is active, that it is time to avenge the murder of his father."

The news brought a deeper frown to her cousin's brow. "You don't need him!"

Gwaethe held up her hand. "Enough! I won't have you dismiss Kain. He is our rightful leader, and he *will* step into the role if I have to drag him by his hair."

Surprisingly, Isiloe stayed silent, but Gwaethe knew it wasn't the last she would hear from her cousin about Kain. While Isiloe left to fetch breakfast, Gwaethe lay back on the pillows, twisting the ring on her right hand. She closed her eyes and visualized Kain as she had last seen him - waving to her, his arm around his wife - a picture of contentment. Her focus shuddered as she allowed doubt to creep in. Why should he forsake Alique and his new home for his sister and the elven nation? He had the Kingdom he had known since birth and fought for, he had his parents and siblings, and he had Alique, the most amazing woman Gwaethe had ever met. She cringed at the thought of the human woman who made her feel lacking, even though Alique did nothing but be herself. Kain's wife was beautiful; smart, brave and tougher than anyone Gwaethe had ever met.

"Why are you weeping?"

Gwaethe started as Isiloe re-entered the room and was amazed to feel tears on her cheeks. "It is nothing," she said as she wiped them away. "I was just thinking of Kain and Alique."

"Pah! And *that* makes you cry?" Isiloe said, placing a tray on the bed beside Gwaethe.

"Why would Kain give me a second thought when he has Alique by his side? She will bind him tighter than ever now they are wed."

"That may be so, cousin, but you are his blood. He will not turn his back on you so easily. I hate to say it, but he seems a man of honor. Perhaps he will do the right thing eventually. If you still think you need him."

Gwaethe sighed. "I hope so, for I feel so alone. I know it is not the case," she said, seeing Isiloe bristle, "but sometimes I think you are my only support. I have Faenwelar set against me and half of the elves with him. My own faction will not accept me as their leader. And Kain would gladly forget he has elven ties."

"He cannot deny his blood, and you are more than capable of seeing this through. You are the most honorable, brave, and wonderful leader I could ask for."

Gwaethe froze at Isiloe's words. Her cousin never gave praise. Never. Her heart swelled, and she immediately felt uplifted. "Thank you, Isiloe," she whispered.

Isiloe leaned over and hugged her. "Let us not speak of this again," she said, straightening. "You are everything that is good amongst our people, and you will prevail. Now eat your meal."

Isiloe left Gwaethe smiling, despite her injuries, despite her self-pity of moments before. She was truly blessed to have such stalwart support. Isiloe would see her through all this. In that moment, she realized why Isiloe rejected Kain. Her cousin clearly saw herself as Gwaethe's main supporter, and to have Gwaethe wishing for Kain's help might be an insult to Isiloe. She would have to be more careful in future.

Regardless, she *needed* Kain. He could fulfil a role neither she nor her cousin could. Gwaethe took a sip of sugary tea and a bite of fresh buttered bread and closed her eyes. She pictured Kain, this time as he had appeared in battle; fierce, eyes ablaze, upon his black charger, sword cutting left and right. It was a powerful vision, and she felt her ring warm. She had had the ring since birth, but Kain had only had his armband for six months. The two amulets could be used to communicate but Gwaethe had only been able to contact her brother once over the last eight weeks.

Brother! Silence greeted her, so she tried again. *Brother, I need to talk.*

Gwaethe breathed deep and renewed her concentration on Kain's fierce eyes. *Do not ignore me. I need you.*

What is it? I'm busy.

A vision of Kain, shirtless, came to her. A blonde woman, Alique, snuggled against him. Gwaethe felt her face heat at being privy to such an intimate moment. She shifted in the bed and pain blasted from her thigh.

Kain's voice stabbed her mind. *You're hurt!*

There was a skirmish with Faenwelar's Sis Lenweri. I took an arrow in the thigh. I will live.

Where are you?

Far to the northwest. We have taken refuge in a hunting lodge but move out today. I need your help.

Faenwelar is on the move?

Yes, and I need to discover his intent. We were almost wiped out yesterday. I think he must be planning something big. He has infiltrated the Kingdom again and caught us by surprise. Vorasava is here and intends to move north today with thirty men. Can you come and bring reinforcements?

Anger radiated through the link. *I would have to leave Alique, and I don't think she will agree.*

Bring her. We could use her skill.

I can't risk her again. She has only just recovered.

Gwaethe wrestled with her own anger. He would always choose Alique over her, and so he should – Alique was his wife – but it hurt nonetheless to compete for her brother's loyalty.

It is your choice, Gwaethe replied, *but I cannot say what will happen if you do not come. Head for the Vorasava hunting lodge. You will find our tracks from there.*

She took off the ring and placed it in a pouch around her neck. It would only work against her skin, and she had no desire to speak to Kain further. He would decide to help or not, and she had the distinct impression less was more where her half-brother was concerned.

She finished her breakfast and gingerly climbed from the bed. Her clothes had been brushed and aired, and a new pair of leggings supplied. Her bandage was bloody by the time she dressed, and nausea made her stomach roil. How was she to travel today?

As she hobbled around the room, collecting her belongings, there was a knock at the door.

"Come."

Jacques entered. "Should you be dressed for travel, Princess?"

She stumbled, and he was suddenly right beside her, his arm around her waist. Head spinning, she held onto him until the world settled. Her stomach felt even worse. "I have to be moving. I'm headed home to collect reinforcements. You should be glad to hear that."

"I'm glad to hear you've given up on the idea of pursuing Faenwelar, but you need another day of rest at the very least."

Gwaethe couldn't think clearly with him so close. She shook his arm from her waist. "I think I know what I need, Captain."

"Well, *I* think you're a stubborn woman who believes the world will stop turning if she isn't in control," he snapped.

"I do not care what you think. I have responsibility for the *Lenweri*."

"Did you ever think that responsibility means you need to take even greater care of yourself?"

His words made her pause. She took a deep breath to center herself, to stop the fuzzy thoughts that were all she seemed to be able to muster in his company.

"Thank you for your advice. I will keep it in mind." She collected her weapons and pack, and limped to the door, praying she wouldn't disgrace herself by falling. Her thigh hurt like a demon, and the bandage around it became soggier with each step.

Gwaethe met Isiloe outside her door, and her cousin helped her out of the house to *Rassar*, her golden stallion. His silver mane and tail gleamed in the weak morning sun and he tossed his head as she approached. Gwaethe rested her forehead against his silky neck for a moment.

"Are you sure you are well enough for this?" Isiloe asked. "We could wait another day."

Gwaethe shook her head and breathed in Rassar's horsey scent. It never failed to calm her. "Another day closer to whatever Faenwelar has planned. I will heal on the road."

"At least let me change your bandage," Isiloe hissed.

"I will, but wait until we are on the road." Gwaethe mounted and turned to Jacques. "I thank you for your aid, Captain, and wish you success in your mission. Until we meet again."

Vorasava gave a small bow. Gwaethe urged Rassar away from the hunting lodge, her band riding behind her. She could feel the Captain's eyes on her until she passed through the first trees. Battling dizziness, she swayed in her saddle but jerked herself upright when Isiloe rode alongside.

Her diminutive cousin nudged her horse close, but not close enough to hurt her thigh. "I wish you would reconsider," she said. "I am worried about you."

The pain was so bad, Gwaethe could hardly speak. "Just make sure I do not fall," she said through gritted teeth. "We will ride for an hour, and then you can tend me."

* * *

Jacques was certain he had done the wrong thing in allowing Gwaethe to leave. She should be abed for days yet, but the stubborn Princess had only one thing on her mind and that was Faenwelar. He could have made things easier for her by agreeing to travel with her, but the best thing had really been for her to return home. It would be a blow to her pride, but better that than coming at Faenwelar with a depleted force. At least now she could enlarge her party and have the chance to report back to her elven comrades.

He watched until she disappeared into the forest, then returned to his men, anxious to be on the road again. They would head north into elven territory, passing beyond the Kingdom lines. With help from the Goddess, they'd locate Faenwelar's headquarters and discover his strength and intentions. By the time Gwaethe was ready to continue her mission, his men would be in and out with whatever intelligence they could gather. The confrontation with Faenwelar would come later, when a larger force was assembled

For now, they would ride north, traveling straight into the Usetar Mountains, while Gwaethe journeyed to her mountain home to the northwest. He just hoped she would have no further trouble until she was safely home.

CHAPTER THREE

Gwaethe's party rode west from the hunting lodge and, by dusk, had almost reached the western road that led into the Usetar Mountains. The day had been an ordeal the like of which Gwaethe had never endured. The pain in her leg never subsided, despite taking powders and leaves to control it. She felt too sick to eat, but Isiloe kept offering her watered wine. She rode in a haze of exhaustion and pain, relying on her cousin to keep them safe and prevent her falling from her horse.

Of their party of seven, three were detailed to act as scouts, riding ahead and to the east, on the lookout for *Sis Lenweri*. It was risky to have so many away from her, risky when she would need everyone to defend her if they should be attacked. But they had no choice. They had to know if danger threatened. Gwaethe hoped those deployed as scouts were up to the job.

Isiloe roused her from her musing when she grabbed Gwaethe's reins and pulled her horse to a stop. "We camp here."

Gwaethe shook her head. "There is daylight left. We go on."

"Perhaps tomorrow can be a longer day, cousin," Isiloe said, "but for now you need rest."

Isiloe dismounted and gestured to one of the others, a tall elf with heavy shoulders and a becoming smile. He helped Gwaethe down, and it was a measure of her exhaustion that she didn't protest.

Let her have her way. I am in no condition to make these decisions.

Isiloe got her settled in a clearing off the track, laying furs on the ground and pulling them over Gwaethe. She detailed the others to set up camp. Gwaethe was soon warm, but it didn't last long as Isiloe drew back the furs to change her bandage. Isiloe muttered under her breath as she peeled the soggy dressing away, her hands gentle despite her anger.

"How does it look?" Gwaethe asked, flinching as the cold air sent pain from the wound to her knee and beyond.

"Nasty," Isiloe snapped, "but clean. I do not think it will fester." She bathed the puncture where she had removed the arrowhead, starting a fresh red ooze, then dried it. She sprinkled dried herbs on a clean bandage and packed the wound, binding it firmly.

"You should have been a healer, Isiloe."

"Nonsense! Anyone can tend wounds. It takes great skill to lead an army and win a battle."

Gwaethe studied her cousin, wondering what Isiloe would do if there was peace. "Do you ever imagine having a husband and children?"

Isiloe's eyes widened. "No! Why?"

"You have much to offer. I see a nurturer in you and wonder what kind of mother you might be."

"Hush! You may as well ask *yourself* that question. I have not seen *you* laying your sword at the feet of any man, giving up your life for a husband."

Gwaethe pulled her leggings on and tried to ease back beneath the furs. "I do not have time for such fancies, though perhaps I owe it to my people to procreate one day. We should all do our best to produce heirs, especially members of the royal house. Mother will no doubt arrange a marriage for me when the time is right."

Isiloe nodded. "Yes, that way you do not have to waste time worrying about it." Her eyes narrowed. "Who do you think it will be?"

"Mother has spoken of Quenulor Joralei. He is from an old family and is nice to look upon. We would have handsome children." Gwaethe saw Quenulor in her mind's eye but didn't tell Isiloe she simply could not imagine laying with him, making a family with him.

Isiloe nodded. "He is fine. I have had my eye on him for a while. But I will not have my eye on him from now on."

Gwaethe laughed. "Go ahead, Isiloe. If it is not Quenulor, it will be someone else. He may as well go to someone who is interested in him."

Isiloe dropped her gaze and fumbled the medicine supplies as she packed them away. "Let us return home instead of following the Kingdom captain. I would like to see Quenulor again, if I have your blessing."

"I will not change my mind, Isiloe. Tomorrow we turn north and follow the path of Vorasava wherever it takes us."

Isiloe shook her head. "If I didn't know better, I would think you had a thing for the Captain. He is rather good looking for a human."

"I have but one goal; to find Faenwelar. If Vorasava can help us, that is all I am concerned about."

Isiloe fell silent but she bit her lip, a sure sign something worried her.

"What is it, Isiloe?" she asked, reaching for her hand.

"You will laugh at me."

"Tell me."

Isiloe closed her eyes as if summoning courage, and Gwaethe's stomach tightened.

"I am frightened."

Gwaethe let out a breath. *Is that all?* "We are all frightened. There is no shame in that."

"You don't understand. I am not frightened of danger. It is change that makes me tremble; change that will come and sweep away all I know, all I love, all that keeps me sane."

"The world is always changing, Isiloe. The mountains rear up and erode, some years are hot and others cold. Our loved ones die, and even the trees grow old and fade. There is nothing more certain than change, and we must adjust or spend our whole lives fighting it and losing." Gwaethe smiled sympathetically at the distress on her cousin's face. "I do not know about you, but I would rather not lose every battle. I would rather fight as little as possible."

"Then why are you fighting Faenwelar?" Isiloe asked. "Is this not just another change we must endure? How do you know his way is not right, that we *are* destined to take back all the southern lands that were stolen from us?"

Gwaethe stared at Isiloe, daunted by the question. Was Faenwelar on the side of right? *No!*

"Imagine a world where all that was important was wresting land away from the humans," she said, "where peace was a thing only dreamed of. No. We have enough land for all. Most importantly, we have the great forests where we can roam, and build our homes, and sing our songs. We don't need the Kingdom lands, and we don't need the loss of life reclaiming them would take."

Her cousin frowned. "How can you be so sure?"

Gwaethe smiled. "Faenwelar killed my father, the king of the *Lenweri*, *your* uncle. That is treason, in the words of the humans, and I *will* avenge his death. Father always lived in peace. I will hold his ideals to my heart. I will defeat Faenwelar if it is the last thing I do, no matter how it is accomplished."

"So that is a change worth fighting against?"

"Now you understand," Gwaethe said.

Isiloe snorted. "But I do not! Oh, I can see the King had the right of it, but how do you tell if a change is worth fighting?"

"First of all, dear cousin," Gwaethe said, "ask yourself if you can influence it in any way. If not, then it must be borne. If yes, that is when you have the difficult task of deciding what is best. That is far harder."

"Which is why you are the leader of our forces and I just a lowly captain," Isiloe said.

Gwaethe drew her forward for a hug, something Isiloe rarely allowed. It felt good to get this close to her prickly cousin. "I would never call you lowly. You are my rock, and I trust you with my life. You have proven yourself more times than I can count. Do not ever doubt your value."

Isiloe pulled back and didn't meet her eyes. "Thank you. Now I must see to the others." She stood and stalked off, disappearing into the mist creeping out from the nearby forest. Tomorrow would be another difficult day, but Gwaethe was glad she had been given the chance to penetrate the thick skin that kept Isiloe such a mystery.

* * *

Jacques sat staring into the fire, wondering how Gwaethe had fared that day. It must have been tough for her and tomorrow would be another day of pain. He had experienced injuries like that and riding with them was complete agony.

The wound had still been oozing blood when she departed, but he had held his tongue, knowing nothing he said would change her mind. He didn't know why he cared so much, except fighting together made for loyalty of sorts. *Yes, that must be the reason.*

Exmund appeared before him and saluted. "Your meal is ready, Captain."

"Thank you, Exmund." Jacques barely heard him.

"Sir? Are you well?"

Jacques came to himself. "Oh… yes, I was just wondering how the Princess is faring. That wound was not the sort I would want to travel with."

"No, sir. How far away is her home, sir?"

"At least a week's ride, although in the mountains it's hard to estimate. You can ride a long way in difficult mountainous terrain and not get very far."

"I expect they move quickly, the elves. They're used to the forest and the mountains."

Jacques smiled. "Yes, quite so. Have the scouts returned?"

"Yes, Captain. They're ready to make their reports."

Jacques rose. "Let's eat then." He accompanied the young aide to the larger campfire where the cook was serving the evening meal. While he ate, his scouts reported their findings.

"We passed the site of the ambush some miles back. Looks like a slaughter house with blood and bodies scattered through the scrub there. It appears the *Sis Lenweri* were lying in wait and took off due north after the fight."

"Did they have injured?" Jacques asked.

"Yes, Captain, a handful of injured going by the blood trail."

"North, you say?"

"Yes, sir. They could be heading for Amitania, the lost city."

Jacques considered. "Is there a trail through the mountains there?"

"Not that we know of, sir. There could be one we don't know about."

"How far ahead are they?"

"Nearly a full day, Captain, and for elves in the forest that means two days for us. We'll never catch them."

"I can deal with that," Jacques said. "I'm more concerned about where they are headed and what they intend. I don't want them to know we're following. That's what you're there for. If they see us, our mission has failed."

"Pardon me, Captain, but hasn't the elven princess alerted the *Sis Lenweri*?"

"No," Jacques said. "It's one thing to have elves on your tail and another to have Kingdom soldiers discover your scheme. We still might keep the element of surprise."

The scout nodded. Jacques dismissed them then set men to stand sentry duty.

* * *

The next morning, Gwaethe's thigh muscles were so stiff she struggled to rise from her furs. She had spent a restless night between the pain in her leg and thoughts of Jacques. Where was he, and what would he say when he learned of her deception? All she knew was he was somewhere to the east, heading due north. She limped to the campfire and sat watching as Isiloe checked the wounds of all her comrades.

Again, Gwaethe wondered how she would cope without her cousin. With any luck, she would never have to find out. "Good morning. I hope you had a better night than I."

"I stood sentry all night, cousin, so I doubt that is the case," Isiloe said, yawning.

Gwaethe glared at her. "I would speak with you, Isiloe."

The diminutive elven woman tied the bandage she was working on and crossed the clearing to kneel before Gwaethe. "What do you want?"

"I thank you for standing guard over us, Isiloe, but you will be no good to me if you fall over from fatigue."

"I will doze on my horse today and sleep half of tonight. There is no need for you to worry."

Gwaethe studied her cousin, noting the dullness of her gaze and the slump of her shoulders. "We have a long way to travel and perhaps fighting as well. You cannot afford to use yourself so. I won't allow it."

Fatigue dropped from Isiloe as her eyes fired. "Then heal, and I will not have to bear the burden of undertaking my tasks and yours." Isiloe stomped across the campsite and over to the row of horses, swishing their tails in the early morning sun.

The rest of their group avoided Gwaethe's gaze as was their habit. Family disagreements were to be overlooked, not entered into. She could make up with her cousin later. It was just the fatigue talking, and she knew she put too much pressure on her. It was just that Isiloe was so efficient in everything she did. She was also too generous when it came to her job.

Gwaethe ate a quick breakfast then helped the others break camp and load their packs on the horses. Her leg was feeling better, now it had loosened up, and she managed to mount without assistance, using a small log to stand on. Isiloe still glowered at the world and took her place at the rear of the column.

"Move out," Gwaethe said, riding to the head of the group. Two scouts had already left, ranging to the north and east, so there were five of them. Gwaethe was content to ride with only her musings for company. She mostly kept to herself. Apart from Isiloe, she did not speak much with the others. It did no good to become too friendly with those she commanded, especially when on a mission. Gwaethe prided herself on her leadership, and you couldn't lead if you became emotionally involved. On a raid, losing a comrade was bad enough without losing a friend also. So, she kept to herself with only Isiloe for support.

They moved steadily but quietly through the sparse trees and on to the denser forest where lay the road to the Usetar mountains. It was beautiful country, with pine and spruce more in evidence as they rode further north. Birds called to each other and flitted back and forth on the branches overhead. It was vital to keep a watch on nature, for it might give warning of another ambush. Gwaethe glanced behind to find Isiloe dozing in her saddle. As she turned forwards, one of the scouts rode up.

"The Kingdom soldiers are due east, Princess," he said, touching his hand to his heart. "Do you wish for me to approach and make ourselves known?"

"No!" Gwaethe said. "Keep them in sight but stay hidden. Report to me if they alter their bearing."

The scout nodded and rode back the way he had come.

Gwaethe's heart pounded at the thought of Jacques's anger when he discovered she had not returned to her home. *He will soon understand I will not go running home just because a man should suggest it.* Gwaethe snorted to herself. How amusing it would be to confront him, to test and push him until he burned with fury. And he would. Jacques Vorasava appeared to be a man in charge of his emotions, but Gwaethe suspected he had a temper when pushed far enough. She might quail to think of him angry at her, but she also looked forward to showing him he must respect her position as elven leader.

* * *

Jacques pushed the men as hard as he dared the second day out from the lodge. They had to stay on the elven trail, and the longer they took, the less chance of discovering the *Sis Lenweri* plans. Amitania was a definite possibility as an elven stronghold. If he lost the trail, he would head there and discover if Faenwelar had any presence in the dead city. Again, his mind wandered to Gwaethe and her injury. He should have made sure she was on the mend before allowing her to leave. Another day of rest would have served her well. Now she was no longer with him, he wanted to know she wasn't dying of wound sepsis or blood-loss. He could only hope Isiloe would keep her cousin safe.

They pushed on, through the dense forest, following the narrow game trail the elves had taken. The path frequently zig-zagged from one game trail onto another, the tracker earning his pay. Jacques sent scouts ranging ahead to the north, west and east and they brought back valuable information which kept the soldiers on course. He had felt eyes upon them all morning and sometimes saw movement from the corner of his eye, but when he studied the forest to the west, he saw nothing. It was always the west that prickled his scalp.

"Jumping at shadows," he muttered.

"What did you say, Captain?" Exmund asked. The Corporal was Jacques's aide as well as the company medic. He was a busy young man but handled everything with no fuss. Jacques had noticed Exmund when he first joined the army and had followed his career, deciding to take him on as his aide when he was raised to captain. Jacques had never regretted it.

"I was merely talking to myself," Jacques said. "Goes hand in hand with seeing things."

"Are *you* seeing things too, Captain?"

Jacques looked across at him. "There have been odd times when I thought something moved at the edge of my vision. Those blighters are damned sneaky. If they can catch Princess Gwaethe by surprise, then we should be on the lookout."

"I keep seeing movement to the west," Exmund said, "but surely our quarry is far to the north by now?"

"We have scouts out," Jacques said, "but keep your eyes peeled, all the same."

"Right you are, Captain," Exmund replied, "best to play it safe."

After the chat with his aide, Jacques saw nothing untoward and almost convinced himself he was imagining things earlier. He did send another three men out to scout though, just to be sure.

They reached the foothills of the Usetar Mountains on dusk. The trees had become sparser as they began to climb the gentle gradient. Small boulders littered the landscape making the going more difficult. Jacques called a halt and had the men take extra care setting up camp, laying sticks around the perimeter and making sure there was clear ground around them even if it meant they were squashed together.

The horses were picketed close by, which led to the pungent odor of dung as a dinner-time accompaniment. He doubled the guard and halved the shift times, much to the disgust of his men. However, it seemed they had all felt watched that day, so grudgingly accepted their turn at guard.

Jacques took his own duty at midnight. He wouldn't have the men griping that their captain didn't pull his weight. It was quiet as the grave for his entire duty. Nothing moved, except for the night creatures, and he no longer felt the watcher. It unsettled him more than he had been during the day. Was he so tired his senses had let him down? When his shift ended, he couldn't sleep and lay in his tent listening to the night sounds, trying not to imagine the creeping sounds of elven feet.

Morning dawned, wet and misty. Jacques crawled from his tent to grumbles from his men about the hard night and the even harder day ahead. There was no sun to warm them, and the autumn chill had seated itself in their bones. He ordered another cup of tea for everyone and then gave the call to mount.

The mountain foothills weren't steep, but there were many small ravines along with hardy brush, the occasional larger tree and the ever-present boulders. Rocks tumbled down at the slightest touch, making the footing treacherous. He ordered the group to spread out along the foothills, looking for any sign of a trail that might lead straight through at this point.

As the morning wore on, the light drizzle became a soaking downpour, creating rivers of mud and rocks. Jacques did his share of searching, cursing the Goddess and all other gods for sending the cold torrent.

He was about to call off the hunt and head west when he spied a gap in the mountain where a sheer rock wall had been forced up from the earth in centuries past. He dismounted and led his horse to a fissure just wide enough for a horse to squeeze through. Water dashed through the hole and into the depths of the mountain, taking dirt and rocks with it.

Jacques pulled back and went in search of his men. It took another hour to round everyone up as he couldn't use his horn for fear of being heard. They huddled under a large tree as they discussed their options.

"I know it's risky, men," Jacques said. "We'd be riding into a crevice full of mud and water. We could get buried. I'll need a volunteer to scout the crevice and confirm it's wide enough."

Sergeant Dodlan, second in command, nodded. "No point getting in there and finding it too narrow, Captain." He turned to two of his men and, after a short discussion, the soldiers mounted their horses and rode in the direction of the fissure.

"Seek whatever shelter you can while we await word from the scouts." Jacques sat at the base of the tree and Dodlan joined him. "What's your counsel, Sergeant?"

The older man took a moment to consider. "I'm the last one to enjoy confined spaces, sir, but our only other option is to go over the mountain and that would take time we don't have."

"And we'd face similar risks of landslides," Jacques said. "I like the idea of escaping this cursed rain." He shuddered as a rivulet of water ran down his neck.

"Then, as long as the scouts' report is favourable," Dodlan said, "we go through?"

Jacques was buoyed by the sergeant's support. "Yes Dodlan, I believe we should."

Dodlan slapped his hand to his shoulder and stood, moving off to speak to his men. Exmund took his place, a frown on his brow.

"I know what you're going to say, Corporal. This plan is risky but with careful strategy we can manage the risk and make up some time."

Exmund nodded. "I trust you, sir. If you say it's safe…" His voice trailed off, his frown deepening.

Jacques placed his hand on Exmund's shoulder. "I didn't say it was safe, son. Often there is no right decision, and this is one of those times. It will be confronting in that mountain, but I'll see us through. You can depend on that."

Exmund stood. "I'll take some men and find dry wood for brands. Even if elves can see in the dark, we can't."

Jacques waved him away and fell to agonizing over the best course for them to take. Before he had convinced himself, Dodlan appeared before him.

"Scouts have returned, Captain," he said. "The passage is wide enough and, further in, there are signs the elves recently passed through. Water is running down the side of the mountain and into the fissure but, as long as the heavens don't open up, we should be safe."

"We go through, then," Jacques said, blocking out the thought of the water and concentrating on the days they would save with their subterranean passage.

* * *

Gwaethe loved the rain. Her mother had told her she was born in a downpour, and her first bath had been in that torrent. Consequently, she wasn't affected by the increasing rain as they rode north. She merely pulled up her hood and wrapped herself in her cloak; both of which were rainproof due to the special solution they were treated with. All the elves wore these cloaks. Living in the forest meant they had to adapt. Fashioning rainproof cloaks and hoods was a centuries old occupation for the *Lenweri*.

Isiloe grumbled behind her. She was no fan of the wet, especially when it stopped her from catching up on much needed sleep.

The heavy showers became a steady downpour, and Gwaethe's thoughts turned to Jacques and his men, battling toward the mountains. They would have to find a pass over the range, and mudslides were a real danger in this weather. Perhaps it was time to rejoin the soldiers and see if she could help. Jacques would be furious. She ignored the voice that told her she was just finding excuses to see him again.

"I think we should turn northeast," Gwaethe said. "I am afraid of what will happen to the soldiers if they try to cross the range in this." She held up her palms to the raindrops.

Isiloe snorted. "Let them try and see how far they get. Better still, they can ride down on a mud slide if they are stupid enough to attempt a crossing."

"Lives could be lost, cousin. I think we should intercept them."

"Rescue, more like," Isiloe said. "They would not be so silly, would they?"

"They are chasing Faenwelar's band of traitors, Isiloe. They will continue until they find them. If I know the Captain, he will not rest until he has the culprits or at least knows where they are headed."

Isiloe growled. "These humans will be the death of us."

"We always intended to meet them on the other side of the mountains. What we did not plan on was this weather. We need them, cousin, and I do not intend to let them perish."

Isiloe frowned at her, mumbling under her breath. Gwaethe was glad she could not hear what was said. "You are right, but are you recovered enough to effect a rescue?"

Gwaethe's leg throbbed, but the wound had stopped bleeding, and she was much stronger after a good night's rest. "I am fit enough. We will negotiate Rocky Pass and then turn to the east. With luck we will meet Vorasava soon after."

Isiloe grunted but kicked her horse into the lead, and they entered the foothills of the western Usetar Mountains. Rocky Pass was a little-used passage through the range, being narrow and only useful for travelers without wagons. Gwaethe often used it as it wasn't as deep as the other passes, negotiating the mountains where the range narrowed. In good conditions it took less than half a day, but today they wouldn't be through until near dark. Gwaethe chewed her lip as they entered the pass, impatient to complete this stage of the journey and ensure Jacques's safety.

The rain didn't let up; rather, it became heavier. The *Lenweri* rode in a torrent of cold mud and small rocks, the horses slipping and sliding whenever they had to traverse a slope. It was the worst weather Gwaethe had ever seen for a mountain crossing, the muddy wash getting stronger by the hour.

"Keep an eye out for mud slides," Isiloe shouted back.

Gwaethe relayed the message down the line of riders, glad they were all back together after calling the scouts in.

"Stay close, nose to tail." She scanned the pass, on the lookout for the movement of rocks which might herald a mud slide.

Isiloe did the same, all the while muttering under her breath. Gwaethe smiled, glad of something that lightened her mood. With the light failing, she thought ahead to where they might stop. They had to get clear of this pass for fear of slides. The country on the other side of the mountains was full of rocky outcrops. There might be a small cave or two they could use, if they cared to risk a rock fall. It was either that or spend the night in the rain.

With the last of the light, they cleared the pass and spread out onto the rocky northern hills of the Usetar Range.

"Ride east!" Gwaethe said, hugging the northern edge of the range and picking her way through the rocky mounds. Over the course of an hour, they discovered three small caves, not much more than ledges under outcropping rock shelves.

They selected the largest two and split their force between them. There was no wood for a fire, and, as Gwaethe huddled with Isiloe and the other female elf in their party, she began to wish for warm clothes and a hot meal in her belly. Instead, they ate nuts and dried forest fruit; nourishing but somewhat bland to taste.

The torrents cascaded over the front of their ledge and around the sides, sending spatters of muddy water into their refuge, but it was better than nothing. Gwaethe began to imagine the groan and rumble of rocks falling; or perhaps it was not her imagination.

"I can hear a roaring," Isiloe said. "Do you think it is the rain or …"

For once it seemed Isiloe did not wish to voice her concerns. She was always the harbinger of doom, but on this occasion neither of them needed to hear their worst fears. Gwaethe only wished she was not imagining the soldiers trapped in a slurry of mud and rock. She needed them whole and hearty, especially a certain captain. Her face heated at the thought of him, tall and lean, dark, with a dangerous edge; as if she pushed him too hard, he would show her who was in control. A shiver ran down her spine as she imagined him on top of her, arms above her head, pinned by his body, his hard lines dominating her feminine curves. Not that she had many of those, but what she did have she would gladly press against him.

It was scandalous, the way she was thinking at this moment. Isiloe would disdain such ideas toward any man, let alone a human. And, yet, no elf had caught her attention as this human had. There had to be a reason. She didn't believe anything happened without a purpose. It might be simply the two of them bringing Faenwelar down, but Gwaethe hoped secretly she might have more pleasure with Jacques than simply catching the treacherous *Sis Lenweri* leader.

She fell into a fitful sleep, her mind very much on Jacques Vorasava.

CHAPTER FOUR

Jacques stared at Sergeant Dodlan's robust shoulders as he rode near the back of the line. They were in single file on horseback, their knees brushing the walls of the fissure. If they made it out of this it would take months to dry out, and that included their horses' feet. The poor creatures snorted and fussed as the torrent flowed around their hoofs on the gentle downhill slope. Had this been the right decision? The water was getting faster the further in they went.

The bobbing brands up ahead stopped.

"What's the matter?" Jacques asked.

"A cavern, sir," Dodlan said, his words reverberating off the stone walls.

The men ahead of Jacques moved forward and to the sides until Jacques reached the end of the fissure. The passage opened out into a large cavern, and the torrent emptied into a dark lake in the center.

"Spread out and explore the other side," Jacques said. He pushed past the men in front of him and rode around the eastern edge of the cavern. It wasn't long before he discovered the first passage leading out.

"There's a way out," Dodlan called from the western edge, just as another shout went up from those exploring the northern wall.

Jacques continued around the cavern, discovering another three tunnels before he joined Dodlan. "That makes six passages out of here," he said, "unless someone has found more. And I saw no elven tracks."

"Six is enough, Captain," Dodlan said. "How did the bastards erase their trail, and how do we choose?"

"At least they look drier than the one we've been traveling," Jacques said, his mind skipping ahead to another difficult choice. He swept his flaming brand over his head to examine the lake. The torrent streaming in had increased and the lake would overflow soon, sending water into the exiting passages.

"I'd like to suggest the easternmost passages might lead along the range," Jacques said.

"We don't know that, Captain," Dodlan said.

"True," Jacques replied, "but we have to start somewhere." He looked around. "That leaves the northwestern, northern and northeastern passages. Which one?"

"There's no way we can be sure, Captain," Dodlan said. "All those may lead out of this place, or they could all be dead ends. Let's keep it simple and continue to head north, and hope for the best."

Jacques turned to Dodlan. "I like that idea, Sergeant. Also, the northern passage exits at the same level as the passage we entered by, whereas the other two are lower. If there's a flood, we'll be safer in the northern one." He walked over to his horse. "Mount up, same order."

They passed into the northern passage which was wider than the one by which they had entered the cavern by. Jacques breathed easier in the increased room. He had never been a fan of enclosed spaces. The ground beneath their horses' hoofs was dry, but, where Jacques had hoped to find some trace of the *Sis Lenweri*, he saw none. "Look out for anything that indicates the elves came this way."

As they moved away from the cavern, the sound of rushing water dwindled until the passage became eerily quiet. The thump of horse hoofs and the occasional snort of the beasts were the only living sounds. The ceiling rose higher above them until the light from their torches struggled to reach it. The sandy floor beneath their feet sloped gently downhill and the passage widened to the extent that Jacques could no longer touch the sides with his outstretched hands.

But the silence played on his nerves. "Keep your ears peeled for any change."

Jacques praised the Goddess for the easier footing. At least he didn't have to worry so much about his horse slipping. It was certainly better than a route over the mountains through the treacherous passes. By his reckoning, it must be nearing dark outside, but they would push on unless there was another cavern to rest in. That way they might catch the elves.

After four hours, Jacques heard rushing water again.

"Stop!" he said. "Listen."

They halted and strained seconds ticked by.

"Water, sir," Dodlan said. "It's coming from the direction of the cavern! That lake must have filled!"

"Move!" Jacques called. "Fast as you can. Look out for side passages. We might need a way to escape if that water is as fast as it sounds."

They broke into a trot, the thudding of the horses' hoofs echoing off the stone walls. The rush of water could still be clearly heard over the noise of their passage, but it was too dark to push any harder. Jacques ground his teeth at the pace. The sheer rock walls on either side drew closer and he felt squeezed, his breath burning in his chest. If the water caught them… He shuddered. Dark, rushing water; enclosed spaces; nightmare. Despite their best efforts, when they called a halt a while later, the sound of rushing water was louder.

"It's catching us!" Exmund said.

"Seems so, lad," Dodlan said, "but we're not finished yet."

"Keep pushing forward," Jacques said. "If you see a side passage that goes up, get inside it as far as you can. Otherwise just get out. We can't be far."

Jacques hauled his horse to the side and allowed the men behind him to go ahead. He was never going to be accused of saving himself at the expense of others. They pushed on, Jacques in virtual darkness at the back of the pack, following the lights ahead, the sound of the torrent growing louder. Despair ate at him. It couldn't end here, inside a mountain, drowned. He thought of his parents, his father paralyzed, dependent on his mother and a son who would never return. What would they do without an heir?

And Gwaethe. He would never see her again in this life. He wanted to see her again, even if it was just for her to tell him he'd been foolhardy entering the mountain. He wanted to see the moonlight play over her fine features and experience again the pleasure of her alien regard.

It surprised him he didn't regret the loss of his career. It was the people he thought of; his parents, Gwaethe, Exmund and his men.

He became aware of a lightening of the passage. Daylight! They had been in here longer than he thought. Yes! It was daylight.

Dodlan's voice barely reached him with the roaring of the water behind. "Captain! We're saved!"

The men were charging forward, cantering now the light was better. Jacques raced after them. The opening was not in sight, yet it was brighter. They must be close. He didn't look back, just hurried the men in front of him, urging them faster.

His horse slipped and crashed to the floor of the passage, throwing Jacques from the saddle. Pain blasted through his skull as it hit the stone wall. Darkness beckoned, but to allow it to take him now would be death. His horse had bolted, and the men hadn't noticed. Jacques pushed himself to his hands and knees and crawled along the passage toward the light and the retreating men. He tried to stand twice, but his legs gave way. The pain in his head crashed at him in hideous waves that threatened to take him under.

He wouldn't make it out in time. A rivulet of water raced beneath him, the first sign the flood would be there in seconds. He dragged himself up, half-standing and half-leaning against the rock. Using the wall for support, he inched along, the water around his feet getting higher all the time. The flood swirled around his ankles, upsetting his balance, and he had to concentrate to stay on his feet. He struggled on, the water rising up his calves, pushing, making his knees give way.

And then he saw it in the gloom. The root of a tree ran down the wall through a crack in the roof. He reached for it, but it was too high. If he could latch onto it, it might provide enough of a hold to secure him against the floodwater. He jumped and missed, agony smashing through his skull and blinding him. He jumped again, ignoring all but the lifeline that beckoned to him. This time his fingers closed around the root and he held on.

He shut his eyes against the pain in his head and tightened his grip as the water rose to engulf him.

* * *

After a miserable night, Gwaethe threw off her fur and rolled out from beneath the rock ledge. The others were doing the same. Her leg reminded her, sharply, to take it slowly. She drew in a deep breath and looked around.

The rain had eased to a miserable drizzle. Multiple mud slides had altered the landscape overnight, but they had survived in their small caves. It had been incredibly risky but necessary. Isiloe was not to be found. Gwaethe cast around for some sign of her cousin, only to find her clambering down from on high.

"It is too dangerous, Isiloe," Gwaethe said. "You will bring the mountain down on all of us."

Isiloe glared and folded her arms under her breasts. "Do you not think I know how to move without disturbing rocks?"

"And what would I say to your mother when I brought your body home?"

Isiloe shrugged. "She knows what I do carries risk." Isiloe's mother, Rasalar, sister of Orionkael, had been a soldier in her day and still trained the new recruits.

Gwaethe sighed. "What did you find?"

"There is nothing as far as my eye can see to indicate the humans. I do not know where they are. I did see a great torrent of water gushing from the range several miles to the east, but I cannot see the opening. The range dips to the south a little there."

The hairs on Gwaethe's neck stood up and fear rippled in her gut. *A river from the mountain?* Gwaethe could not remember the existence of such a feature. The astonishing amount of rain they had experienced over the last day, might have found its way through the mountain. If anyone had tried to travel through via the same passage…

No, he would not be so imprudent as to take *that* path.

Gwaethe ordered camp struck, and they mounted up without breakfast in their stomachs. They nibbled on nuts and dried fruit yet again as they rode east along the northern edge of the Usetar Range, picking their way through the numerous rivers of mud that had brought down great chunks of the mountains. They had gone a mile when they saw a group of mounted men coming their way.

Gwaethe pushed her horse into a canter, and the rest did the same, Isiloe cursing under her breath about foolhardy cousins. She moved as fast as she dared. The country was already treacherous with its boulders and loose rocks, but the recent slides hid soft mud and holes that could break a horse's leg. She leaned over and breathed encouragement into Rassar's ear. The golden stallion snorted and shook his mane. Gwaethe smiled at his spirit.

She soon confirmed the group of men was indeed Jacques's soldiers. Panic struck her as she searched among them and failed to find him. She rode into the middle of the humans, instantly ensnaring the young corporal, Exmund, with her gaze.

"Where is he?" She flung her arm out, pointing at a white mare. "That's Jacques's horse!"

"He didn't make it out of the mountains, Princess."

Exmund's eyes were wide, half crazy.

"What do you mean?" she snapped. "What were you doing in those mountains? Where is he?"

A large, older man rode his horse forward several steps. "I'm in charge here, Princess. My name is Dodlan. It's as the boy said. The Captain was bringing up the rear when the torrent caught us. We all made it out, but something must have befallen him. The passage was caving in as we rode through it. When we made it to safety, the Captain's horse charged past, but he wasn't on it. I immediately turned back to find him, but a massive gush of water beat me back. It was too dangerous." The man's hands fidgeted with the reins and his eyes were downcast.

Gwaethe felt a keening begin in her chest and bubble its way up to her throat. She couldn't allow that. She took herself in hand and looked to those around her. "Grab shovels. We will dig until we find him." Turning back to Dodlan she said, "Take me to where you exited. We are not leaving without him."

Dodlan flinched. "It doesn't seem likely he survived, Princess. Even if we dig him out, I can't believe he could be alive."

Gwaethe fought harder than ever to keep her nerve. "We will find him." With that, she kicked her stallion into motion, Isiloe and Dodlan catching up with her, and the rest streaming out behind.

Within two miles, they had found the scene of the disaster, and Gwaethe quailed at the thought Jacques was somewhere under all that mud and rock. Water still ran from a pile of rubble at the base of the range, and it had brought down rocks too large to move.

She rode back to where Dodlan watched with the other soldiers.

"Sergeant, I know this region and its dangers," Gwaethe said. "I believe we can find Captain Vorasava alive. Will you hand the command over to me?"

"Princess, this is highly irregular," Dodlan said, leaning across the pommel of his saddle. "The men won't follow you."

"They will if you do, Sergeant." Gwaethe looked to the weak sun, slowly climbing to its zenith. "Give me until sunset. I promise if he is not found by then, you may have your command back."

Dodlan frowned. "I want to find him as much as you do, Princess. If you think there's a chance then we owe it to the Captain to try." He dismounted. "Listen up men! The Princess will oversee the rescue of Captain Vorasava. Follow her orders as you would mine or the Captain's. We need to work fast."

Gwaethe nodded to Dodlan. "Thank you, Sergeant." She turned to the men. "I want ten horses moving large boulders with ropes." She put Isiloe in charge of the horses and singled out ten large men to help. The rest moved the smaller rocks. By mid-afternoon they had cleared the entrance of the tunnel, so a small person could enter.

Gwaethe climbed over the slippery hillside where Jacques's men were arguing over who should enter. "All of you are too large," she said. "I shall go."

As usual, Isiloe hissed behind her. "Let me."

Gwaethe lifted her chin and turned to her cousin. "I will not allow another to take this risk."

"You have proven yourself time and again," Isiloe said. "There is no need."

"There is every need." How could Gwaethe explain her compulsion to be the one to find Jacques when even she didn't know why she felt the way she did?

While Isiloe pondered her next objection, Gwaethe knelt beside the hole and reached inside, patting over all the surfaces and finding only mud and rock. "Dig some more," she said, standing and moving to the side. The men looked at her as if she had lost her senses. They had long given up on finding their commander alive. The thought of such a vital man lost under all that mountain made her gut clench. He could not be dead. She looked to Dodlan who stood to one side. "Sergeant?"

Dodlan frowned but nodded. "You heard the Princess. Get digging."

The men grumbled amongst themselves but moved to enlarge the hole. The sun came out from behind the clouds, sending light into the opening for the first time. But it would be short lived with sunset only a matter of an hour or so away. "We must find him now," she said. "The light is almost gone."

That brought more mumbling. Gwaethe could understand the fatigue the men must feel. The Gods knew she wasn't much better, but it simply was not an option to give up now.

"You know this is a waste of time," Isiloe said, her voice barely a whisper. "He is dead under all that. We should push on to the real mission."

"And you think these men will gladly fall in with us if the Captain is gone?" Gwaethe gripped Isiloe's upper arms. "They will go home. A monument will be erected here, and our chance will be lost."

"Let them go home. We will survive without them."

"We have to find him. There is no other way."

"You have lost your heart to this human," Isiloe sneered. "How could you forget what he is? Do you think he would do the same if you were trapped?"

"I do not care."

Gwaethe turned away and walked to the edge of the hole again, peering into its depths as the sun appeared from behind a cloud. A shaft of sunlight speared into the crevice, and she saw something glitter.

"Wait! I see something!" Gwaethe said, pushing men out of her way and kneeling in the mud. "Captain! Jacques! Do you hear me?"

The light had found a brass button, and Gwaethe hoped it was attached to a uniform. "There," she said, "dig there."

The soldiers fell to removing more mud and finally uncovered Jacques's arm, complete with uniform and brass buttons. A cheer went up, but Gwaethe held back this time, fearing the worst. Isiloe stepped into the breach and reached past what must have been his shoulder.

"His head is clear," she said. "He must have got into a gap at the last moment." She backed away. "Dig him out. Quickly!"

The soldiers set to digging again while Gwaethe hugged herself, biting her lip to try and control her emotions. He was a human commander, nothing to her except what he could offer in way of military advice and aide. Nothing, nothing, nothing! No matter how she argued with herself, her heart just didn't listen. The seconds seemed like hours and she held her breath as Jacques was pulled muddy and unrecognizable from the tunnel.

Exmund knelt beside his leader, his fingers at Jacques's throat. "There's a pulse! Weak, but definitely a pulse." He looked around at his fellow soldiers. "Build a fire!"

Gwaethe watched as Exmund gently bathed Jacques's face with clean water and then had two men move their leader to a tent which had been hastily erected. She shook all over, and her leg ached like a demon. Arms around her guided her over to the fire that had been lit. Isiloe's arms. She sat on a rock and wrapped herself in the fur her cousin brought, huddling inside, keeping her eyes on the tent into which Jacques had vanished.

She had no right to feel this way, and she had no reason to be beside him, watching his chest rise and fall and reassuring herself he was alive and well. She had precisely no right, but that was where she wanted, needed to be. Except she couldn't stand, couldn't find an ounce of strength to move. A warm goblet of mulled wine was pressed into her hands, and she drank without thinking. Slowly, the heat of the liquid defrosted the cold in her core, and she looked up, searching for her cousin. Isiloe stood before the tent, speaking with Dodlan. Snatches of their words floated to her.

Unconscious…condition…let her know…more in the morning.

It wasn't enough. Gwaethe had to know how he fared. She stood and walked toward the tent but the sergeant blocked her.

"He is still being tended to, Princess. I'll let you see him when he's awake."

Gwaethe couldn't take her eyes from the tip of Jacques's shoes, visible through the gap in the tent flaps. "Did he say anything?"

"Nothing," the sergeant said. "Look, don't get your hopes up. He was in the mud a long time."

At that, Gwaethe did meet Dodlan's eyes. "He will awake, and he will be well." Her voice verged on the shrill, even to her own ears. She had to get herself under control. This was unseemly behavior for an elven princess. She took a deep breath and tried again. "I must see your captain, Sergeant. I will not stay long."

Dodlan frowned, as did Isiloe. What did her cousin expect? That she would not check on a man so important to their cause? Gwaethe stood firm as she waited for the sergeant's response.

He nodded. "Go ahead, Princess, but only a few minutes."

She pushed through the flaps and into the tent where lanterns gave the space a cozy glow. Jacques lay wrapped in blankets, his skin pale, even bluish. His chest rose and fell slowly, but Exmund raised devastated eyes to her.

"I don't think he can make it, Princess," he said. "He's cold, so cold. I think his body has shut down."

Gwaethe had seen this time and again in the mountains of her homeland. And she knew how to help him. "Empty the water skins and fill them with boiling water, then place them around his body. He must also be raised off the ground to keep out the chill. You must try to get warm water and broth into him; it will warm him from inside."

Exmund charged from the tent leaving Gwaethe alone with the Captain. "You will survive, Jacques. You need warming, that is all." She knelt beside him, ignoring the jabbing pain of her leg, and rolled him onto his side. Supporting his shoulder, Gwaethe rubbed his back, which was deathly cold. If not for the rise and fall of his chest, she would swear she held a corpse. She rubbed harder, alternating between the back rubs and chafing his hands together. Where was Exmund with those water bags?

As if her words had summoned him, the corporal burst back into the tent along with Isiloe, carrying six water bags. They pulled back the blankets, and Gwaethe helped place three bags along his front and three along his back. Then they covered him again with the blankets. Exmund disappeared to get the broth, and Isiloe sat beside Gwaethe. For once her cousin was silent.

Gwaethe couldn't bring herself to speak as she watched the rise and fall of Jacques's chest. Was he getting stronger? Did he have more color in his cheeks? Would he awake only to expire from being cold and —? She stopped herself before she could imagine any more horrible scenarios. She noticed a dribble of water from the corner of his mouth and bent to examine it. The liquid held a faint pink tinge. She had heard of drowned elves having blood in the fluid that ran from their chests.

She reached over him and began to thump his back. More liquid ran out; this time it was redder. She pounded again, and Jacques groaned.

"Captain! Can you hear me?"

He groaned again, but Gwaethe kept pounding on his back until a great gout of liquid shot from his lips. He coughed and coughed as Gwaethe rubbed his back. "It is alright, Jacques, you will soon be well and ordering your men about. You have been through a terrible ordeal, but you will recover and soon."

Isiloe snorted. "He will not recover if you keep pounding on his back. You will break a rib if you keep that up."

Gwaethe glared at her, but her response had to wait as Exmund returned with the broth. She and the Corporal rolled Jacques onto his back and propped him up against his saddle. He did have more color! Gwaethe stared as Exmund spooned the warm broth past Jacques's bluish lips. He was swallowing the soup. It had to mean he was better.

"What do you think, Corporal?" she asked, hating the desperation she couldn't hide and earning a sharp look from Isiloe.

"It's too soon to say, Princess, but he does appear stronger, and his breathing is better." Exmund fed his leader until a coughing fit stopped him.

Again, Gwaethe soothed Jacques, laying a hand on his brow and finding it warm. "Do you think he is developing a fever?"

Exmund frowned. "Please, I'm not a healer, just a bumbling medic trying my best."

"Would you people hold it down?" Jacques said. "I need rest, not jabbering."

A hot wave of relief had Gwaethe fanning herself, and a tear escaped to splash against her boot. "How do you feel?"

"Weak as a kitten but glad to be alive, Princess. What are you doing here?"

"You should be very glad she is here," Isiloe said, "or you would still lie beneath the mud."

Jacques sought Gwaethe's eyes. At least she had managed to get her ragged feelings under control.

"Does she speak the truth?" he asked.

"I feared for your party when the rain did not let up," Gwaethe said. "I came looking for you and came upon your men this morning. The mountainside had collapsed, and you were buried."

Exmund cleared his throat. "Princess Gwaethe insisted we dig until we found you, Captain. We all thought she was wrong to hope, but here you are."

Jacques swallowed thrice before he spoke. "It seems I owe you my life, Princess Gwaethe," he said, his voice husky, his gaze spearing her as though he would drag all her darkest secrets from her.

She straightened her spine and threw back her shoulders. "Your men should not have abandoned you."

"They followed orders when they rode away," he said. "I would never wish for more lives to be lost in the search for me."

Gwaethe sucked in a breath. "It was not an option to abandon you until there was no hope, until you were found dead or alive. You are important in the fight against Faenwelar, and your recovery fills me with gladness."

Isiloe snorted. Gwaethe turned on her. "Leave us!" She glared at her cousin until Isiloe and Exmund left the tent.

"One day she will go too far, and I will have no choice but to discipline her," Gwaethe said.

Jacques smiled. "She is very loyal, despite her impertinence. I think she is safe."

"We were discussing you and your men, Captain," she said. "I cannot believe you approve of them giving up."

"And I can't believe you chose to come looking for me instead of going home. You were seriously injured and still are. I'm angry you chose to lie to me."

"I did not lie. I changed my mind!"

"You never intended to return home, did you?" Jacques asked, fixing her with piercing blue eyes that almost made her squirm.

Gwaethe's chin rose. "I am an elven princess, not one of your soldiers you can order around and take to task. You should be very glad I came looking. I do not appreciate your attitude."

Jacques frowned. "Very well. We'll discuss this later." He paused to study her. "How are you?"

Suddenly Gwaethe felt every one of the days and nights since her injury, but she would not show him the extent of her weariness. "I am recovering slowly. Isiloe is taking care of me."

"But you don't make it easy for her," Jacques added. "Never mind, Princess, you are free to leave now, and I will spend the next days recovering and then decide the fate of our mission. It seems doomed before we start."

Gwaethe rubbed suddenly tight muscles up the back of her neck. "I am not going home, Jacques. I cannot."

CHAPTER FIVE

Exhaustion lay deep and hard in Jacques's body. He couldn't even lift his head from his saddle, and breathing hurt like fire. He wanted to cough and cough, but he hadn't the energy. And now Gwaethe was here and telling him she was staying. Telling him like he had no choice in the matter.

"You aren't well enough to be here, Princess."

"You aren't either, but you will go on and complete your mission. Why shouldn't I?"

Jacques snorted. "The way I feel now, I might be dead tomorrow."

She grasped his hand and squeezed. Hard. "Please do not say these things. You are strong and must prevail."

"Must prevail so I can help you?"

She dropped her eyes. "It is not only that... I care about you, Jacques. Since the time we first met, there has been friendship between us."

More than friendship. But that could not be allowed to run its course. A flirtation with an elven princess was foolish. He shouldn't waste his time on her. "The friendship of comrades, Princess. You will return home, and I will make my decisions. You can leave at first light."

Anger flared in her dark eyes. "I am going nowhere. This mission means everything to me. I just know Faenwelar is planning to strike, and I fear if he is successful this time, he will win this civil war. That will only lead to him becoming stronger against Thorius."

Jacques frowned. "You think he is after you now?"

"I do not know. It makes sense for him to unite before he takes on the Kingdom again. My faction would have no choice but to fight for him. He knows I would never allow my people to war against the humans, so he must kill me. Perhaps Kain as well."

"Ah, yes, our half-breed elf," Jacques said. "I wouldn't count on *him*, Princess. He seemed rather lukewarm about his elven heritage last time I spoke to him."

"Kain will do what must be done for elves and humans to have peace."

"*You* have to believe that, but I don't. As far as I can see, Jazara is as 'Kingdom' as they come; and now he has a Kingdom wife. You're being pushed out."

"He will never turn his back on us," Gwaethe said, her dark skin pale, her fists bunched by her sides. "Blood ties cannot be denied, even by my brother. He will come to his senses before too long."

"Why would he?" Jacques's cheek stung as Gwaethe slapped him.

"How dare you assume to know how my brother will act? How dare you?"

Jacques rubbed his face. She was strong for a slight woman. "So much for needing my help, Princess. Do you think the way to my heart is through violence?"

Gwaethe snorted. "I care nothing for your heart." She stood, fury in her gaze. "And that was not violent. You have seen nothing, Captain." She swept from the tent, leaving Jacques wondering at her reaction.

The Princess had one hell of a temper when you poked the right areas. He hadn't meant to upset her. His question about why Kain would help her had been an honest one. Jazara was devoted to Alique Zorba. He had known nothing of his elven heritage for thirty years. Jacques imagined it would be supremely difficult to come to terms with the revelation your father had been of another race, let alone a king of that people. He couldn't see Jazara tossing his wife aside to go haring off to defend Gwaethe, a half-sister he had only just met. If Jazara had any hope of regaining his lost footing in the King's eyes, he would think carefully before weighing into Gwaethe's battle.

Which brought him to consider his own predicament. He couldn't continue his mission feeling as ill as he did. He had been plucked from death's door and yearned to return to Brightcastle and regain his health. But this mission could raise his standing with the King if it was successful; it might even lead to a promotion. After all, *that* was the goal, the thing that drove him to get up in the morning and take on whatever he must to get noticed. Ramón Zorba, Guardian of Brightcastle, and Princess Benae had faith in his skills as a leader and had recommended him for this mission when others might have been chosen.

If he rode back to Brightcastle now, the King might send someone else back out, and his chance would be lost. Yes, it was best to continue the mission if possible. But Gwaethe and her elves could not be allowed to take part. He had to convince her to go away, to return home, and not involve herself until she was asked to.

* * *

Gwaethe threw herself down on the log beside Isiloe. "That man is the most infuriating human I have ever had the displeasure to know."

Isiloe snickered. "I could have told you that, cousin. If you had allowed him to die under the mountain, you would not have had to endure him."

Gwaethe cast a sideways look at her. "I almost wish I had."

"He may still die. I have not seen many pulled from the mud and survive, but then it is not a common occurrence."

"I do not wish death on anyone, besides Faenwelar and his leaders." Gwaethe sighed. "I will have to apologize."

"To Faenwelar?" Isiloe's eyes were almost standing on stalks.

Gwaethe laughed. "No, to Jacques."

"You are not making sense. He should be down on his knees offering to be your slave for rescuing him. He owes you his life."

"That may be so. But I just slapped him..."

Isiloe laughed, nodding, her eyes even brighter than usual. "I can almost believe we are related now."

Gwaethe glared at her cousin. Trust Isiloe to be completely unhelpful in this delicate situation. She had slapped the only man who might be able to help her, and he was ill, might even be on his death bed. She closed her eyes against tears at the thought. *Stupid, stupid.* She was making a mess of this when she was usually so in control.

"It is not amusing at all," she said. "He is set on sending us home. It will be most difficult to convince him to help now."

"You are determined to order the world to your own desires," Isiloe said. "That task was always to be a difficult one. However, I am sure you will find a way." She smiled broadly; something Isiloe almost never did.

Gwaethe was lost for words, opening her mouth and closing it several times before she decided she had nothing to say to Isiloe's summary. Her cousin was right. She did like the world and those in it to fall in with her plans; and they usually did. Had she met an immovable object in Jacques? Was he a man she could not mold to fit her desires? And, if that was the case, how would she defeat Faenwelar? She could not return to Selinore without success and hope to keep her position of leadership. Already there were those disgruntled about a female leading the *Lenweri*. Kain was supposed to be in place by now, or at least helping her, a visible male figurehead, even if she was the true leader.

She sighed. Who was she deceiving? Kain would never have agreed to be a puppet. But at least leadership of the *Lenweri* would have stayed within her family. Now it might well pass to Faenwelar if he demonstrated strength and direction.

"What should I do, Isiloe?" she asked. "If I return home it will be seen as a defeat. There may well be rebellion against us." She studied her cousin. "Is there *any* male in our family who could stand against those who will call for a new leader; a male leader?"

Isiloe frowned. "Our uncle is the only male of the blood of Orionkael besides Jazara, and I cannot see *him* as King. Most of the time he cannot even be found." Isiloe referred to their uncle Melandrach who lived alone in the forest and would only emerge for celebrations. He was so reclusive, Gwaethe often forgot his very existence.

"Melandrach would never be accepted. Most have never met him, and those who have think he has lost his mind. I am not certain they are wrong."

"Uncle Mel is as sane as any of us," Isiloe proclaimed, eyes blazing.

Gwaethe smiled. Isiloe and Melandrach had always been close, though for reasons only known to them. Perhaps her cousin had sensed a kindred spirit in the reclusive older elf. Isiloe's choice of the warrior life had ensured she could never isolate herself from others, but she had always been a loner. But musing on Isiloe and Melandrach was not going to get Gwaethe any closer to the decision about what she should do tomorrow when Jacques tried to send her away.

"We cannot return home, that is clear," she said. "If we do, we must be prepared to be challenged unless I can convince Kain to step forward as leader."

"And where is your brother?" Isiloe asked.

"I spoke to him when we were at the lodge, but he was…unhelpful. He would not commit."

"He may yet help. I think you should contact him again."

"I will, as soon as I decide what to do."

"I never thought of you as indecisive, cousin, but lately…"

Gwaethe scowled. Isiloe really did take liberties sometimes. Who did she think commanded this force? "Mind your tongue. My decisions do not just affect me." Trouble was, she *had* been dithering about Kain and Jacques and the right course to take in both cases.

"I have decided I must confront Jacques and tell him in no uncertain terms that we are traveling with him, that I cannot go home, and why. He will understand, and, besides, there is nothing he can do to force me to leave."

Isiloe's face screwed up trying to follow her reasoning. *Wonderful!* She had not even managed to convince her cousin.

"First thing in the morning, I want our group assembled for a trek, and I will tell them we will be accompanying the captain."

"Are you sure this is wise?" Isiloe stood and Gwaethe followed suit. "What if the human makes you back down? You will lose the respect of our people here."

Gwaethe squared her shoulders and lifted her chin. "It is the right thing to do. You will see. Now go to your rest and tell the others to do the same."

Isiloe moved away from the campfire, and Gwaethe went to look in on Jacques. She poked her head through the tent flaps to find him asleep, though he moaned and tossed his head from side to side. As she drew back outside, she said a fervent prayer to her favorite God that Jacques should make a full recovery; then said one to the Goddess whom the Kingdom citizens worshipped.

She tacked on a plea for the Goddess to ensure Jacques listened to her on the morrow.

CHAPTER SIX

Jacques groaned as he awoke the next morning. Even in the dim light of the tent, his eyes protested the glare. How would he face the trek today? Again, he wondered if he should just turn back, but the same arguments assailed him. This was his task, his unit was intact, and the mission remained unfinished. It was even more essential to pursue the *Sis Lenweri* than it had been when he left Brightcastle. The rebel elven leader was enacting his plan, and it seemed Gwaethe and her elves were the target. He should at least return with more intelligence than they currently had.

His head ached just from the effort of thinking. There was also an unpleasant task he had to perform this morning. Gwaethe must be sent home. She would not want to go, but her force was too small now, only seven of them. About the only use they could be to him would be as scouts. He readily conceded the elves moved more stealthily than any human. But as much as he liked Gwaethe, he could not allow her to interfere in his mission. She was injured, as were the bulk of her force. The sooner they parted ways the better.

He stood slowly to a great deal of crashing in his head. It was as if a monkey played the cymbals inside his skull. He breathed deeply, in and out half a dozen times, before the pain dimmed.

"Captain!" Exmund swept into the tent, and Jacques scrunched his eyes up at the flash of light from the cloudy morning outside. "You should not be up and about yet. You had a difficult night and need your rest. Here, sit down at the table and eat something before you fall over."

He *did* feel weak, but he was hungry. *That* was a good sign. As he walked slowly to the breakfast table, a coughing fit struck him, seizing his chest and not subsiding until all he saw was spots of light. He all but fell into the chair. Exmund sponged his face with a damp cloth.

"I told you, sir," he said. "You should be abed. Have some food, and I'll tuck you up nice and warm."

Jacques's heart beat faster than it had ever done after exercise, and the stuff he had coughed up scared him; all brown and green. "Is there more of the potion you said would help stop the fouling of my lungs?"

"There is, Captain, but you must also rest. Another day and we shall see how you fare. Then we may be able to return to Brightcastle."

"Brightcastle isn't our destination," Jacques wheezed, after another coughing spell. "We're riding for Amitania."

Exmund stood before the table like a trout starved of oxygen, his mouth opening and closing. "Please, Captain, think this through. You might die on this trek. It's not worth your life."

Jacques pulled himself together, breath by breath, not inhaling too deeply as that seemed to set off the coughing. He waited until his heart slowed to near normal then took a drink of the watered wine served with breakfast. It soothed his throat, made it easier to swallow the dried bread and cheese. "Get that potion and send the princess to me."

His aide stood there shaking his head until Jacques fixed the man with a stare that brooked no argument. Exmund left the tent with an indignant snap of the flaps.

Moments later, he was back with the medicine, and Gwaethe strode in behind him. She folded her arms across her chest as the corporal fixed the drink, studying him with expressionless eyes. There really was no one as good as an elf at hiding their true feelings, except for Isiloe who had none of the usual elven reserve. He did some studying of his own, allowing his eyes to slide over her long-muscled thighs, past her neat waist and up over a voluptuous bosom not at all hidden by her tunic. When his eyes reached hers, they blazed back at him.

"Stop ogling me like a tavern wench!"

Exmund served the medicine and slipped from the tent.

Jacques gave a small laugh. "I see you're in no better humor this morning. You do look well-rested though, Princess. Are you ready for the trek home?"

She took in a deep breath and blew it out slowly, her eyes still angry. "How are you? I'm glad to see you up and eating, though that coughing sounded terrible. Exmund thinks you should still be in bed."

"He's probably correct, but I can't sit here any longer. You're right that Faenwelar is up to no good. I intend to discover where he is and what his intentions are."

"I shall help you."

He shook his head. "Let me handle this. All of your party are injured except for Isiloe. You're too few to do anything. I'd feel better if you just went home." He should have known it would come down to a fight this morning. He just didn't have the strength in him to argue. *Damn her, catching me as weak as a kitten!*

"I can help," Gwaethe said. "None of the injuries are serious. I think you need elven support to make sure you don't go stumbling into a trap."

"Oh, like you avoided doing the same thing yourself," he snapped. "You don't trust me, I understand that. Unfortunately, you have no choice."

"*You* have no choice about leaving me behind. If you do, I shall just follow, so you may as well agree now and save yourself the aggravation later. I may even save your handsome neck again."

That pulled him up short, but she looked as though she already regretted the comment.

"I am sorry, Jacques. I didn't mean that last part about your neck being handsome. We should keep this on a professional footing. There is no point in getting involved."

"Are you involved, Gwaethe?"

Her eyes darted around the tent. A frown marred her brow. Finally, she sighed and shook her head. "No, I am not. There is no room for you in my life except as a colleague. Let us be civil to each other though."

Jacques was surprised to find himself disappointed in her words. He had never found himself so intrigued by a woman. On some level, they understood each other, even though they were from different races. Despite what she said, there was something between them, and he wished she had been born human. But there was no future with her, not if he wanted to rise to the very top of his profession. If he had ever doubted it, the rejection of Kain Jazara after his elven heritage was revealed should be proof enough of that.

"Quite right," he said. "What shall we do about this impasse? I still believe you should return home."

"I cannot. Should I return home in defeat, I think it would be very bad for the *Lenweri*. There is only me to lead them unless Kain should step forward. I cannot wait for him to do that. If I fail, I am afraid they will turn to Faenwelar. He will know I am on shaky ground, being female, and he will know there is no one else standing in his way." She stared at him, and he saw the desperation that drove her and threatened to undermine her.

"Very well, but there should be no doubt about who is leader of this mission. I have the greater force and the support of the King. You will defer to me in all things."

Gwaethe drew herself up. Jacques wondered if the condition would be too much for her to swallow. It was necessary though. Could she accept him as her commander? Could Isiloe?

She closed her eyes and shook her head, her lips moving but no words coming. Finally, she opened her eyes. "You shall be leader. What would you have me do?"

Jacques let out a long breath. "I thought your elves might act as scouts. You move silently through the forest and should know the country better. Especially since we trek to Amitania."

Her head snapped up. "You think that is where we shall find them?"

"Amitania, by all accounts, is the ideal staging ground for their forces, even though much of it is ruined." Jacques spoke of the Thorian city that had slipped into decline centuries ago. "It's close to the seats of Kingdom power while still being in the northern forests. I think it very likely the *Sis Lenweri* might use it as a base."

"Right under the nose of the Thorian King," Gwaethe said, her eyes narrowed. "It is something Faenwelar *would* do. I had assumed he would keep his base in the far north."

"I could be wrong, but I think it worth exploring."

"Then that is what we shall do." Gwaethe turned on her heel and was gone.

Jacques pushed himself to his feet, wondering how he would ever survive the day ahead, let alone the trip to Amitania.

* * *

Gwaethe led her force along a little-used game trail in the forest. It was almost a week since leaving the hunting lodge and they were within a day and a half of the fabled city of Amitania. She had to admit the human soldiers had learned quickly how to move with stealth. And finding this trail had been a boon. The trees hung silent above them, their tops lost in the thick mist that sent its tendrils reaching for the riders. The humans cast nervous glances up at the fog as if expecting it to pull them into the trees. They were superstitious about everything to do with Amitania, even this forest. She preferred to call the city Elvandang, its elven name, but had refrained out of respect to Jacques.

It *was* eerie, even to an elven princess who had spent all her life in the forest. Heavy mist had the effect of dampening noise, and the silence began to play on the nerves after a time. Isiloe no longer dozed but scanned the forest constantly, and Jacques rode hunched in his cloak, his eyes flicking left and right.

It had been difficult since they left the scene of the landslide. The captain had been too ill to sit on his horse but had insisted on riding. Gwaethe didn't know how he had endured the days in the saddle. Each evening when they called a halt, he had slipped from his horse, rolled himself in a blanket, and fallen asleep.

Exmund was worn to a frazzle, trying to make sure his leader drank the medicine he swore would stave off the fouling of Jacques's lungs and that he ate enough food to get better. So far it seemed to be working as he got stronger every day. Still, he seemed to sleep in his saddle often, and his face still held the gray cast of the gravely ill. She admired him more than she would ever express. He could have given up and gone home to heal, but he had not even considered that. Jacques led by example and that was commendable.

He also argued all the time. Everything she suggested met with a list of reasons why it would not work. She had spent hours explaining her ideas and outlining their advantages during the trip. He protested everything from the selection of their camps, to the trail they should use, and their objectives on arrival in the deserted city. How he had the strength to debate, she simply did not know. And her sixth sense where Jacques was concerned was telling her he was about to appear beside her for the fifth time that day.

"What do you want, Captain?" she asked, not even looking to check it was him.

"How do you do that?" he snapped.

"It is always you who comes to argue with me," she said, sliding her gaze his way. The gloom hid the pallor of his skin, but his cheekbones seemed more pronounced, his cheeks hollower. Her heart ached at the thought this trip might be killing him.

He blew out a short breath. "Someone has to do the planning. You seem to think the important bits will just happen. Have you had any contact with Kain?"

"He comes."

"And?"

"He is around three days behind us," Gwaethe said, filled with happiness that her brother was riding to her aid. She should be resentful that she must depend on a male, but her life had been so hard since the loss of her father. She was sick of shouldering the responsibility for all that happened with the *Lenweri*. It was good to have someone else to rely upon.

"We'll have to be careful if the *Sis Lenweri* do inhabit Amitania," Jacques said. "Three days is a long time to await back up."

"Of course," she said, only half listening.

"Have the scouts brought any news?"

"They have not yet entered the city but will on the next pass. Soon it will be time to make camp. There is a suitable place an hour ahead." She cast her gaze over him again. "You need rest."

Jacques shook his head. "If I stop now, I'll never get going again."

"Jacques!"

"You of all people should understand the need I have to see this through, Princess."

"This need you have is driven by ambition. It is not the same for me at all. I want this for both our nations."

"So noble, Princess, but why do you assume there is no good in my motivation? If it serves me *and* our people, how can that be bad?"

She clenched her hands on the reins, and Rassar threw up his head. She soothed him with a pat on the side of the neck. "Because when it suits you, your help will vanish. All your King must do is give the order, and you will ride away."

Ha! That made him pause and think. Gwaethe could almost see the wheels turning, examining and discarding arguments as he realized she was right.

"You're overthinking this," Jacques said. "I'm here now to help your cause. Just accept that and be done." He turned his horse and rode back down the line.

* * *

Jacques sat wrapped in his cloak and a blanket, staring at the fire, willing sleep to take him. His chest ached, and he desperately needed rest. The Goddess only knew how he had come this far. His body healed slowly; too slowly. He wondered if tomorrow morning would bring the same hacking cough that brought up matter full of blood, the smell of which turned his stomach. Was there a little less each day? He hoped so, but he knew in his heart he wouldn't last long in a battle.

The knowledge weighed heavily upon him. He should have turned back after the landslide. A less stubborn leader would have known his limits, and now he was less than a day from his objective. But would the *Sis Lenweri* be there? He kept telling himself a battle was not the aim, but one could arise any time if they were spotted.

His eyelids had begun to droop when he saw Gwaethe across the campsite. She sat on a rock, sharpening her sword. Jacques watched her body move in the rhythm of running the blade over the whetstone. He had done the chore every day of his working life, but, when Gwaethe did it, she looked like poetry in motion. His mind wandered, imagining a time when they could be together, when she would wait at home for him to return from a mission. He imagined her in his bed often enough, screaming her satisfaction as they made love. He got hard thinking of it. But, of course, sex between them was forbidden.

Everything but a professional relationship was prohibited. It didn't stop his traitorous mind from playing out scenes in his sleep. It didn't stop him from watching her every move when he thought she wouldn't notice. Jacques knew he had to move on, had to focus on the mission and working with Gwaethe to accomplish the removal of the *Sis Lenweri* from Thorius. At least they could work together on that goal.

* * *

At midday the next day, Gwaethe drew her horse to a halt as Isiloe cantered toward her. Her cousin slid to a standstill with barely the rustle of a leaf.

"Greetings, cousin," she said, placing a fist over her heart.

Gwaethe mirrored the gesture. "What news, Isiloe?"

"As we thought, the city is held by our enemies, but I cannot tell how many without further surveillance." She rubbed her eyes, keeping them closed for a time as if they hurt. "We cannot enter the city from this side as it is heavily patrolled. My advice is to circle around to the north and enter from the western side. That is the least patrolled as the outer wall in that area is mainly intact."

"Pass the word down the line. We stay in the trees and circle to the north and west —." There was a masculine clearing of the throat behind her.

"Are you forgetting who's in charge here, Princess?" Jacques asked.

Damn the man! He is the most silent human I have ever encountered! She turned to him and shock hit her at the pallor of his skin. How did he go on in that condition? "I am sorry, Captain. I keep forgetting you are here and need to be consulted."

"Well, don't forget!" Jacques said, his brows drawn, and intense blue eyes angry. "You're here because of me. I would think *that* was rather hard to forget."

Isiloe hissed. "Do not disrespect my cousin! You owe her your life!"

A flush crept across Jacques's pale cheeks and pulled up the hood of his cloak. For once, Gwaethe allowed Isiloe to put Jacques in his place. His barbs hit deep when they were aimed at her. She wished they didn't, but it was a fact of life.

"I would ask you, Princess, to ensure in future you defer to me in all decisions. I will, of course, consult you on anything major."

Gwaethe stared at him just long enough to see him adjust his seat. Good! Let him squirm! "I apologized, Captain, and I will endeavor to remember."

Jacques nodded curtly and turned his gaze to Isiloe. "You've advised coming at the city from the west?"

She dipped her head. "I have seen our enemy but have no idea of their numbers."

Jacques took a deep breath, which turned into a coughing fit he tried to suppress. "Send the scouts to blaze a trail through the forest to approach the city from the west. We need to find a suitable base to work from. We'll follow two hours behind."

Isiloe nodded, after getting approval from Gwaethe, and moved off down the line, stopping every few riders to relay the plan and selecting more men to act as scouts. Gwaethe clucked to get her horse moving. Jacques fell in beside her. The path was narrow, so their legs brushed together from time to time. It made her very aware of him.

"We should find a clearing and rest for an hour while the scouts search," she said, desperate for something to say to break the uncomfortable silence.

"Always talking about rest, Princess," Jacques said. "Are you tired?"

"Exhaustion hangs on you like a cloak! You need to look after yourself. You nearly died!"

"I think I might still be dying."

That remark was telling! He never revealed weakness to anyone. "Then stop this and go home. I will take the troops and do the job. Kain will soon be here to help. They will listen to him even if not to me."

"I can't do what you ask."

"Oh!" If Gwaethe had been on foot, she would have stamped one. The man was infuriating! "You are so stubborn! Will this mission benefit from your death?"

"Of course not! But I feel in my gut time is precious. If we don't discover Faenwelar's scheme now it will be too late. It's high time we eradicated the High Prince and his ilk from Thorius, from this entire region, no less."

Gwaethe froze at his words. Just what did Jacques mean when he spoke of Faenwelar? The High Prince led more than half of the elven race. They couldn't afford to exterminate all *Sis Lenweri*. "Eradication is a strong word. Tell me you will have mercy on his followers."

"Mercy? On the elves who wage war on Thorius? I have been given no such brief. I'm to find and destroy. Surely you see there is no wisdom in picking and choosing who amongst his followers is worthy of living?"

Gwaethe ignored the cold stone that had formed in her gut at his words. "When Faenwelar fought my father and mortally wounded him, it was elves loyal to Father who helped him escape to raise the alarm. There are those who will return to the fold if given the chance. We must only defeat Faenwelar and his closest supporters. The rest will be mine!"

Jacques shook his head. "I remember when you told me you stood on shaky ground, that being female meant you couldn't guarantee the loyalty of even your own faction. How can you hope for the *Sis Lenweri* to return to your side if Faenwelar is defeated?"

"I hope because it is my only choice. I must bring the *Sis Lenweri* back into the fold because it is the elven people's only hope for survival. We can't afford to lose half of our race. I won't stand by and see them slaughtered."

"Then we have a problem."

"*You* have a problem if you think I will help you slaughter elves!"

"Just a minute, Princess," Jacques said. "You've asked me for help in finding Faenwelar. I'm offering that help, but am bound by my orders from the King and General Formosa. I'm to locate Faenwelar's headquarters and report back to the crown. At that point, the Kingdom forces will move in to destroy the High Prince, and there's nothing you can do to stop it."

She fought to keep her composure. How could she have been so wrong about this man? She stopped her horse, turned in the saddle, and grabbed hold of his arm.

"I will fight you tooth and nail if you kill one more elf than you have to," she said. "You may take my word on that."

* * *

The campsite filled with men and elves who went about the daily chores of the warrior when stopped for any time: sharpening weapons, building campfires, sleeping, boiling water for tea or porridge. Jacques stood to one side, wondering what the next days would bring and second guessing his choices thus far. He should be home in front of a roaring fire now.

Gwaethe approached. "Get rest while you can." Her tone was brusque, strained after the harsh words they had exchanged.

He looked upon her exotic beauty and was seized by a desperate urge to kiss her. *This will never do! Our relationship must be professional only!*

"Would you take a walk with me, Princess?" He didn't wait for an answer but left the clearing, heading back up the path they had previously taken.

After a handful of paces, he heard the light fall of her steps behind him. He walked on a little way further to be sure they wouldn't be heard and then turned to her, surprising an uncertain expression on her face. He looked at her, lost for words, wondering if this had been wise.

Gwaethe's face changed from uncertain to baffled then outright annoyed. "Is this some human game, to lure me out here and just stare?"

Jacques shook himself from his daze and reached for her hand. Her whole body stiffened. "I don't mean to play games. All I seek to do is clear the air between us."

She frowned. "There is always clear air between us, Jacques."

"I don't think there is," he said. "From the first time I saw you, I felt drawn to you, and I think you felt the same."

Her frown deepened. "Where are you leading with this? If you are seeking to confuse me, you have succeeded."

"I need to place our relationship on a footing we can both live with. It must be professional, not personal. There can be nothing physical between us. We both know it would never work."

Gwaethe positively scowled. She stepped toward him, bringing them so close he felt her warm breath against his face. "So, it will not work?" she said, raising her hand to slide it down his cheek.

He nearly choked on his spit. "You know it." He sounded like a bullfrog, hoarse with lust.

Her hand worked its way round to the back of his neck, her firm grip ensnaring him. "You brought me out here to let me know you are not interested in a romantic attachment with me, to advise that whatever desire we feel for one another will never amount to anything."

Jacques released a long breath. *Thank the Goddess!*

"I knew you would see sense," he said. "This thing between us will only get in the way of what we must do. As much as we might wish there could be more, it can never be."

She leaned even closer, if it were possible to do so. "I could change your mind so quickly you would never know what happened," she breathed. "You have convinced yourself you can ignore the attraction that simmers between us, but what if I wish no such thing?"

"Surely, Princess…Gwaethe," Jacques said, his heart already pounding fit to split his chest, "you jest."

Her lips met his; it was a chaste kiss, but one which swept all thoughts of professionalism from his mind. She held him there, lips fused to lips, her body pressed against his until she must feel his arousal clearly and undeniably. That virginal kiss stirred him more than the kiss of any other woman he had enjoyed in the past.

Her lips fell away, but she kept her face just inches from his. "I never joke about matters of the heart." With those whispered words, she was gone, back up the path to the clearing they had chosen for their stop.

Jacques watched the sway of her hips until she was lost in the gloom and then slowly followed.

* * *

Gwaethe stood before the campfire, sipping on her tea and wondering what had possessed her to be so provocative with Jacques. She had acted like a camp tart! Not that she knew about such things. She had little experience to fall back on, just a casual flirtation here and there with elven suitors. They had soon discovered her people and her job meant too much to her to sacrifice for love. Her career and commitment to the elven nation meant she rarely indulged in affairs of the heart. The flirtations and agony of love were not for her. And so, she had scared all suitors off; until now. Now this human told her they could not be involved, and she had kissed him, she had initiated contact and enjoyed it. Gwaethe had wanted to deepen the kiss, but that would have been too forward, and Jacques might have rejected it. She couldn't take rejection from him; she wouldn't open the door to the possibility.

But why had she kissed him at all? Was it because he had written off the possibility of anything deeper between them? It had hurt when he said that, as if he could decide not to pursue his feelings for her. *He has feelings for me!* Something inside her had spoken to him and been acknowledged. Why then did he try to reject it? If he accepted her, finally, what would that do to her life, to his life, and to the cause they worked toward? Their relationship at its deepest could only ever be sexual, could not extend to the deep and loving feelings of a life couple. There was no place in this world for that.

Gwaethe was tempted by Jacques. She felt more deeply for him than she had ever felt for any male. He had integrity and ambition which she understood. He had sensitivity which she needed in a mate. But would he ultimately avoid any entanglement with her? And would she have been wiser to agree with his assessment of their relationship? Why had she thrown down the gauntlet?

She watched him as he returned to camp, his eyes flickering everywhere but at her. She had unnerved him and that, in the end, was her desired outcome. Perhaps now he would realize he could not keep her at arm's length, could not relegate their relationship to the purely professional. It was complicated and neither of them really knew where they should draw the line; at least she didn't. She resolved to explore this with Jacques over the coming days.

* * *

Jacques had put Gwaethe's extraordinary behavior to the side and guided his band into position on the western edge of Amitania. Gwaethe insisted on calling it *Elvandang*, but since the city was first built by humans, Jacques didn't see the sense in giving it an elven name.

They had found a cave large enough to accommodate their entire band, but the horses had been moved to a clearing further back in the forest. He worried about them being discovered by the elves who held Amitania.

They had experienced few concerns in their journey, their scouts helping them to avoid two patrols of *Sis Lenweri*. From tonight, they would infiltrate the city, or the elves would, with humans for support and backup. All except Isiloe would be involved; with her white hair, she was instantly recognizable as Gwaethe's cousin. Jacques worried for Gwaethe and her band of five other elves and knew he would feel helpless when they entered the city.

In another two days, Kain would be on hand to help, but he would only be of assistance if they decided to storm the city and capture Faenwelar. Jacques still didn't know what to do. His brief was to find the *Sis Lenweri* High Prince and ascertain his intent, but surely capturing the rebel elven leader would go a long way to winning favor with the King?

Gwaethe approached. "All is in readiness, Captain. We enter in two groups of three. Isiloe will remain behind with you. Know that she is my representative. You will please listen to her advice." She stared unblinking, waiting for his response.

"I'll listen to her." *Doesn't mean I'll take her advice.* "Be careful, Princess."

That brought more staring from the stunning elven woman. She knew how to put a man off kilter.

"We will join the patrols, get the lay of the city and where the center of power is likely to be. No one will notice the small differences between my people and the *Sis Lenweri* at night."

Jacques nodded. "I wish you a safe night and look forward to speaking with you at dawn."

Gwaethe inclined her head and left, immediately joining her group before melting into the darkness. The humans detailed to patrol the outer perimeter had already departed and would communicate with the elves via night animal noises. Half his men were involved; five groups of three. If they heard the distress calls of the rabbit or the frog, they would reform into one larger group and enter the city, while two men were dispatched to alert Jacques.

* * *

Gwaethe crouched in the deep shadow of a stone wall and strained her ears for sounds of approaching elven patrols. It was eerie in the city, piles of rubble obscuring all but the widest streets, and little light spilling from the windows of residences. The odd quiet unnerved her. If here was a city of thousands of elven soldiers, why was it so still and silent? Was it always like this, or did her enemy know she was coming? A worm of fear slid its way up her spine and lodged in the base of her skull. They were so few, and their enemy many and ruthless. Faenwelar cared nothing for the destruction he wreaked on his society. It was clear all he cared for was ultimate power. That was why he had killed her father.

Her heart ached at the reminder. If Orionkael was alive, Gwaethe would not be in this position. He had lived and breathed leadership. She, on the other hand, was not ready to lead the *Lenweri*, and Kain was not prepared to govern either. So what would the outcome be? She shook the thoughts from her mind. She could not allow them to undermine her confidence. It would be as it always was; one step at a time would see her move forward and solve the towering problems of her people. But she was so tired of always being the one to take the lead, and even Jacques, whom she was counting on for help, had a very different agenda.

The soft scuff of leather on stone alerted her to the approach of a patrol, and she hissed to warn her two companions. As the group of *Sis Lenweri* passed their hiding spot, Gwaethe stood and tagged onto the end, hoping the three extra elves would go unnoticed. Now all they had to do was locate Faenwelar and gain intelligence around his next move.

CHAPTER SEVEN

Years of campaigns had taught Jacques to stay busy once a mission was underway. He sat at the front of the cave, making notes on a map of Amitania. True, it was a copy of an ancient map from a time when the city thrived, which was why there needed to be adjustments. Broken walls provided new escape routes, and any streets with rubble might trap them when they finally entered in force. Yes, there were many changes that needed to be made to this old map.

Isiloe rode back and forth between the cave and the human patrols, bringing information as it came in. There had been no news of Gwaethe or her scouts. He reminded himself she was a soldier, trained for just this mission. She had all the necessary skills. Why then did this nagging worry eat at him? Normally he'd be out with his men, but he'd be a liability in his current state of health. Someone would end up having to rescue him, and they couldn't afford the distraction. Besides, this was merely an infiltration for the purpose of gaining information, not an all-out assault.

He would sit here, collect the intelligence, and plan for the time when they could eradicate this troublesome High Prince and his band of elven scum. Jacques frowned at the thought. Gwaethe believed some, perhaps many, of the *Sis Lenweri* could be brought back into her elven faction. Was she right? Or would those elves recovered cause more trouble in the future? Would it, as he believed, be better for the *Sis Lenweri* to be wiped out in the interests of future peace in Thorius? Gwaethe had drawn a line in the sand on this issue, and there would be conflict in future if Jacques stepped over it. He respected Gwaethe, but he doubted his King would see things her way. And he would be stuck in the middle!

That was why he had tried to speak to her about keeping their relationship on a professional footing. It was the only way they might negotiate through this difference of opinions; of philosophies. But she had refused to agree, as if they could pursue a fling while digging the Kingdom out of this hole? They couldn't, and she would see that eventually.

The trouble was, his mind became jumbled whenever Gwaethe was near. Just the sound of her voice did wild things to his heart, not to mention other body parts. Jacques had lost count of the number of times he had told himself to forget her; that she had no place in his life other than professionally, and that his destiny was serving Thorius with everything he had in him. His parents would arrange his marriage to a suitable woman of noble birth. He would be the second man in his family line to lead the King's army - General Vorasava II - earning himself everything he had ever wanted from life.

Isiloe returned with the latest information which she relayed concisely. He couldn't fault her work. "Thank you, Isiloe. That will be all."

"I am worried."

"About what?" Jacques asked, only half his attention on her words.

"It is too quiet," she said. "There should be more movement and light, more of the small noises that make a city."

"It's abandoned, Isiloe, I assume that accounts for the quiet."

She shook her head. "By all we have learned, there are thousands of elves in there preparing for war, and yet it feels almost deserted."

"They'd hardly want to give themselves away," Jacques said, thinking on the run. "Perhaps they have a blackout in place?"

"That is certainly the way this place feels, but I still don't like it."

Jacques took a long breath. "Hopefully the conditions make it easier for Gwaethe and her band."

Isiloe shook her head again and turned away. Despite her silver hair, she disappeared into the trees in the blink of an eye.

Her words left Jacques unsettled. He respected elven instinct, especially when it related to their own people. If this was unusual then he would be wise to take Isiloe's intuition into consideration. He looked to the east, trying to ascertain how close they were to dawn. The moon had slipped beneath the tallest trees, and there was the faintest lightening of the sky. There was no need to panic. He would wait until it was light, and all the patrols returned to the safety of the cave. They would know more when they had information from those who had infiltrated the *Sis Lenweri* watch.

An hour later, the only elf who had returned was Isiloe. Jacques paced back and forth across the opening of the cave, scanning the trees for signs of movement. Isiloe stood with him, still, though grumbling to herself.

Jacques stopped and turned to the diminutive elf. "And you are certain no one heard anything from Gwaethe and her band after they left?"

Isiloe hissed at him. At least it stopped her muttering. "How many times do I have to tell you? I have questioned all the humans, and there was no report. They are all gone."

"Maybe they have successfully integrated themselves into Faenwelar's forces. We may hear from them during the day."

Isiloe looked at him with undisguised disdain. "There are two females in that band. Females are rare in *Sis Lenweri* soldiering groups. In full light, Gwaethe and her companion will stick out like a crimson cloak in the snow. We must go in and rescue them!"

Jacques held up his hand. Amazingly, Isiloe fell silent. "Panic will help no one. The Princess is resourceful and may at this very moment be hiding within the city with her comrades."

Isiloe opened and closed her mouth like a trout out of water. "Yes, perhaps." Her eyes were wide; fear blazed from them. Jacques had never seen Isiloe fearful before, and he had seen her in battle, had seen her captured by his own forces. "But I fear the worst." She snapped her mouth shut as if speaking her fears would bring them to fruition.

"*Ramar* Isiloe," Jacques said, "we will wait all day if we must, but I will have faith in Gwaethe for at least this day. If there is no sign of her over the next twenty-four hours, then we must revise our plans. Until then, you must wait."

Jacques walked to the back of the cave, determined to rest, so he could lead his force into the fray if needed.

Jacques knew there was something wrong. All day and night had passed without hearing anything from their scouts. His men had patrolled the perimeter of the city during the hours of darkness, and no communication had been made to them from within. They had spied several *Sis Lenweri* patrols in the perimeter of the city, but none had contained their elves.

He had agreed to Isiloe accompanying his men in order to ensure they didn't miss anything, and had made Exmund stay with him instead. His aide had spent hours thumping his chest to clear the foul liquid that welled from his lungs each day. It had helped, for he breathed easier already. *I must get my health back.*

It was also good to be encamped instead of on the road. He already felt more alive than he had on arrival. But dawn had brought no sign of his elven band. Today the King's army should arrive and, with it, Kain Jazara. Jacques was not looking forward to telling him he had lost Gwaethe. Also, he must spare some of his men to meet the army when it arrived.

"What are his aims?" Jacques mused, gazing at the few towers of Amitania tall enough to see from their vantage point. The tallest tower was still intact but was obscured from where they sat.

Isiloe appeared in front of him. "I have an idea."

She never called him 'Captain', or Vorasava … or anything really. "Yes, Ramar."

"I will infiltrate the city on my own and discover where they have Gwaethe. I know I can find her and bring her out."

"No, I can't spare you. I'll have soldiers here over the next day and will need you as the only elven intelligence I have at my disposal."

She frowned. "I will be back by the time they arrive, and I will have the others with me. I know I can do this."

Jacques wished he had as much faith as Isiloe. "Absolutely not. I need you here. If you wish to help, relieve one of the sentries." He cast his gaze back to the city, and, when he turned again, she was gone.

Jacques chose a force of ten men to escort the army to Amitania. That left him with twenty as protection. Isiloe would accompany the escort to aid Kain Jazara. He looked forward to seeing those two butting heads again. Jacques secretly thought Isiloe hated Kain because he was a rival for Gwaethe's affections and loyalty. Isiloe saw herself as Gwaethe's right hand, so Gwaethe's insistence she needed Kain must seem like a rejection to Isiloe. Personally, Jacques thought the elven princess needed both of her kin, especially now with all the chaos Faenwelar had caused.

He went in search of the escort party which should be almost ready to leave, Exmund hot on his heels. Sergeant Dodlan saw him coming and met him halfway.

"The elven woman, Isiloe, is nowhere to be found, Captain," the man said.

Jacques cast his eyes to the heavens. He should have predicted this might happen. She was so headstrong.

"We can't worry about that now," Jacques said. "You're in charge here, Dodlan. I'll go and meet the army in your stead." He retrieved his horse and led his small force southwards through the forest.

He rode wrapped in his own thoughts and with a sense of impending doom. Would they underestimate the *Sis Lenweri* again? They had before, and it had been at great cost even though the King's men had prevailed. Now, they would fight in a tumbledown city against an enemy who knew the terrain well. How many soldiers would Kain Jazara bring with him and would they win the day? He refused to listen to the nagging voice that worried about Gwaethe. She could take care of herself.

Around midday, the scouts returned with word they had contacted the army. It was being led by General Formosa, another man Jacques was acquainted with. Josef Formosa had risen to power after the revelations of Kain Jazara's elven blood. He had a fiery temperament, and Jacques worried at such a delicate operation being entrusted to an untried leader. Kain was also present, so perhaps he would keep Formosa under control.

He ordered a brief camp be made while they awaited the army. He longed for a nap but chose instead to take a bite of lunch and a mug of tea. Exmund clucked around him like a mother hen, making sure he was warm and had enough to eat.

"I'm well, Exmund. See to yourself. We'll be on the move again soon enough."

The young man moved off grumbling, and Jacques smiled to himself. He felt lucky to have such a devoted aide.

They didn't have long to wait before the soft thud of hoof beats floated to them through the trees. Formosa appeared on his white stallion, surrounded by his usual group of followers. Kain Jazara rode a black stallion but kept to himself out on the left flank. Jacques was astounded to see that Lady Alique, and another woman, rode with him. The last time he had seen Lady Alique she had been close to death. How could Jazara risk his wife on a mission like this?

He approached the General and dismounted. "Greetings, General Formosa. I'm glad to see you. I trust you had a safe journey from Wildecoast."

Kain dismounted, but the General stayed on his horse as did his men. "Quite safe, Vorasava. It's good to see you again. What's the state of play?"

"We've confirmed *Sis Lenweri* in the city, General. They are keeping a low profile. We've infiltrated their ranks with our own elves."

"Thorius has elven warriors, does it? I think not. What is the news from your so-called elven scouts?"

Jacques ground his teeth. "I've not heard from them since they left."

Kain stepped forward. "Gwaethe?"

"I'm sorry, Jazara, but she's with them."

Kain glanced up at Formosa and then back at his lady. Alique, a gifted healer, was Formosa's cousin but also, of course, Gwaethe's sister-in-law. Jacques imagined it must be difficult for Lady Jazara to juggle the two roles when Formosa held so much antipathy for the elven race. "You've heard nothing?" Kain asked.

Jacques shook his head, his gut tightening. From Kain's words, he assumed Gwaethe hadn't communicated with her brother via her ring. "Isiloe has gone in after them"

Kain groaned. "We need to get moving before this blows up in our faces. They must know we're coming or at least suspect some force if they've captured Gwaethe. I just hope they don't know who they've got."

Jacques had been hoping the same thing. If the *Sis Lenweri* knew they had the elven Princess, there was no telling what their next move might be. "We can't let them escape with her. We need to surround the city and squeeze them from all sides. How many men do you have?"

The General cleared his throat. "Look at you two! Devising strategy without any regard for who leads this force. I expected better of you, Vorasava!"

Jacques swallowed his pride and bowed. "Sorry, General. Go ahead."

Formosa cleared his throat again. "That's better. To answer your question, I have six hundred men with me, three hundred archers amongst them. I also have a band of engineers, so, if we must tunnel or pull down a wall, we are well equipped. We have enough food with us for three weeks and more on the way. When I got wind of your plight, I convinced the King we should move quickly to secure Amitania. This time, I'll get Faenwelar or die in the attempt." The men surrounding Formosa nodded.

Jacques was somewhat surprised at the level of preparation that had gone into Formosa's mission. Perhaps he had underestimated the man? However, by the look on Kain's face, *he'd* rather kill Formosa than take orders from him.

"Very good, General," Jacques said. "If you don't mind, I suggest your men dismount and secure or muffle any equipment that will make noise. Also, if they could tie sacks over the horses' hoofs it would be ideal. The usual rules of stealth apply."

Formosa scowled at Jacques, but turned to relay the information to his aides. "No talking and cold camp, men. We'll feast when we are victorious." The aides left to spread the word.

Jacques joined Kain Jazara. "The Princess and five other elves entered the city the night before last. They were to split into two groups to join patrols, get the lay of the land, and gather any intelligence they came across. They didn't return."

"I haven't heard from Gwaethe in two days. I thought it was odd."

Jacques glanced at Alique then back to Kain. "I can't guarantee the safety of your good wife and her maid, Jazara. I can't believe you allowed them to accompany you."

Kain gave a snort of laughter. "Allowed? Once she knew where I was to travel, there was no denying Alique. Believe me, I tried to stop her, especially after what happened six months ago. She's barely healed."

Alique had been injured in the last *Sis Lenweri* battle and had hovered between life and death for over a week. Jazara needed his head examined for bringing her! "Just keep her out of the way. I won't have her death, or her maid's, on my conscience."

"Good luck with that, Jacques."

"I mean it, Jazara. I already have Gwaethe and Isiloe missing."

Kain nodded grimly. "I understand, believe me."

Jacques paced back and forth, unable to quell the unease that dogged him. "What if the Princess is spirited away to the north and we can't get her back? What if they kill her?"

Kain gripped his forearm. "You and I are not going to allow that to happen, Jacques. Gwaethe is too important. I can't even think about losing her when I've only just found her."

"Funny way you have of showing it," Jacques snapped.

Kain gave him an odd look. "What is it to you? This hasn't been easy you know. But what would a noble like you know of the trials of others? I'll just bet no one has ever stained your bloodline."

"I understand more than you think." Jacques couldn't say more without revealing his regard for Gwaethe. He had pondered more than once how his parents might deal with an elven daughter-in-law. But, as quickly as that speculation arose, he killed it, knowing Gwaethe and he were not destined to be together.

"Sure you do," Kain said, his tone disdainful. "What intelligence do you have on Faenwelar?" He spoke quietly for Jacques's ears only.

"Very little. The city is dark at night and minimal patrols are out. During the day there is smoke from cooking fires and the sound of sword play from the center of town. I've been trying to bring an old map I have up to date, based on the information my men have gained from surveillance from outside the city."

"We don't know much then," Kain said, staring off through the trees. "Formosa won't be much help. I've never met a more impulsive man. You'd think being made general would have sated his ambition, but he has a fire in his gut over the *Sis Lenweri*."

"They almost killed his cousin," Jacques said.

Kain shook his head. "If that was the cause, I'd be the first to join him. I've put my revenge on hold for now, but with Formosa it's not about revenge. I don't understand what drives him."

"I think I do." Jacques wasn't about to explain to Kain what drove Formosa. Ambition had an ugly side, especially when it ran unchecked. Jacques hoped he would be able to rein in his own zeal if he had to.

"So, what do you recommend we do now?" Kain asked

"As I see it, we have two priorities," Jacques said, his voice still low. "Neutralize Faenwelar and get Gwaethe back. Formosa is unlikely to agree with the second, so it may be up to you and me to see it through."

Kain extended his hand. Jacques seized his forearm in the warrior's grip. "I'm with you," Kain said. "Whatever happens, we need to see Gwaethe safe."

"Mount up!" The call begun by Formosa was echoed down the line, just loud enough to reach a dozen horsemen and be relayed along.

Jacques was impressed with the discipline of the King's soldiers and said so.

"I trained them," Kain said, "they'd better be good." His grim visage said more than words how much he missed overseeing the army; how much he resented relinquishing control to a lesser man.

Jacques mounted and led the army forward through the trees, Kain by his side. Six Brightcastle soldiers moved forward to scout, and the remaining formed a guard around Jacques, Kain and the ladies. Formosa needed no extra guard with his cronies dispersed around him. He rode on the right flank in silence, aloof from Kain and Jacques.

There was not a word spoken as they traveled north through the forest. They picked the wider game trails and paths rather than forging new ones. There was less noise that way. Jacques would not have believed six hundred men and horses could travel so silently. They took their meals on horseback and were within an hour of the city when night fell.

Again, the word was passed down the line, horses were fed and tethered; water was fetched from the streams that ran close by, and a cold, dark camp was prepared. Men simply lay beside their mounts, wrapping themselves in their blankets and cloaks. Jacques was thankful it was autumn, not winter, for this would not have been possible in the colder months. It would still be an uncomfortable night, however.

Jacques, Kain, and Alique stayed up later than the rest. They sat in a huddle, trying to plan for the morrow.

"Lady," Jacques said to Alique, "it's good to see you so well. The last I saw, you were clinging to life after the battle with the *Sis Lenweri*. Now you're back fighting them."

"It's kind of you to say so, Captain," Alique said, "but I'm far from fully healed." The beautiful blonde lady did indeed look tired, and

Jacques had noticed her maid, a young woman called Julli, helping Alique with everyday tasks. "I fear I may never be my old self. But I'll be healthy enough to do my job, and that's all that matters."

Kain growled beside her. "If anything happens to you on this trip, I won't be responsible for my actions."

Alique laid her hand on his arm. "I learned my lesson last time, my dear. I will stay well back, look after the injured, and mind my own business." She appeared the obedient wife, but Jacques knew it was far from the truth.

"I certainly hope that's the case, Lady Jazara, and you won't suddenly go haring off after Gwaethe or some such mission." Jacques bore the brunt of Alique's disdainful stare for his remark, but considered he had to make it clear she had her place; and it was not at the front.

"I've said I will mind my place, Captain; now let that be the end of this discussion."

Jacques was aware of Kain's smirk as he was put soundly in his place.

"I do, however," Alique continued, "want to know how you will rescue my sister-in-law, Gwaethe. She means the world to us and must be returned in the quickest possible time."

"I assure you everything will be done to achieve this. Your husband and I have already discussed the matter and are completely in agreement."

"In agreement on what?" Josef Formosa had approached close enough to hear their discussion.

Alique looked up at her cousin. "Princess Gwaethe must be fetched back from the *Sis Lenweri*."

Josef smirked at her. "Of course, cousin, the Princess shall be saved if at all possible. She is not, however, my priority."

Alique started to stand, but Jacques raised his hand and stood instead. He turned to face Formosa. "Princess Gwaethe is the key to a harmonious relationship with the elves, General. I intend to see she is rescued with all haste."

"Well, *I* intend to see the *Sis Lenweri* driven from this region and as many as possible never draw breath again, *Captain*," Formosa said, blue eyes narrowed and hands on hips. "And before you remind me you have orders from the King, let me inform you those orders are now superseded by my own."

Jacques looked Formosa in the eye. What he saw there made his blood run cold. "And they are?"

"My orders are to seek out the *Sis Lenweri* and their leaders and wipe every one of them from the Kingdom." Formosa paused to let his words sink in. "So you see, Vorasava, your little intelligence gathering mission is ended. As far as I'm concerned, you can stay or go as you please, but if you aren't with me then you are against me." He stepped closer until Jacques could feel his breath on his cheek. "Don't get in my way."

Formosa turned and stalked off. Jacques turned back to the others, not surprised to find them angry.

"I can't believe how he has changed over the years," Alique said. "He was always pompous, but now I fear he is out of control."

Kain frowned. "His rise to the rank of general has gone to his head. The King could not have made a worse choice. And this has come to pass because of my elven heritage."

"No matter all of that," Jacques said. "How do we combat him? How do we ensure he doesn't make this a whole lot worse than it already is?"

Kain stood. "You and I, that's how." He turned to Alique. "You must try to stay close to him. He will tolerate that, and you may get wind of his intentions before he can act on them. Jacques and I will oversee the larger mission and influence it where we can. And we'll launch our own operation to rescue Gwaethe and the others."

"Jazara, you must have men loyal to you in the army," Jacques said. "Men who will work with you if you ask them?"

Kain walked back and forth across the small area in which they stood. "I'm not sure how many. Some will support me."

"This is delicate, man," Jacques said. "We'll never get Gwaethe out if he goes in there aiming to annihilate. It's fighting on the run, not reasoned strategy. We need more time to plan."

"We have no time. Get the map out, and you and I will try to salvage something from this."

They talked deep into the night. By the time he closed his eyes, Jacques had more hope that, in Kain, he had a man he could count on to get his elven princess out of Amitania.

CHAPTER EIGHT

The cell was cold, wet, and dark. Gwaethe did not mind the dark, but the scuttle of roaches and the squeak of rats was beginning to grate on her nerves. Was it only two days since she had infiltrated the patrol? It felt more like ten. She and her fellow elves had underestimated the cunning of the *Sis Lenweri*. When the patrols had reported at dawn, Gwaethe and the other five elves had been immediately seized and brought before High Prince Faenwelar and his son Prince Gorin.

As Gwaethe had looked upon the *Sis Lenweri* gathered in the central square, she had seen many who had been loyal to her father. Some she knew had helped him escape when he had been attacked by Faenwelar while on a peace mission. None of them had met her eye, and none of them had raised a hand to help as she was tied to a pole and flogged; scourged until her back was afire and bleeding, flayed until she screamed for mercy.

Her pride shriveled at the memory of being broken, shattered by the son of her father's enemy. Yes, it had been Prince Gorin himself who had taken the whip and doled out her punishment. Her hands curled into claws as she relived every lash, felt the pain again and again, heard the laughter from her hateful torturer. And no one had tried to stop it. Had she been wrong? Were all the *Sis Lenweri* beyond saving? Was this the end of the elven race? The thought of it brought a sob deep from her chest.

I have been wrong to trust them, she thought. *Wrong*. She was on her own with no one to speak to. The elves who were with her had been murdered before her eyes. And what for? For believing in peace? For loving Gwaethe and following her? She had not been able to save them. The only way she had been able to bear the flogging was thinking she was sparing her comrades by doing so. She had gladly chosen the scourging, when given the choice. But she had not known the rules. She had not known Faenwelar's evil intent.

When the lashing stopped, the real torture had begun. Gwaethe was turned to face the crowd, and her five comrades were marched in front of her. Their throats had been slit one by one, and their bodies thrown from the wooden platform into the crowd. Gwaethe could still see the shock on the faces of the *Sis Lenweri*. The bodies, blood draining from ruined throats, were raised by the High Prince's guards and paraded through the crowd, while Faenwelar warned them this was what happened to traitors.

And while all this had transpired, Gwaethe was powerless to stop it. Indeed, it was their faith in her that had led to their deaths. She was to blame. So many were dead because of her. And while she screamed, they had died, their bodies defiled, their deaths used to secure Faenwelar's power.

She had been so enraptured by her own lofty beliefs that she had underestimated her enemy. She had imagined Faenwelar would fight fairly, with honor and with dignity. He had taught her the folly of her beliefs, and now it was too late for the elves he had killed. She had no idea of her own fate, but she didn't much care. For the rest of her life, she would hear herself beg for mercy while none was shown to her comrades. The certainty that she had led them to their deaths lay within her, a cold hard rock in her gut. She would forever carry that and would never forget what they had sacrificed for her. And it was all for nothing.

Faenwelar was strong, evil, and insane. He wanted Thorius, and he would take it. There was nothing she or Kain could do to stop him, even with all the might of the King behind them. How she wished she had her ring, so she could warn her brother, but it was the first possession they had taken from her. Perhaps he knew the insanity of Faenwelar. Perhaps her brother was not a romantic like she had been.

It didn't matter anymore. Faenwelar had plans for her, or he would have killed her yesterday with the others. She didn't care. Everything that had ever mattered to her had been taken. Her father, her faith, her self-belief, and her ability to protect the *Lenweri*. She lay on a mossy stone platform in the cell welcoming the gut-wrenching pain of her wounded back, for it was the one thing that told her she was still alive. Gwaethe lay and let herself slip into hell.

She walked amongst the trees, but they were not the trees of her world. They had tortured trunks and stunted branches. Their leaves were spotted and decaying. They lay under a grey sky, and a cold drizzle fell. Even in the dream, Gwaethe's back was afire, the only thing that warmed her. All else was frigid.

She wondered why she was here in this dead forest, in this dead world. It could not be her world, just as her back could not really belong to her. Who would flog an elven princess?

Gwaethe kept going, coming to tree after dying tree, feeling as if she was walking through ever deeper mud. She was being dragged down until she felt like falling to her knees. *What?* She was on her knees, and her fingers clutched the moss of a tree trunk, the grey muck pushing under her nails. Tears wet her face as fog swirled around her. The pungent smell of decay forced its way up her nostrils.

She stared at her hands, at her ring, without seeing it. Something was wrong, but what? A man's voice called in the distance, speaking with a Kingdom accent, but the words were unclear. Did she know that voice? A memory niggled at her, but, when she tried to concentrate on it, the mist in her head pulled it away.

The voice grew louder, and then Jacques appeared, walking toward her, his body covered in wounds. He had been in a battle, his uniform torn and dirty, his face paler than she had ever seen it.

He stopped when he saw her. "Why are you here? This is the place of the dead."

She craned her head up to look in his eyes. They were no longer blue but a muddy grey. "Perhaps I am dead then," she said.

His eyes searched over her. "I see no wound."

Gwaethe's heart ached. Her Captain was dead, and none of her dreams would ever come true. But, if she was dead, it hardly mattered. Perhaps they might have a life together, here.

"I was flogged, Jacques. They captured me and flogged me. I remember wanting to die because living with what I have done will be too hard."

"What have you done but loved your people and believed in peace?"

"I was stupid and naïve. I believed Faenwelar would fight with honor. I was wrong, and he tortured us." She paused. "We cannot win against that evil."

Jacques smiled, his eyes full of sadness. "We can win, Gwaethe, if you don't give up."

"I have already given up." She dropped her gaze, too ashamed to go on.

His hands pulled her up to stand beside him, and he placed her palms on his chest. For the second time, she noticed her ring. "All is not lost, fair Princess."

Her ring! They took it from her, but it was back. In this world, it was on her finger!

Gwaethe pulled her hands free and grasped the ring as Jacques turned away.

"Jacques! Wait, don't leave me, we have so much to talk about."

He didn't seem to hear but kept walking, growing fainter until he vanished into the mist.

Gwaethe couldn't move, her feet stuck to the floor of the forest. "Don't leave meeeeeee!" Tears rolled down her cheeks and she shrieked at the treetops, the sound lost almost as it left her throat.

Sister.

Kain! It was Kain's voice! *Brother, I am lost.*

Hold on! Jacques and I will get you out. Where are you?

95

I am in an underground dungeon on the eastern side of the city. I am on my own.

Isiloe?

Gwaethe sobbed. So, her cousin was missing. *Not here.*

Just hold on, Gwaethe. We're coming!

His voice was gone as suddenly as it came, and Gwaethe was jerked back to wakefulness by a hand on her shoulder. She opened her eyes.

"Ha, I thought you were dead," her jailer said, handing her a plate of forest fruits and nuts. "Would not look good for me if you were." He set down a pail of water and left the cell. The door shut with a squeal of the hinges.

Gwaethe sat up, her heart pounding after the dream. She had used the ring in her trance state and spoken to Kain. Or had she? Had the whole thing been a dream or not? She had heard of dreamers and their ability to communicate from the dream state but had not experienced it herself. And how had Jacques come to her? Was he well? Kain had mentioned he was coming for her with Jacques, so the Captain had to be well. Unless her dream had been something of a premonition?

She shook her head. There was no use trying to understand it all. For now, Gwaethe would have faith in her brother and Jacques, and hope Isiloe was safe. And she would examine every inch of her cell. Surely walls this old had to have a crack somewhere she might escape through.

CHAPTER NINE

Jacques looked across at Kain as they paused in the shadow of the southern wall of Amitania. The man was cold iron, forged in a mold that had since been thrown away. Jacques had never met a soldier so unmoved by fear. He himself had never been able to approach battle so calmly, especially against an enemy he didn't know or understand.

The *Sis Lenweri* were even more foreign than Gwaethe's faction; intent on war and domination when the elves had traditionally been peace-loving and forest-dwelling. He hated not being able to predict their tactics. Kain, on the other hand, seemed to make up strategy as he went along, flowing from one situation into the next as though he thrived on danger and uncertainty.

A soldier's life was always unreliable, but when your enemy was foreign and the territory unknown, it was more uncertainty than he liked to deal with. He shook himself out of his musings and tried to focus on getting Gwaethe out of her predicament. Through some magical communication Kain had with Gwaethe, he had been able to confirm his sister was alive.

Thank the Goddess! She had come to mean something to him, more than just a thorn in his side, a prickly elven woman he had to deal with to get what he wanted.

She had honor and principles and wanted peace for her people; that meant peace for the Kingdom as well. He found his thoughts wandering to her even when she wasn't around, found himself worrying if he would ever see her again.

Jacques had Exmund with him, and Kain had brought with him a sergeant, Jer Blas, who was an experienced tracker. It was up to their small team of four to free the Princess, for General Formosa had not been willing to mount a rescue mission. He distrusted all elves, which was not uncommon among the Thorian populace. He treated Kain with unconcealed contempt and animosity. Jacques secretly thought the General was glad to get them out of the way, so he'd be free to make all the decisions without interference.

So be it. If they rescued Gwaethe and Isiloe, it would do a lot for the cause of peace. Jacques was not stupid enough to think, as the General did, they would be better off if the elven race were wiped from the face of the world. He was, however, uncertain how many of the *Sis Lenweri*, freed from the influence of Faenwelar, would come back to Gwaethe. In his mind, if they tried to integrate the traitors back into elven society, Gwaethe would never know whom she could trust. So they really had nothing to lose from allowing the General to have free rein in the coming battle. Let him make his mistakes, and, just maybe, Jacques could swoop in, save the day, and earn a promotion. Yes, it was certainly possible this battle might be the stepping stone to greatness that Jacques needed.

But for now, they must rescue the only elven leader he trusted. He sat against the wall, and Kain followed suit, the others bracketing them.

"We can use the coming battle as cover," Jacques said. "Follow our army in and find Gwaethe by using the battle around us as confusion in which we can operate."

"We'll be pulled into the fighting," Kain said.

Jacques nodded. "Yes, but all will be chaos. There will be risks, but we should be able to make it with care and not a little luck."

"You like relying on luck?"

Jacques grinned. "Every soldier needs lady luck, Jazara. You of all people should know that."

Kain stared at Jacques then turned to his sergeant. "Make your way to the north-eastern quarter of the city. Take Exmund with you and send him back with anything you find: enemy location, movements; you know what I need."

Jacques suppressed the flare of anger he felt at Kain ordering his man about. Exmund wouldn't wish to leave his side. "Go with the Sergeant, Exmund. It will be dangerous, and you'll find yourself alone at times." He reached into his pocket and withdrew a small whistle. "Blow on this if you become trapped or lost and I will come for you."

Kain scowled at him. "Don't make promises you can't keep, Vorasava."

Jacques fixed Kain with a cold glare that had cut more men down to size than he could count. It made no impression on the half-man. "If I say I'll come then I'll keep my word, Jazara. You can count on it."

"And what if you're dead?"

"I can't afford to die. There is too much at stake." Jacques shook Exmund's hand, and the two men left quietly, following the outer wall until they were out of sight.

Jacques felt an unexplained urgency to be moving out as well, but he waited for the count of one hundred after he lost sight of Exmund and Blas. There was no point in blundering into something because he was too anxious to find Gwaethe.

He tugged on Kain's shirt sleeve and pointed forward. They hugged the shadow of the wall on the outside, stopping where there was a break in the wall and listening before crossing the breach and heading further north. They didn't speak, both because they didn't wish to give away their position and also so they could hear the approach of enemy fighters.

Two hours into their trek, Jacques pulled Kain to a halt, his finger to his lips. He had always had exceptional hearing. Someone approached from the north. They found a hiding spot behind rubble from the wall and hunkered down to wait. Exmund appeared, running toward their hideout, and threw himself over the pile of debris, landing on Kain.

Kain had his knife to Exmund's throat before Jacques could blink an eye. The aide froze but not before a trickle of blood oozed from his neck.

Kain pulled his knife away, wiped it on Exmund's shirt, and sheathed it. "What news?"

Exmund swallowed several times before he spoke. Even then his voice was merely a croak. "A large group of elves has engaged our forces an hour to the north. Blas is working his way around them but has been forced into the city."

"Who has the upper hand?" Jacques asked.

"The elves did last I was there, but the fighting was ferocious. They've improved their hand to hand combat skills and have piles of rubble blocking off escape routes. Then they scale ropes to the roofs and regroup to attack again with bow and arrow."

"Nasty," Jacques said. "Our men need to learn on the fight if we are to prevail. Is there a way through? Over the rooftops?"

"Not the roofs, Captain," Exmund said. "We'd be spotted in an instant."

Jacques didn't like the sound of it, but they had no choice. They had to advance to the hot spot. Hopefully by the time they caught up, the fight would have moved on.

"Lead the way, Exmund."

The aide rose and jogged away, keeping a low profile, Jacques and Kain following.

By the time they arrived at the site of the battle, the fighting had worked its way toward the center of the city. The outer wall was a mass of rubble at this point, so Jacques led the others into the outer streets, hugging the alleys and staying out of sight of the low towers that abounded in the decaying city.

They moved silently up a narrow passage, ears strained for the smallest sound of approaching enemies. Without warning, Sergeant Blas jogged past the end of their alley, heading east, casting a glance back over his shoulder. Jacques looked to Kain who nodded and waved them forward to the end of the alley. He edged around, took a look, and held up five fingers. Three swords were drawn as one, and Jacques moved to the eastern wall of the alley where he would be seen first by the enemy. He crouched on the balls of his feet, ready to move.

The five elves saw him and made directly for him, silent in their attack. Jacques met the first head on, astonished to find a talented rival on the other end of the sword. He blocked and parried. Elves had never been sword fighters and certainly not skilled! He shoved the thought away and concentrated on wearing his opponent down. Jacques was superior in ability; it was only a matter of time before he found an opening. Trouble was he was short on wind after his lung issues, and he was horribly afraid his poor stamina would undermine him.

He flicked an eye to the side, registering Kain and Exmund fighting side by side against the other four elves. One elf went down, but that was all Jacques had time to see. He had to concentrate harder than in any fight before. His opponent sensed him tiring and redoubled his efforts to get past Jacques's defenses. Pain burned in his left bicep as the flesh was opened by a glancing blow. By now he was panting, his skills reduced to desperate slashing. So far, he had fended off all except that one slice, but his endurance was almost gone.

It was getting difficult to see through the sweat. Was that blood running down his forehead? When had he been hit there? Jacques fell to the dirt of the alley as his right knee gave out. He threw up his sword to protect his head and neck. Blood blinded him, and his breath rasped from his throat like a dying man.

Something hit him, pushing him farther to the dirt, but there was no pain, only a weight on top of him. He wiped the sweat and blood from his eyes in time to see Jer Blas lift the body of his elven opponent off him. Blas stuck out his hand and pulled Jacques to his feet.

"Are you alright, Captain?" Blas asked.

Jacques still struggled to get his breath. This damned illness clung to him like a limpet on a rock. "I will be, thanks to you, Sergeant."

"Let me look at the cut on your head," Blas said, only to be pushed aside by Exmund.

"I'll tend the Captain, Sergeant," Exmund said, leading Jacques back up the alley and seating him in a recessed doorway. "Those cuts need stitching." He went to work, cleaning and suturing the cuts on Jacques's forehead and upper arm, while Jacques waited for his breath to return.

"Not too good, Exmund," Jacques said. "I was nearly done for back there. If Blas hadn't come when he did…"

"Well, he did, sir," Exmund said, applying a bandage to Jacques's arm. "No use worrying about what almost happened."

"How are you?" Jacques asked. "Any injuries?"

Exmund let loose a soft chuckle. "Fighting alongside Jazara might be about the safest place in any battle," he said. "The man's a demon fighter. All I did was watch his back while he killed four of them. I think I got one or two blows in, but, honestly, I don't think he needed me. Next time, I'm watching your back, Captain."

"Very well, Exmund, I'd be grateful. I just can't seem to get my wind. It was that more than anything that had me on my knees."

Kain approached. He had shed his own uniform and dressed in the brown and green tunic and leggings of one of his fallen elven opponents. He appeared totally unscathed.

"Are you well, Vorasava?" he asked, holding out another tunic and leggings for Jacques.

"I wouldn't say well, but I'm alive. It was a close-run thing though. If Blas hadn't come along…well I won't think about that." He looked at Exmund who smiled back.

"Must have been your lady luck, man," Kain said. "Put this on. It might make us less conspicuous. You too, Exmund." He gave the corporal another set of elven garb, took a long swig on his water bottle, then sat down and sharpened his sword. He looked completely at ease, while Jacques could have happily found a hole and crawled into it. Well, *that* wasn't true, he needed to find Gwaethe, but he could certainly do with a rest.

Jacques knew real fear for the first time in this conflict. How could he hope to prevail when he couldn't fight? He would end up letting someone down.

"I've failed you, Kain," he said. "I thought I could assist you in this mission, but it seems I might be more of a liability."

Kain snorted. "I've been told what you endured under the mountain," he said, squatting beside Jacques. "That would have killed most men. You won't be letting anyone down."

Jacques smiled, but only for the benefit of those with him. "You need someone who can watch your back. That's not me at the moment. I'd watch your back as the enemy drove a sword through it, unable to get there in time."

"We have no choice but to go on," Kain said. "We're halfway to the target. You can be the leader you need to be, just don't give up now. To give up is to die."

Jacques frowned at his companions as he studied each one. Exmund looked back with open and complete trust. Jer Blas simply waited to hear Jacques's decision as all soldiers did. Kain watched him with an intensity that unsettled him, as if waiting to see if Jacques would pass the test. Well, damn, he *would* pass this test.

"I see I must continue with you all," Jacques said. "I merely wished for you to realize none of you can count on me to be there when you need me most."

Exmund saluted. "We'll be there for you, Captain. You've pulled me out of more scrapes than I care to list. About time I did the same for you."

Kain grinned. "A good man you have there, Vorasava. He speaks for all of us. We'll do this together, and – by damn – we'll succeed. Now, are you ready to continue?"

Jacques nodded and rose, Exmund there to see he was steady on his feet. They formed up, Jer Blas in front, followed by Exmund with Jacques and then Kain bringing up the rear. Jacques was impossibly buoyed by the words and support of his companions. His step was suddenly light, despite the pain in his head and arm and the tightness in his chest. He *would* prevail, and so would they all.

* * *

Gwaethe paced the length of her cell and back like a chicken in a coop. She cringed at the likeness, but it was how she felt. She would never have imagined calling herself a chicken before this mission, but everything had conspired to make her feel like the lowliest of beasts. She had given in to fear and pain, and still had not saved her comrades. Faenwelar had taken her pride from her, and the only way she might redeem herself was to take his life. She could not see how to accomplish the feat right now, but she *would* find a way.

Anger burned within her, more so with every hour. The moss-covered stone she had lain on appeared to have soothed her tortured skin, and as her back hurt less, the wound to her integrity, her very soul, tormented her even more. That she should be in this prison, powerless, while the *Sis Lenweri* were free to bring their terror to all in Thorius and beyond… It was intolerable!

She had searched the cell, feeling stone by stone, and found not a crack to escape through. But she had a plan. When the guard came next, he would not find her feeling sorry for herself but ready to fight. That was what she did best, and no upstart High Prince was going to rob her of her freedom or the ability to avenge her father and his people.

And so, she paced the cell in the darkness, stretching her muscles and staying alert to any sound that might herald the arrival of the guard. She would be ready if it was hours before she had her chance. Kain was out there and so was Jacques, but she would not allow them to rescue her. She was more than a weak female who waited for others to help her! She was an elven princess with right on her side, and someone would pay for the hurt they had done her.

Her chance came three hours later at another meal time. Gwaethe lay on her pallet and played dead. Even her breathing would be difficult to detect in the deep gloom. A tentative finger poked her ribs, but she steeled herself not to respond. A toe kicked her calf, and, again, she remained completely still. When a hand clutched her chin, Gwaethe reared up and punched the elf in the side of the head. She was rewarded with a grunt. The guard fell, clutching his face, and Gwaethe kicked him in the side of the head, rendering him unconscious. She swapped tunics with him, used the leather ties from hers to bind his wrists, then ripped a sleeve off her old tunic and stuffed it in his mouth. The guard was still unconscious but may not be for long. They would miss him, but his silence for the moment might buy her precious time. She also picked his cap up from where it had fallen and jammed it on her head. The keys to the cell were in the door. She locked it and took the keys with her when she left.

The hall was dark, but a torch flickered at the far end. Gwaethe crept along, making scarcely a sound, eyes fixed on the stairs beneath the torch. The cells she passed seemed empty. She shuddered at the thought she might have been left to die down here, and no one might ever have found her. As she reached the stairs, a cool wind swirled around and past. Faint voices echoed from above. Gwaethe had no plan beyond pretending to be *Sis Lenweri* and, if that failed, fighting her way out. She would take as many of the traitors with her as possible.

Step by step she ascended until sixty stairs lay below, and she could peek above a landing. It was deserted and led to another row of cells. Cobweb-covered weapons, chains, and spikes hung on the walls of the landing. Another set of stone steps led upward, but she didn't know whether to enter the hall or continue up.

Footprints disturbed the dirt in the hallway that led to the cells, and moans echoed to her from that direction. Her heart told her to try and free those souls. Who would be in prison here except enemies of the *Sis Lenweri*? They might aid her. On the other hand, she could not count on their help, and her head screamed at her to escape this dungeon.

But she had the keys, and they might free many in this dark place. What kind of leader was she if she ignored the plight of her subjects? Swearing softly to herself, Gwaethe entered the hall and crept to the first cell on the right. She choked on the stink coming from it; death. The next was the same and the two after that. Despair dragged at her, told her there was no point in risking her freedom for dead allies. The fifth cell held life! A cough and a sniffle made her enter a key in the lock, but she had to try five keys before the lock moved. The door swung in, and Gwaethe peeked around it. Two elves sat against the far wall, their unblinking eyes just discernible in the gloom.

"If you can walk, you need to come with me now," Gwaethe said.

"Why should we?" one of the elves asked. "Are we the next to be tortured?"

"Why not?" the other rasped. "We'll only die a slow death here. At least the alternative might be quicker."

Gwaethe clenched her teeth against frustration. "I am Gwaethe Arenil, and I am here to rescue you. Come with me and fight the *Sis Lenweri* who did this to you."

The first elf who had spoken stood slowly; rather, he pushed himself upright against the stone wall. "I am Ruven Magbalar, Princess, and I have heard fell things of your rule. Why should I follow you?"

"You sit here in a dungeon being starved to death, and you ask me that? My cause is the cause of peace, not war. It is the cause of acceptance, not dominance. Faenwelar killed my father. He wants to take back the lands the men rule over, but I say we should be making peace with the men. We don't need our old low lands when we can live in the forests, the mountains."

"How long will it be until the men turn their eyes to our forests?" Ruven asked. "They have ever been discontent with what they have; always seeking to extend their territories."

Gwaethe stepped closer. "There is no time for this. I must do what I can here and escape. Already I risk much by freeing you. Will you aid me or not?"

The other elf stood with help from Ruven. "I am Théoden Leovaris, Princess. I helped your father escape when he was attacked by Faenwelar. I will aid you."

Gwaethe shook his hand and helped him from the cell. "Take the stairs at the end of this hall, Théoden. Go up but be cautious. There are weapons before the stairs. Arm yourself."

Ignoring Ruven, she continued opening cells, frustrated at the time it took to find the right keys and then to explain who she was. Faenwelar had slandered her name amongst these elves, and not all had supported her father, but, in time, she might win them over. For now, it was enough that she could offer them freedom. When all the cells had been opened on that floor, she had more than twenty willing followers and the same number who would follow her until a better offer presented itself. They were a ragged lot, having starved for days if not weeks, but Gwaethe hoped their palpable hatred of Faenwelar might overcome their frailty.

She followed her small force up the steps, having removed an old sword from the wall. It was heavy, and Gwaethe had never been an avid student of the blade. Most elves shunned the sword in favor of a knife or bow, but she would make the weapon sing if pressed. Her ragtag army was quiet and ascended without incident. She began to hope they might escape without raising any alarm, but then cries rang out from below, quickly followed by a clash of weapons just above.

As cries of pain echoed down the stairwell, Gwaethe gathered those around her into a rear fighting force. She cursed herself for a fool, for she and her comrades were stuck on the narrow stairs between two stone walls, blocked from ascending and with a certain foe fast approaching from below.

"Prepare to defend our position," she cried and peered into the darkness below, trying to catch sight of what was coming at them. An arrow sliced above her head. "Down!"

More arrows hummed above them, but most bounced off the stone. Gwaethe was finally able to see their attackers. They were elves, not human! "If you desire to escape this with your lives," she said, "you must fight as if you are possessed by demons. I will promote all who survive, and you will be honored among the *Lenweri*."

Ruven stood beside her. "If we survive, I may hold you to that promise, Princess," he said.

Gwaethe hissed. "Do not call me that! Not here, not until we win free."

Ruven nodded and turned to face those below, wielding a mace as though he had been born to it. How he had the strength, Gwaethe had no idea. A space opened above them, and they backed into it, slowly ascending as arrows flew at them. Some hit their target, but more hit the stone and became ammunition for those in her force who had bows.

Tripping over their fallen comrades and dodging arrows and elbows, Gwaethe and her rear guard ascended the stairs, occasionally casting their eyes behind when there was a lull. The leaders were thinning, and the light above strengthening into something near daylight.

"Push forward while we can!"

Gwaethe raced up the stairs and rallied her fighters for one last push. They were all tiring. They hacked their way through the last of the attackers and stood panting in a large circular anteroom with five wooden doors leading out of it. The door closest to her smashed open against the wall; and she came face to face with Jacques.

Gwaethe's first impulse was to throw herself at him and never let him go. She gulped down the frenzied greeting that fought for release. "Jacques…Captain Vorasava, well met."

He bowed, allowing her a view behind him to a tall, lean man whose dark eyes pierced her all the way to her soul.

"Kain! Thank the Gods!"

Kain inclined his head. "You're a sight for sore eyes. Isn't she, Vorasava?"

Jacques was staring at her as if taking inventory. He had no right to that kind of regard! "There has never been a more welcome one."

The clash of weapons reached them from the stairwell.

"Pull back, defenders!" Gwaethe shouted. "Help is here." She grabbed Jacques by the arm and pulled him with her to the wall. His face was ashen, and she was certain only sheer strength of will kept him on his feet. "Silly man," she hissed. "You should be home where you can heal, not leading a sortie."

He frowned at her and pulled his arm from her grasp. "Your words are wearing thin, Princess. We've been through all this before. I'm where I need to be." He paused as his gaze raked over her. "Are you unharmed?"

Gwaethe averted her eyes lest he see the darkness that dwelt inside her. A darkness that hadn't been there when last they spoke. "I will be well, just as soon as I kill Faenwelar. Have you located him? What is happening?"

Jacques watched as the few remaining *Sis Lenweri* who reached the anteroom were dispatched. "We four are your rescue party. The Kingdom army is within Amitania, seeking the High Prince. Battle with the *Sis Lenweri* was joined yesterday but we have only been involved when we needed to make our way through skirmishes to reach you."

Gwaethe's heart sank. "I see how it stands."

"Princess, don't jump to conclusions," Jacques said.

"Your General will not work with me," she spat. "His approach to Faenwelar is completely unilateral with no regard for the wishes of the elven people." Fury boiled within Gwaethe, threatening to take over. She would find this Kingdom general and make him see he could not disregard the *Lenweri*. He could not treat all elves as one, as enemies.

She drew a deep breath as the skirmish before her was settled. Kain approached and held an object out to her. "My ring!" She received the precious object and placed it back on her hand. *Thank you, brother.*

Kain nodded. His control of mind speak was not as developed as hers, but he would learn. "I found it on the finger of one of the elves I fought."

"What now?" Gwaethe asked, and then something occurred to her, turning her blood to ice. "Where is Isiloe?"

Kain's jaw clenched, and Jacques looked at his boots.

"Where is she?"

Jacques faced her. "Isiloe asked to be allowed to enter the city to find you and the others. I refused her. The next thing I heard, she had vanished. That was two days ago."

Gwaethe turned and began pacing back and forth across the anteroom. All manner of possibilities swamped her mind but upper most was what Faenwelar had done to her comrades. That must not happen to Isiloe. It could not already have transpired; she would know if Isiloe was dead.

Jacques stepped in front of her. "She is clever and resourceful, Princess. She will win through with nary a scratch."

"You didn't see what they did to the others," Gwaethe gulped, as a sob almost choked her. "I was given the choice of being publicly flogged as an example, or Faenwelar would kill my supporters one by one. I agreed, of course, and the High Prince took great delight in showing his subjects even an elven princess wasn't above punishment." Memories flooded back, and shame took her words. "They broke me, and it was all for nothing."

Jacques tried to gather her into his chest, but Gwaethe spun away. She couldn't accept his comfort; she had to hold strong, or she would be no use to anyone. The hurt in his gaze was almost her undoing.

"Faenwelar killed my comrades anyway, and no one in the crowd stood up to him." She faced Jacques square on. "You may be right, Captain. Perhaps there is no one of the *Sis Lenweri* worth redeeming."

And then Gwaethe spotted Théoden Leovaris, his head held high, his dark eyes daring her to shame him. She looked around at her makeshift troop. All of them had heard her declaration.

"Am I correct, *Sis Lenweri*? Can you be redeemed? Will you stand with me for peace, or will you run back to Faenwelar? You have seen how he treated you, how he had me flogged and my followers killed. He killed my father, the true king, and now he will sacrifice elven lives in order to recover the lands of men."

Gwaethe had expected Théoden to be the first to step forward, but it was Ruven Magbalar who joined her.

"I will fight on the side of Gwaethe Arenil. In her I see a way forward that doesn't mean death. Do we need the lands of men? Can we be happy in our mountains?" He turned to Gwaethe. "If you swear to safeguard our mountain home, I am behind you, Princess."

Thirty other *Sis Lenweri*, all who had survived the stairwell battle, slapped their fists over their hearts. Gwaethe knew hope for the first time in weeks. "Now we find Isiloe and Faenwelar."

CHAPTER TEN

Jacques left the prison complex and stepped into the light of mid-morning. He was exhausted after a day and night of running, hiding and fighting. More than that, he was a mess of conflicting emotions and hated it. How could he do his job when he allowed his feelings to rule him so completely? The sight of Gwaethe had struck at him, the wave of relief so strong that Exmund had seized his arm in support when he swayed. Until that moment, Jacques hadn't allowed himself to dwell on the possibility of never seeing Gwaethe again in this life.

But she had been cool and dismissive, and now he was uncertain she harbored any strong feelings for him. Aloof and stern, his elven princess appeared a different person to the leader he had dealt with in the past. He swallowed a lump in his throat, reprimanding himself for being such a stupid sap. *You should be thinking of yourself and this battle, how to get the best outcome for Thorius!* And that included salvaging some success from the fighting.

The Goddess only knew what Josef Formosa was doing! Jacques stifled a half-crazed laugh. Perhaps the Kingdom general had already died in the fighting, and he and Kain would be free to steer things their way. But Kain was out of favor, and Jacques was merely a lowly captain.

Pull yourself together, man! His illness ate at him from the inside out, his lungs burning and waves of nausea washing through him whenever he pushed too hard.

"Exmund, my potion." He drank a long draught, and the liquid burned within. Jacques focused on the burn as he breathed deep, but not too deeply, lest the coughing fits seize him and never let go.

Kain came back to where Jacques and Exmund had halted against a rock wall.

"You're pale as a snow wolf, man!" Kain said. "Are you sure you don't need to return to camp?"

"How could I? There's no one to serve as escort."

Kain straightened. "I'd do it. The battle can wait. I haven't forgotten your support of me in the last campaign."

Gwaethe joined him. "Brother, I do not think the battle can wait. Faenwelar must be stopped before he escapes to fight another day. And we must find Isiloe."

"The Princess is right," Jacques said. "My health is of minimal importance alongside finding that monster." Gwaethe's gaze warmed just a shade at his words.

Kain turned away and scanned the area of Amitania visible from their vantage point. Sounds of battle came from the northwestern sector of the city. He turned back to the elves who stood with them.

"We'll work our way toward the fighting, angling north and checking the buildings we pass. Any who will join our cause may do so. Take all weapons you discover if you can carry them. Our aim is to upgrade our fighting ability. Also, I want all of you to wear a headband, so we can differentiate you from Faenwelar's *Sis Lenweri*."

The elves thumped their chests with their fists and proceeded to make the requested head bands. Ruven and Théoden sorted the elves into two parties with themselves as group leaders. When Jacques looked to Gwaethe to judge whether she was angry that Kain had taken over, he found a smile on her lips that puzzled him. She was the obvious elven leader here, yet she had ceded to her half-brother? What was more surprising was the fact that their new comrades appeared to have accepted Kain too.

Kain grasped his upper arm. "Are you certain you can keep up?"

Jacques ignored the burning in his chest and nodded. "I have to."

Gwaethe appeared beside him, her arm sliding around his bicep. "I will watch over him, brother. You lead."

Kain nodded before leaving them with Exmund.

"Princess," Jacques said, "you should be with your people, not me. Exmund will suffice."

Her dark eyes bored right through him. "You are important, Jacques. I will not leave you behind. I will watch over you and ensure your feet stay on the right path, no matter what happens."

Jacques couldn't decide precisely what she meant by that, and his mind was not willing to expend any more energy on her cryptic words. With Gwaethe on his left and Exmund on his right, Jacques trudged after Kain and their new elven friends.

* * *

Gwaethe was more conflicted on the inside than she would ever reveal. First there was the gritty, enigmatic man she had volunteered to guard. She felt so much for him but feared he would never allow her closer than she was right now. She had no right to be pursuing a relationship with a human when she was so vital to her nation's survival. And yet she cared for him, felt protective of him, especially when he was so ill. It was a miracle he had survived the landslide, let alone was on his feet. She couldn't lose him!

His arm under her fingers was tough as granite but beneath all that was a vulnerability that called to her. He held himself aloof, but she sensed he was susceptible to her. Which led her right back to the impossibility of this whole situation.

And Kain! This was what she had long hoped for; that he would step into shoes befitting of an elven prince. He was a natural leader, and the elves who had pledged themselves to her had not questioned when Kain stepped up to lead them. Yet, it rubbed her the wrong way. Why could she not lead them in her father's place? These would follow her, she was sure. They had pledged themselves to her, not Kain.

Gwaethe shook her head, tossing away the fog that seemed to

have enveloped her mind these days. Nothing was as it should be. She prayed for a miracle, and, when it occurred, she was angry! Later, there would be time to bring female elves to the fore. Now, it was vital she create the conditions for success and that meant a male rival for Faenwelar. Kain was everything she and her people needed right at this moment.

They progressed through the city, searching each building they came to and finding the occasional elf who was old or injured. Some readily joined their cause, but others came at them with whatever weapon they could lay hands on. Their company grew to fifty, all wearing headbands. They had agreed any who engaged in combat against them be killed. Gwaethe loathed the waste of life, but if these elves had been swayed by Faenwelar, there was every chance they would condone the torture she had been exposed to.

She began to wonder where all the female elves were. Even Faenwelar needed them for the efficient functioning of his army. And then they came upon a large ruined hall filled with female *Sis Lenweri*. The females hissed as Kain and his elves moved into the hall. Most of them were obviously pregnant, some large with child, which made no sense to Gwaethe. Kain found her eyes and raised his brows. She shrugged and stepped forward.

"*Sis Lenweri!*" she said.

The hissing intensified. Gwaethe folded her arms across her chest and waited. Eventually they hushed.

"I am Gwaethe Arenil, and I have come to offer you a choice."

An older female draped in a flowing green kaftan approached Gwaethe. "We know who you are, Princess. You are a mouse hiding in the forest while we, *Sis Lenweri*, are lions who will chase the invaders from our lands."

"We shall see," Gwaethe said, again studying the female elves. "Why are so many of you with child?"

The woman sneered again. "The High Prince has found an answer to the elven breeding difficulties. Our females don't fight as yours do. We make children. When our men go to war, if we are not with child, the women accompany them. This way, we are not separated for any time. Our children stay home to be minded by the elders."

Gwaethe took this in, a sinking feeling inside. These elves were so different from her own. And there were so many of them. While she and her *Lenweri* females had been learning fighting skills, the *Sis Lenweri* had been making babies.

"Are any of you willing to come with me? To be true *Lenweri* again? You will no longer be incubators but real elves with aspirations and feelings. You will not be subordinate to the males."

"Faenwelar will cover us in glory. We are more numerous by far than your faction and do not want to fight. Let the males seize the lands while we guide from the rear. That is how we have decided it should be." She paused, studying Gwaethe's company without fear. "What will you do with us?"

Gwaethe had been asking herself the same questions. By their prior agreement, these elven females should be killed. They carried dozens of new fighters for Faenwelar's cause. But she would not waste such innocent life. If she did, she would be no better than the High Prince.

She walked with Kain and Jacques, away from the females.

"What will we do with them?" She asked.

Kain's dark gaze was troubled. "They're pregnant women. We can't slaughter them. It would be the end of our quest for peace."

"You and I are in agreement, brother, but what are we supposed to do with so many pregnant women in a war zone?"

Jacques cleared his throat. "I agree they should be spared, but we can't allow them to return to Faenwelar." He wiped his hand across a face grey with exhaustion. "I say we give them a choice. They come to us as allies or prisoners. If it is the latter, they remain prisoners until their babes are born, at which time we ask them the same question. If it is still no, their newborns stay with the *Lenweri*, Princess, and the females are free to return to their males."

Gwaethe's heart lightened at his suggestion. "It is a good suggestion, Jacques, and will buy us time."

"Time and, perhaps, new followers," Kain said. "These *Sis Lenweri* females may be brought over to you yet if they are treated with care."

Gwaethe cast her gaze over the females, noting the hostile looks she received from more than half of them. "They will give us much grief, but it may be worth the trouble in the end. We must reunite our factions somehow."

"Must you, Princess?" Jacques said. "I suspect that will be an almost impossible task."

Gwaethe heaved a great sigh. Hadn't the two of them been through this already? "The *Sis Lenweri* can be saved, Captain; at least as many of them as possible."

"You can still say that after they watched you flayed? And killed the others with not a protest raised?"

"War is war, and I shouldn't judge them. Faenwelar is a tyrant. Given the chance, they will come to me in time."

Jacques stared deep into her eyes, and Gwaethe lost herself for a moment in the boundless blue of his irises. She wished with all her heart she had the time to wallow in this moment of connection. "They will come to me, you shall see."

Jacques sighed. "Not if Formosa has anything to say about it. We must find him and judge the lay of the land."

Gwaethe turned from him lest he realize the longing in her had nothing to do with the *Sis Lenweri*. She addressed the females before her.

"You will stay here for now. We leave elves loyal to our cause to guard you." She found Ruven and Théoden and nodded to them. "While we are gone, decide on which side you will stand. Those who pledge loyalty will live as free elves with my *Lenweri*. Those who do not will live as our prisoners."

Her words were greeted with loud murmurs and angry muttering.

"Make your decision, for I will expect an answer when I return." She drew Ruven and Théoden aside. "If you face physical threat from

117

these females, control them but do not threaten their lives or that of their unborn children." They nodded and turned to select the elves who would remain with them.

Gwaethe nodded. "I have faith in those two. They will stay true to their word." She turned to find Jacques glaring at the two elven leaders.

"Possibly," he said.

"I had my crisis of faith in my people back in the cell," she hissed. "I will not doubt them again." Gwaethe turned from Jacques and strode from the hall.

* * *

A flurry of snow drove between the buildings as Jacques strove to keep up with the force ahead of him. Gwaethe was at his side, Exmund on the other. He hated to be a burden, hated to feel as weak as this. He was a leader, and that was what he wished to do. But the foul poison that burned his lungs would not release its grip. Exmund did a mighty job of mixing the potion that kept him alive, but its effects dwindled more swiftly with each draught. It seemed the mountain might yet be the death of him.

A coughing fit wracked him, and he stopped, desperately drawing air into his damaged lungs. When it passed, Gwaethe gazed at him with fear in her eyes, her hands bunched into fists and her shoulders tense.

"You are not getting better," she said.

Jacques made to deny it but then nodded. "If I don't get help soon, I'll die here."

"Alique is here," Gwaethe said. "If anyone can help, it is she. We will rest overnight and find Alique on the morrow."

Jacques clutched her forearm. "Your place is with Kain. Exmund can see to my needs." He gritted his teeth. Admission of weakness was something he never did. But she was his friend, and he would not hide before her or lie to her.

She stepped closer. "I care for you. If we are separated, I may never see you again. That would not be tolerable." She called to those ahead. "Halt!" Jacques watched with pride as she selected six elves to guard them and spoke to Kain. The larger force continued while Gwaethe and her six surrounded Jacques and Exmund.

"Find a deserted building and make a fire. Captain Vorasava must rest."

In minutes, a small house was located, and a fire was built in the center of the front room. There were windows, just holes really, out to the street and enough guards to watch for intruders. Exmund cooked a meal and made more of the medicine while Gwaethe settled Vorasava on a blanket.

"I must protest, Princess," he said. "You should be leading this sortie, not playing nurse maid to me."

She sat beside him, her arms around her knees. "I have not told you this, but now seems a good time." She closed her eyes, and, when she again opened them, she speared him with her gaze. "I have great affection for you, Jacques. I will not see you die. I will do everything I can to save your life. You know this."

He didn't understand. "I have great affection for you too, Princess."

"Call me Gwaethe!"

He paused. "Gwaethe, I'm a sick man. Perhaps there is nothing that can be done for me. Are you trying to say you love me?"

Her head rose, nose in the air. "It is possible I feel this for you. Do you feel the same?"

He huffed out a breath. "I …well…you know I have the greatest respect for you, and you are very attractive."

"That is not what I asked."

"We can't be together." It simply would never be tolerated, and he had other goals. Grand plans of running the Kingdom army. But if he died, none of it would matter. Was it better to focus on now than save himself for an uncertain future?

"I don't know if I love you," he said. "I never allow myself to imagine us together. Do you?"

She sidled closer and lay her hand on his cheek. "I think about you when I should not. You ensnared my heart the very first time I saw you. You were different to the other men, more tolerant; a gentleman. You spoke to me, treated me as equal. You are easy to love, Jacques Vorasava."

Jacques drew a deep breath that threatened to send him into another coughing fit. "You're beautiful, Gwaethe. I too think of you when I shouldn't. I imagine you in my bed and in my life. My dreams have contained you since the first time I saw you. But I don't wish to hurt you. A life together can never be."

She didn't seem to hear his last words as her face drifted closer. Her lips met his in an explosion of desire Jacques had never anticipated from the dignified princess. He gasped, allowing her tongue to invade his mouth, taking what breath he had left. The weight of her body pushed him back until she must feel the swelling in his breeches.

Gwaethe pulled back. "I have changed, Jacques. I am not the high and mighty princess I was when we renewed our acquaintance. Prince Gorin beat me and then killed my people. No one stopped him. I was flung into a cell and could have died down there. You and I can be something together. We can make a future our combined nations can be proud of. All we need to do is let go of the past and make our new destiny."

Jacques stood and pulled Gwaethe with him. He led her to a small room in the back and closed the door. He spread the blanket on a pallet of leaves and branches and drew Gwaethe down beside him. Soon, her tunic was unlaced, and her magnificent dark skin was his to admire. Her firm breasts had dusky pink nipples that stood to attention in the chill air. He pulled her breeches off, and she was bared to him in all her glory. He ran his callused hands up her legs from knees to thighs, and Gwaethe gasped. More dusky pink glistened between her legs and Jacques's cock swelled, desperate to plunder the riches before him.

When it was his turn to undress, Gwaethe helped him out of his tunic and breeches, ran her hands over his shoulders, his chest, his thighs, all the way to his straining rod. A droplet of moisture glistened at the tip, and she licked it away.

Jacques groaned. As sick as he was, this was heaven. He could take all she had to offer and die a happy man. And, as Gwaethe's mouth closed over his rod, Jacques indeed thought he might succumb. His breathing quickened, sounding harsh in the small room. His world receded to his cock and Gwaethe's warm, wet mouth as he drew close to his climax. It had been so long and all he wanted was to stay right here in this room with this elven princess. But this was not how he wanted it between them.

Groaning, he pulled himself from her mouth and pushed her back, parting her legs and lowering his mouth to her. He sank into her warmth, his tongue darting between her slick folds. She spasmed around him, and it was all he could do not to plunge himself in and take his pleasure. But this was all they might have, and he would not tarnish it. Gwaethe's hips bucked as his tongue lashed the tight nub of her desire, her head thrown back, her hands clawing the blanket beneath. He plunged two fingers into her, curling them upward, and she exploded, screaming his name. He lowered his mouth to silence her and slid his cock home.

Gwaethe closed around him as though she were made for him alone. The tail end of her completion ensnared his rod, milking from him an explosion like no woman had ever triggered before. She encased him, her muscles a tight sheath of warmth and love he never wanted to leave. As he pulsed within her, he knew he had made a mistake, but did not care.

CHAPTER ELEVEN

Gwaethe woke with the dawn and turned on her side. Jacques was peaceful in sleep, as though all his troubles were laid to rest. A powerful wave of longing swept her as she stared at her Kingdom man. It had been a mistake to lie with him, for now she knew she would not be happy with any other. What they had shared was more than she had ever imagined. She had long ago given up the drive for carnal knowledge. It just complicated things when you were a princess. And so, after several fumbling episodes as a youngster, Gwaethe had been celibate.

Until now. And now she would never be able to walk away from Jacques. Already her belly tightened at the thought of being intimate with him again. She leaned over and kissed his jaw. He rolled toward her and encircled her with his arm, pulling her against his erection. She moaned, threw her leg over his hips and angled herself so his rod slipped into her. This was heaven, and that was before he began to thrust, before she was caught up in another explosion of love and desire too strong to deny.

He rose above her, and Gwaethe opened herself to him, her nails digging into his buttocks to keep him anchored against her. He came deep inside her as she too reached her completion.

"Never leave me," she breathed. "You can never leave." Tears streamed down her cheeks as he emptied himself into her. She must do everything possible to save him, to keep him with her. Even as she said the words, had the thought, she knew their love was threatened.

Jacques pulled back and stared at her. There was passion in his eyes, but also sadness. "This might be all we have, Gwaethe, all we have in this world. But it will be enough."

"It will never be enough!" She pulled away and rose, striding across the room to lean against the stone wall. Despite the cold, she didn't try to cover up. She didn't care if she was cold, if she was exposed to his gaze. Let him see her naked, vulnerable. It was the truth of her!

Jacques pulled on his breeches and brought her a blanket, but she shrugged away. "I don't care about the cold." She turned to him. "Look at me! All I have is for you! I was born for you."

He dropped the blanket and pulled her close. "I'm flattered you believe that, Gwaethe, but what would your people say? This is your one chance to bring them together. How successful do you think you'll be with me as your … I don't even know what I'd be!"

"My love, my everything!"

"Listen to yourself!"

"I love you," she said, pushing herself back to look at his face. "Nothing will ever stop me from loving you. I will not allow it."

Sadness cloaked him. She was so sick of sadness everywhere she looked. This, what they had, should be cause for celebration. Instead, they must slink around in the dark, hide everything she wanted to shout from the treetops.

"Gwaethe, listen, my love." His lips descended to hers as though he could not help touching her. "I cannot see how we can be together, but we can see each other from time to time. It will have to be enough." Even as he said the words, Jacques looked so bleak she couldn't stand it. "Besides, this illness may still kill me. Please don't saddle yourself with an invalid."

Gwaethe glared at him. "I will take you however I can have you. I don't care if you are ill. You already feel better after being with me, don't you?"

Jacques cast his eyes to the ceiling and then took a deep breath without coughing. "I am breathing easier."

"See! That proves we must stay together. Each time you are ill, I will come to you, and you will take me."

He laughed without real mirth. "We must rejoin the others and discover what has transpired." He pushed the blanket at Gwaethe, and she pulled it around her shoulders.

A knock on the door preceded Exmund's entrance. "Captain, Princess, we must leave." He handed Jacques a mug of the medicine. "You seem better, sir. The rest helped?" Exmund's gaze didn't quite meet Jacques's.

"I am better." Jacques downed the drink and collected the rest of his clothes.

Exmund turned to Gwaethe. "Princess, news has come of Ramar Isiloe. She has been found."

"Alive?" Gwaethe only just stopped herself from clutching at Exmund.

"I don't have the details, Princess. I believe she has injuries, but I don't know how they were caused."

"Thank you, Exmund," Gwaethe said. "We will be out very soon." Gwaethe clutched the blanket to her and imagined all the terrible things Faenwelar and Gorin might have done to her cousin.

Jacques arms closed around her from behind, and he kissed her neck. "Don't imagine the worst. She is alive, and she is strong. Isiloe will be a thorn in your side for many years to come."

Gwaethe turned and threw off the blanket. She dressed quickly in her tunic and leggings then drew her cloak around her. "How will we conduct ourselves? Is there to be overt affection between us."

"I urge discretion, Gwaethe. There is no telling the repercussions if we make our feelings known."

Gwaethe studied him. Did he still wish to deny her when this war was over? Could they only ever be bedfellows in secret? Living months or years without seeing each other? Would they each be forced to take partners despite the love they had for each other? She would die inside without him. "I will be discreet for now, beloved, but I have never had to hide feelings as strong as these. I want you with me forever."

She left him then, her heart unsettled at the thought of a future where she must deny him. Outside was a new day, and Gwaethe opened her senses to all that surrounded her; the weak sun spearing its first rays through a gap in the cloud, the chill wind as it whistled through the buildings, a distant shout. She spoke to Kain.

Where are you, brother?

There was silence, but Gwaethe refused to fear the worst. Surely she had lived through enough grief that the Gods would spare her now?

Gwaethe, where are you?

We are where you left us last eve. Where should we head? She would not ask about Isiloe. She was afraid to.

Did my scouts find you?

They did.

Head west to the Grande plaza and enter the palace there. The city is almost ours. Formosa is using the palace as his base.

His presence faded, and Gwaethe spoke to Jacques as he emerged. "We head west to the palace in the Grande plaza. I urge caution, though Kain says the city is almost ours."

Jacques nodded and Gwaethe deployed her guard, then sent them west through the ruined city.

* * *

Jacques strode behind Gwaethe with Exmund at his side. His energy had been restored during the night with his elven princess, but still his reserves were poor. He felt like the most useless excuse for an army captain ever to grace the Kingdom. If he were not so ill, he would laugh out loud at his aspirations for the leadership of the Thorian army.

They moved west through the city, alert for remnants of Faenwelar's force left behind, but encountered nothing more than the occasional injured *Sis Lenweri* fighters. They had all sworn to Gwaethe, but Jacques was not convinced. Dubious new followers were just another headache in an already long list of headaches.

Jacques heard the Thorian force long before he saw them. Shouts and the clash of weapons floated down the streets, and they slowed their pace, unwilling to blunder into fighting. A street away from the plaza, Gwaethe sent two scouts further ahead. They returned to report Kingdom soldiers holding elves, including those newly sworn to her, in huddles in the large open space.

Every nerve in his body went on alert. Formosa was unpredictable, likely to kill first and ask questions later. There was no one with the rank to control him.

"We must get there before the killing starts," Gwaethe said. "If I can speak with him, maybe he will listen."

Jacques didn't like her chances.

They continued, reaching the plaza via the northeastern gate. Kingdom soldiers surrounded them, many with bandaged wounds.

"Halt!"

Jacques stepped up beside Gwaethe. "I am Captain Vorasava of Brightcastle, and this is Princess Gwaethe Arenil. Let us through."

The Sergeant who had spoken saluted. "Captain! We have been advised of your coming. Please follow me."

The Sergeant led the way through the prisoners, many of whom cried out to Gwaethe. Considering she had only taken fifty or so under her wing, there were many more who now wished to change sides.

"What is the state of things, Sergeant?" Jacques asked.

"We believe the High Prince of the *Sis Lenweri* has fled north, but his son has been taken prisoner."

"Gorin?" Gwaethe asked.

The man sneered at Gwaethe but answered. "I don't know his name."

Jacques's hands itched to teach the man a lesson in manners. Instead of violence, he began to ponder how having Faenwelar's son as a prisoner might be used against their enemies.

They approached the stairs of the largest palace in the square, and a group of soldiers blocked their path.

"No elves past this point," the leader said. His men seized their elven guards and pushed them into a huddle.

Jacques curled his arm around Gwaethe's middle as one of the soldiers grabbed her forearm. "This is Princess Gwaethe Arenil! She is not *Sis Lenweri*."

"I have orders for no elves to be admitted, and no exceptions. From the General himself."

Jacques stepped forward. "You will admit the Princess, or I will cut you down where you stand."

The soldier didn't appear to be daunted by Jacques's threat. "Orders are orders, Captain."

"This lady is our ally! Fetch Kain Jazara." Jacques still had his arm around Gwaethe's middle and felt her muscles tense. But she didn't pull away.

"Thank you, Jacques," she said, "but you must unhand me. It will do our causes no good to face the General like this."

Jacques allowed his arm to drop from her side. "What do you mean 'our causes'? I thought we fought for the same cause?"

Her dark gaze challenged his. "Not quite."

Had she discerned his ambition? "I assure you I wish for nothing more than the defeat of Faenwelar's forces. If I am not as idealistic as you about the elves currently on his side, it's only wise."

Her gaze narrowed, and the noise around them seemed to retreat until it was only the two of them. "Never mind," she said. "All will be revealed in time. For now, let us secure the best outcome for my *Lenweri*."

She faced the sergeant who barred their way. "I fought with you at the last great battle against High Prince Faenwelar. I request you bring Kain Jazara, so we may talk."

The man frowned as he held Gwaethe's gaze. "I *was* at that battle. It was a glorious fight."

"Then you must remember me. I ask only that you fetch Jazara. I will stay here with Captain Vorasava until you return."

The sergeant turned and sent one of his men into the palace. Jacques swelled with pride at the way Gwaethe held herself; as though she held court in her own empire. When they had been reunited, he had discerned a change in her, as though she had been through fire to emerge out the other side stripped of all but the most basic elements. Now she appeared to have recovered her poise, the shell she carried around her.

There was a stir, and Kain appeared through the barrier of soldiers. He shook hands with Jacques and then bowed to Gwaethe.

"Princess." His eyes swept the crowd. "I see your elves are here," he murmured.

"Indeed. Can you get me in to speak with the General?"

Kain's throat bobbed, and he looked as uncomfortable as Jacques had ever seen him. "I don't know. Alique is with him. If anyone can convince him it's his cousin."

"Has he done anything irrevocable?" Gwaethe asked.

"Not yet, but he is high on the success of battle. He has Prince Gorin, and Isiloe is in there as well."

"She is well?"

"She was hurt by the *Sis Lenweri*. Gorin started his torture, and when the battle with our forces began, Isiloe was left tied to a pole. Our men found her and brought her with them."

"Is there something you aren't telling me?" Gwaethe asked.

Kain took a long breath and ran a hand through his dark hair. "She is quiet, and her eyes have a wild look."

Gwaethe shook her head. "I know how it is with her. She will be well in time."

"I'll go back in and negotiate to have you join us." Kain turned and pushed his way through the Thorian soldiers.

Gwaethe watched him go, then turned to Jacques. "You need to rest. Come, sit on that fallen pillar, and your man will make you a draught of your potion."

"I should be in there, dammit. I'm an officer of the King's army, and this was my commission from the King himself until Formosa stepped in." But he allowed himself to be led away.

"Hush, Jacques. Leave this to Alique and Kain. They will do all they can."

* * *

Kain stood before General Formosa, a man he had no admiration for, and tried to be respectful. Tried to keep his voice low, without anger.

"I advise caution in dealing with the *Lenweri*, General," he said. "To this end, I urge you to speak to Gwaethe Arenil."

Formosa sneered. "*You* would. I, on the other hand, wish to ensure the Kingdom is safe from the *Lenweri*. And that means no discrimination between *Sis Lenweri* and their so-called peaceful cousins."

"Has the King advised wholesale slaughter, then?"

Formosa's lips pressed tight and a muscle twitched in his jaw. "He has asked me to act on his behalf for Thorius. I will not disclose his orders to me. I don't have to."

Alique placed her hand on Formosa's arm. "Josef, my husband is advisor to the King. He also acts in the Kingdom's interests; he always has."

Formosa frowned as he looked down at her hand. They had to keep the General calm. It was their best chance of getting a good outcome for Gwaethe and her people. *My people.* And Isiloe's life was in the balance if her continued binding was any indication. She remained roped to a pillar before all, just as Prince Gorin was. They were nothing the same!

He hoped Isiloe remained quiet, for a few well-chosen words from her would ignite the general.

"I expect you to be on their side, cousin," Formosa said. "You are hardly capable of forming an unbiased opinion."

"Perhaps I am one of the few capable of such, Josef. If anyone has a reason to be bitter, it is me. I almost died. I still suffer disability. But I love Thorius, and I want the best for it. I believe in Gwaethe and her honor. Please talk with her. You have nothing to lose."

Formosa's jaw clenched, and his eyes darted around the hall filled with his supporters. They all waited to see what the General would do, what they might be asked to do. If Kain was any judge, many would be reluctant to slaughter innocent elves. Many had fought in the battle with Gwaethe's elves on their side. Many were alive because of *Lenweri* aid. Perhaps Formosa, even in his insanity, was lucid enough to understand the risk if he pursued retribution on Gwaethe and her followers.

He turned to Alique. "You are right, cousin. I have nothing to lose by speaking to the elven woman. Have her brought before me."

Kain breathed for the first time in long moments and sent his wife a warm look. He dared not smile before Formosa, just as Alique would not. He held out his arm, and she moved to join him, linking her fingers through his.

"Nice work," he breathed.

She squeezed his hand but maintained her focus on her cousin.

Now if only his sister could convince Formosa to cease his killing, they might all escape this, including the Kingdom.

* * *

Gwaethe strode into the chamber behind the Sergeant, Jacques, and Exmund. It grated she should be relegated thus, but she would swallow her pride and do whatever was needed to rescue her *Lenweri*. She searched the chamber and immediately found Isiloe roped to a column to one side of the raised dais. Her heart stopped as she searched for a sign her cousin was alive. The ropes appeared to hold up her diminutive relative, and her head was slumped on her chest.

A wail pushed itself up from within, and she stopped, fighting the certainty she had lost her closest ally. *Pull yourself together! Don't show weakness!* She knew without doubt Formosa would use her attachment to Isiloe against her if he had a chance. You must be cold, hard; harder than the humans! She resumed walking, keeping her gaze on Jacques's back. He walked with a shuffle, and Exmund stayed close as if to catch him if he fell. When did he get that ill? A deep chill entered her at the thought he might die. Alique must examine him as soon as possible.

But now was not the time for worrying about anything besides extricating them from this scrape. She must make the General respect her. She stopped before him, three steps below. Jacques and Exmund moved to the side. She met Formosa's gaze, her back to most of those assembled. Let them see the blood that stained her tunic since the scourging. It was proof she was on the side of the Kingdom. Shame swept the pride aside and tears welled. She swallowed them down, clenched her teeth, and willed her emotions back deep inside. Despair pulled at her and made her wonder how this could be resolved for the good of all.

Gwaethe inclined her head slightly toward the General, but Formosa merely glared down his nose at her.

"Gwaethe Arenil, you come before me," he said. "Why?"

Anger replaced despair. He *would* respect her! "I come on behalf of my people, the peaceful *Lenweri*. We want nothing but to live in peace in our mountain homes. We seek no Kingdom lands. Only do we seek the death of High Prince Faenwelar."

His son, Gorin, hissed from where he was tied, his cat-like eyes glowing in the dim space.

Gwaethe ignored him, all her focus on the General.

"How can I be assured of the truth of your statements?" Formosa asked.

"I have only ever been a friend of Thorius as was my father, Orionkael. True, there has been no treaty between our nations, but there has never been the need. Until now."

"Faenwelar killed my father and seeks to reclaim lands which were elven centuries ago. My *Lenweri* have no interest in his quest. Indeed, many of Faenwelar's people will return to my fold if they have the choice. They will never have the choice while he lives."

Formosa's eyes were hard as flint. "I cannot agree, *Princess*. I have no knowledge of what your elves want or that Faenwelar's followers could be trusted. I can only agree on one issue; Faenwelar must die."

"Where is he?" Gwaethe asked, her hands clenched into fists at her sides.

Formosa's gaze dropped to the floor. "He has fled to the north, leaving his son as our hostage." The last he roared at Prince Gorin, who hissed and spat in Formosa's direction.

When the uproar had subsided, Formosa continued. "And him I intend to execute this day."

Gwaethe clutched her ring and met Kain's eyes across the chamber.

This is a mistake, brother!

I agree! Gorin alive is more valuable than he is dead. We can use him to draw Faenwelar back. Surely his son is crucial to his schemes?

Gwaethe nodded and turned back to the general.

"I believe that would be a mistake, General," she said. "Alive, Prince Gorin will be a bargaining tool, bait to lure the High Prince from hiding."

"He is no prince! Just as you are no princess!" Formosa roared. "Elven scum should have no titles." His gaze swept across Kain as he said the words, leaving no one in any doubt he was included in "elven scum".

"Regardless," Gwaethe said, her voice ringing through the uneasy murmurs of those present, "I urge caution, General. I urge you not to take any actions that cannot be reversed. The King must decide the next course. You have won a great victory, but it is only one battle in this war. I have fought at your side and will do so again for as long as it takes to defeat Faenwelar. I urge you to take all prisoners to the King, including Gorin. Allow *him* to decide how they shall be used. He will think it wisdom, not weakness."

For the first time, Formosa appeared uncertain. His gaze wandered around the chamber. He met the eyes of every one of his captains and sergeants, before returning his attention to Gwaethe.

"You have some standing with my King, I grant you that. I don't understand it, but it is fact never the less. Gorin shall be conveyed to Brightcastle and kept as prisoner there until his fate is decided."

Gwaethe held herself rigid. That was only part of the solution. Her people must be protected. She thought of all those unborn babes, the future of their race, and resolved to save them.

"However," Formosa continued, "there is still the fate of the other *Sis Lenweri* under our control."

"General, hand them over to me, and I will see them punished or rehabilitated," Gwaethe said. "They will not worry the Kingdom again."

"That is a reckless statement indeed, Princess," he said, stepping down so he was on the same level. "I would be insane to hand these dangerous prisoners over to you. Even in Kingdom hands they will be at best a nuisance and at worst a dire threat. I think it best they be dispatched, and their bodies burned, here and now, before they can wreak further death and destruction."

Gwaethe thought of the elves she had released, who had fought with her. "You cannot possibly decide who lives and who dies, General. There are many here who will support me."

"And that is exactly what is wrong with your plan! How can I predict what actions you will take in future? Why should I give you a ready-made army with which to attack Thorius?"

Gwaethe hissed, and Formosa stepped backward. "You cannot possibly make that decision! It is the King's to make!"

She felt a presence beside her. Jacques!

"She is right, General," Jacques said. "It's not part of your brief to decide policy toward the elves. I urge you to convey the prisoners to the

King and have them tried. You don't want their blood on your hands if all this goes wrong. The King is not a forgiving man." He dissolved into a coughing fit but waved away Exmund who still hovered.

"I think you misunderstand my brief from the King, Vorasava," Formosa sneered. "He has tasked me with vanquishing the *Sis Lenweri* and that is what I intend to do. By any means."

Jacques leaned closer. "You hold the supreme position in the King's army. Why would you wish to jeopardize it by behaving recklessly? The *Sis Lenweri* have shown themselves to be cunning enemies. Don't you think we should be just as cunning?"

Formosa frowned as he stared at Vorasava and then Gwaethe. "I don't trust you," he said.

"You have little reason to mistrust," she said. "I fought alongside you. Your prisoner Gorin had me flogged and then killed my followers. I have no interest in your Kingdom. What I do have interest in is defeating the man who killed my father and my people. You and I are on the same side."

"She saved my life, Formosa," Jacques grated. "When I was buried under a mountain and my men had ridden away, the Princess came after me and forced them to dig me out. Only for her, I would be feeding the worms."

Formosa again studied Jacques. At least in him, there was someone he might respect; if he could respect anyone. "You look like death. Perhaps you should have my cousin treat you. As to the rest..."

He turned and climbed the stairs then faced his supporters. "All prisoners are to be taken to Brightcastle and then onto Wildecoast. See that you gather them all. Leave no one behind."

Formosa left the hall in company with his cronies.

Gwaethe hurried to Isiloe's side. She gently raised her cousin's head and heaved a great sigh when one of Isiloe's blue eyes fluttered open. The other was closed by swelling and bruising.

"It is high time you arrived, cousin," Isiloe croaked, her lips curving into a crooked smile.

"Are you well, Isiloe?" Gwaethe turned to the nearest soldier. "Cut these bonds from her!"

At a nod from Jacques, the soldier did as he was bid. Gwaethe drew her cousin against her and held tight, then helped her over to the stairs. She rubbed her arms where the rope had cut the circulation.

"Don't fuss," Isiloe said. "I will be well. Do you think I would allow *Sis Lenweri* scum to truly hurt me?"

"They did this to you?"

"Gorin got his hands on me, but I think he will hesitate before he does so again. I took down three of his soldiers before he managed to knock me out. When I awoke, it was to the humans swarming the place. I was brought here and tied up." She groaned and rolled her head from side to side. "Maybe I am dying after all. My head hurts like fire."

Gwaethe summoned Exmund and left her cousin to him. As she rose, Alique was there to hug her.

"I'm glad to see you whole, Gwaethe," she said when she drew back.

Gwaethe laid her palm along Alique's cheek. "I am almost whole, sister. Can you tend to Isiloe?"

"Of course, and then I will check on you."

Gwaethe smiled and turned to find Jacques close. "Thank you."

He shook his head. "Why should you thank me?"

"I know you don't believe the *Sis Lenweri* can be saved, but you cast your doubts aside to stand up for me. How did you know what would sway him?"

Jacques ran is hands through his hair. He really did look half-dead. "I didn't. I had a hunch a threat to his career might make him think twice."

"Well, thanks to you we have time."

He raised his hands as if he wished to hold her then dropped them to his sides. "You were magnificent, but I don't know if it will matter in the end." He appeared to crumple, and Gwaethe clutched at him.

Exmund was there in seconds and lowered his leader to the ground, laying his cloak under Jacques's head.

Gwaethe grabbed his hands, patting them. "Jacques, can you hear me?" She laid her palm along his forehead and hissed at the heat. "He is burning up!" She sought Exmund. "Get him the potion!"

"It's not working, Princess. He has been hiding his illness until he could no longer do so. I fear he is close to death!"

Alique was there, her calm voice urging Exmund back to Isiloe while she cared for Jacques. She had him moved to a nearby room where a bed was soon made and a fire set. Gwaethe stood by while her sister-in-law worked on her beloved. The man who would never be hers. When she felt able to leave her patient, Alique drew Gwaethe over to the fire.

"He is gravely ill, Gwaethe. I'm afraid I can't save him. His chest is so full of foul liquid, he can't get air into his body. All we can do is keep thumping him to help it drain." She grasped Gwaethe's upper arm and squeezed. "You care for him?"

She nodded, never taking her gaze from Jacques. "Is there nothing more you can do?"

"If we could get him to Brightcastle, Princess Benae may be able to help. Her healing is superior to mine."

"Then let us take him there!" Her gut rebelled at the sympathy in Alique's eyes.

"I'm afraid it will take too long. I'm sorry, Gwaethe, but I urge you to prepare for the worst."

As if one could ever prepare for that! Alique might be prepared to give up, but she, Gwaethe, never would. Jacques was tough for a human - tougher than anyone she had ever met - and a simple mudslide would not be the end of him.

"Make him comfortable and keep him alive," Gwaethe said. "I will get him to Benae if it is the last thing I do." She strode from the room, determined to get help for Jacques before it was too late. She ignored the small voice that warned against believing in yet another human to save the day.

CHAPTER TWELVE

The first person Gwaethe encountered on leaving the sick room was Kain. She clutched at his arm and ushered him into a corner. "I need to get Jacques - Captain Vorasava - to Princess Benae in Brightcastle with all haste!"

Kain gazed at her, infuriating her with his calmness. "Brightcastle is the better part of ten days ride away, especially as this army travels. From what I saw, the man is hardly up to a hard ride."

She gritted her teeth and clenched her fists to hold in her fury at the situation. "I don't care how impossible it is, you must make it happen!"

"And just how am I supposed to do that?"

"Send a messenger with all haste to Princess Benae and have her meet us."

Kain clasped her hands in his. "Sister, the Princess is heavy with child. There is no way she could travel in that condition."

Gwaethe wrenched her hands from his grasp and turned to lay her forehead against the cold stone of the wall. "I can't allow him to die," she whispered.

Kain's hand found her shoulder and squeezed. "Sometimes we don't have the choice of who lives and dies. I was lucky with Alique. She walked a precipice and came back to me after her head injury."

Gwaethe turned back to him. "Then you know miracles can happen. He is strong."

"And he has already been through so much. Perhaps his body has done all the fighting it can."

She pushed her face close to Kain's. "I will not believe that until he has drawn his last breath. Now are you going to help me or stand there and give me more reasons why I should not hope?"

He let out a long breath. "Of course, I'll help. Allow me to organize an escort for your elves and my men, and we will leave with all haste."

She gripped his sleeve. "No! You must stay here with the General. Without Jacques, he needs you as the voice of reason; the witness."

Kain frowned. "I don't like you to travel alone."

"I will be fine, but there is one more thing I must ask."

"You wish to take Alique with you?"

Gwaethe nodded. "I know she will agree immediately, but I must have your blessing. Will you allow it?"

He rubbed his hand through his hair, dark eyes showing more distress than usual for her brother. Alique was precious to him.

"I can't believe I'm agreeing to this, but yes, you must take her. It will be hard on her as she is barely recovered herself, but I know it's what she will insist upon."

She kissed his cheek. "Thank you, brother. I will ensure no harm comes to your lady. We will take all the most seriously injured with us. Even if we are too late, we must try." Gwaethe returned to the sick room to warn Alique of their imminent departure, then sought her cousin.

She found Isiloe still on the steps arguing with Exmund. "I tell you I am well enough!" When she spotted Gwaethe, Isiloe leapt to her feet, almost knocking Exmund to the ground. "There you are! Tell this… man… I am recovered enough to help with the withdrawal!"

Gwaethe smiled but hid the relief she felt at Isiloe's feistiness. There was no better indication her cousin would make a full recovery.

"I'm afraid there is no point in arguing, Exmund," she said. "Isiloe must be allowed to act as she sees fit. I'm sure there are plenty of other injured you can tend."

"How is the Captain, Princess?" he asked.

Her heart clenched at the question. "We leave immediately for Brightcastle and Princess Benae. I believe she is his only hope."

"Right you are, then. I'll see we have everything we need for the trip. We'll make this the fastest journey from Amitania to Brightcastle there ever was."

Exmund bowed and left, having lifted Gwaethe's spirits.

"Well he's changed his tune toward you," Isiloe said, gazing after him.

"No time to stand around, cousin. We must be on the road within the hour!"

As it happened, it was closer to two hours before they were ready to travel. Three supply wagons were commandeered to convey the sick and injured. Gwaethe's heart bled that she could not take more. There were many gravely injured she had to leave behind to travel when the rest of the army was ready to leave the following day.

Jacques was made comfortable in the lead wagon. Each vehicle contained either Alique, Exmund, or Alique's maid, Julli, who was skilled with potions. Gwaethe worried it would be too much for Alique, but there was nothing for it.

They took the sturdiest horses and three teams of good strong Kingdom men to help the wagons over the rocky passes. General Formosa had complained of the drain in army resources but had been swayed; not by Kain, but by one of his own cronies, a Lieutenant named Dickfos who appeared very sensible. Gwaethe thanked the Gods the man had stepped forward at this time.

The first twenty-four hours out of Amitania were the easiest, though the weather was turning cold. Gwaethe never allowed herself to dwell on failure but kept her mind always on the next leg of the trail, the next hurdle she must overcome. Even though everything within urged her to stay with Jacques and watch his every breath, she steeled herself to check on him only twice a day. The remainder of the time she oversaw each detail brought to her, from hunting expeditions to scouting forays.

As much as she had hoped to find none of the *Sis Lenweri* in their path, remnants of Faenwelar's forces were scattered in all directions. They engaged two to three groups of the rebels each day for the first three days out of Amitania. She thanked the gods for the fighting men Kain had managed to scavenge from the main army force, and for her own elves and new converts. The latter were particularly fierce, as if they tried to prove their place in her army. Gwaethe took note of it all. It lifted her heavy heart. At least something was working in her favor.

Isiloe was almost fully recovered thanks to Alique's medicines, even though she grumbled about having to accept the human woman's help. She worked tirelessly supervising the new elves, her suspicious eye always roving their activities. But she discovered nothing to indicate they were disloyal. She often kept company with Exmund when he had time off his nursing duties. The two were an odd couple but appeared to have found a grudging respect for each other. Gwaethe was beyond understanding it.

The weather steadily grew colder, and they were short on furs and cloaks even after plundering Amitania. Despite all her prayers that the weather stay kind to them, a blizzard struck in the afternoon of day three. They were almost through the last of the mountain passes and carried on until they found a wider path where the wagons could be grouped around a central firepit. The vehicles provided shelter to the men and elves, and the fire kept the sick and injured warmer.

Gwaethe's teeth chattered as she climbed into Jacques's wagon; her last duty for the evening. Alique's maid, Julli, sat with him, and the space was lit by a lone candle.

"How is he?" Gwaethe asked, kneeling on the other side of the pallet. She placed her palm on his forehead. It was the same as it had been since the fever subsided; cold and clammy.

"No change, Princess," Julli said, "but I don't think he's worse either."

Gwaethe smiled. "That is the trouble. We can't tell. Take a break, and I will sit with him."

Julli nodded and left. The poor girl appeared exhausted, and Gwaethe regretted the toll this trek would take on her. Still, there was nothing any of them could do about that. At least some of their injured were improving enough to sit in the third wagon, leaving Jacques the luxury of his own vehicle.

"We are three days out, beloved," she said, smoothing his hair back from his face. "In a week, we will be close to Brightcastle, and Princess Benae will heal you. All you must do is hold onto life until then." An image of what he might look like by then popped into her head, but she shoved it aside.

She ran her hand under the covers and gasped. He was cold! She checked his feet and they were ice-like. Gwaethe didn't hesitate. She stripped her clothes off and slid under the covers, laying her warmth against his naked body. Then she maneuvered her fur cloak over the two of them and hunkered down to wait until her body started to warm him. She rubbed her palm up and down his chest and abdomen and chafed his hands while folding her feet between his.

Slowly, achingly slowly, he began to warm. Desperate fear struck. How long had he lain like this? Dying of the cold. Three days? *No!* Alique would have checked his body temperature. It was likely just this blizzard. The temperature had dropped dramatically with it. He had not been lying in this wagon for three days freezing.

Gwaethe kept up a soothing murmur of sound, so Jacques knew she was there, caring for him. She wanted to be his connection with the living world. *He can hear me.* If only he would stir and smile the smile that warmed her through. *One day he will. Keep the faith.* She fell asleep with the blizzard howling outside.

The next morning, Gwaethe was awakened by Alique during her first rounds of the day.

"He was cold," she said, as she slipped from Jacques's pallet. She quickly pulled on her clothes, careful not to look at Alique.

"You did the right thing, Gwaethe," Alique said. "Cold would have killed him as surely as the muck in his lungs. But hasten, I have asked Exmund to attend to help me turn him."

Gwaethe threw the rest of her clothes on, grabbed the cloak, and fled the wagon, almost knocking Exmund over in her haste.

A sunny, fine morning greeted her, and she hurried to the campfires to deliver her orders for the day. Perhaps they could open the tops of the wagons and get the sun on their patients. It would be good to ride in the sunshine instead of under gloomy cloud. After a hurried breakfast, the camp was packed up, and they took to the trail.

Around midday of that day, Gwaethe noticed a beautiful hawk hovered above them. Several times over the next hour, she almost felt it was peering at her, trying to understand. It was silly, of course. She had put it out of her head when a stranger stepped onto the path before her. He was tall with long dark hair, and his green eyes harbored golden flecks. They were the most extraordinary eyes she had ever seen. She called the column to a halt.

The man approached and bowed. "Well met, lady. How can I help?"

"What makes you think we need help?" Gwaethe countered.

"Just a feeling I have." His visage was handsome if gaunt. There appeared not an ounce of spare flesh anywhere on the man. "Tell me."

Gwaethe frowned and looked around for the fellow's companions, or at least a horse. "Are you alone?"

He smiled, but it did nothing to relieve the severity of his expression. "I am quite alone. You have nothing to fear. Tell me how I can aid you."

For some reason, Gwaethe wished to pour out all her troubles to him. "What is your name?"

"You may call me Anton," he said. "And you are?"

Gwaethe drew herself erect in her saddle as Isiloe rode up. "I am Princess Gwaethe Arenil, and this is my cousin, *Ramar* Isiloe."

The man bowed again, but not quickly enough to hide the surprise in his eyes. "You ride with men and wagons, Princess. That is no common thing. Where are you bound?"

"As if it is any of your concern!" Isiloe snapped, leaping off her horse and confronting him.

Gwaethe sighed and dismounted but signaled the column to continue past them. She detected no threat toward them, though Anton carried an array of knives on his person.

"Leave the man be, Isiloe," she said, placing a hand on Isiloe's shoulder.

Anton hadn't moved a muscle despite Isiloe's threatening advance.

"We are bound for Brightcastle with all haste," she told Anton. "There are several gravely ill soldiers with us."

"So, we cannot afford the time to spend talking with you, stranger," Isiloe snapped.

"Isiloe, hush!"

But Isiloe didn't hush. She turned to Gwaethe, eyes blazing. "But we must get your captain to the healer, cousin. I could not stand you if he passes."

Gwaethe glared at her so hard she fell silent.

"Captain?" Anton asked.

Gwaethe faced him. "Yes, Captain Vorasava of Brightcastle. Do you know of him?"

"I do. What happened?"

"He was caught in a mudslide over a week ago," Gwaethe said. "I believed he was recovering, but he had a relapse and now is near death. It is said there is a healer at Brightcastle who may save him. The others were injured in a battle with the *Sis Lenweri* at Amitania."

Anton went very still. Her words seemed to mean more to him than they should to a disinterested stranger. It seemed this Anton had more to do with Brightcastle, or possibly Amitania, than he had revealed.

"Show me the Captain," he said. "I will help if I can."

Gwaethe led him forward to the wagon and they both climbed aboard as it trundled along. Jacques was still unconscious, his face grey.

Anton sucked a breath through his teeth. "He is indeed a sick man," he said. "Continue on to Brightcastle, and I will find a local healer I know and ask her for a potion." With those words, he turned and disappeared into the trees. As Gwaethe mounted her horse, she again spied the beautiful hawk, winging its way south.

"I don't like it," Isiloe said. "Strangers popping out of the trees and then disappearing. You should not have told him as much as you did."

"Comes a time we have to trust, Isiloe," she said. "I detected no threat from him, although I feel he is a dangerous man."

Isiloe stared. "You are making no sense! I am going back down the line to check our trail. I hope, by the time I return, you will have come to your senses."

Now it was Gwaethe's turn to stare as her diminutive cousin mounted her horse and trotted off. It was good to see her returned to health, but her caustic tongue was difficult to deal with sometimes. She shook her head as she urged her stallion forward to the head of the column. They traveled thus for the rest of the day, and their camp that night was uneventful.

The following morning the weather stayed fine and sunny. Gwaethe began to breathe easier now they were out of the mountains and attacks by Faenwelar's stragglers had ceased. She mused on how Kain might be dealing with Formosa. The General would cause them more trouble before this was over, she was sure.

Around mid-morning, she spied the hawk again. It circled over her band of soldiers and elves, flying in ever-increasing circles as though surveying the area of forest around them. Gwaethe was fascinated as the bird angled its head this way and that, effortlessly gliding over the terrain. She was sure it was the same bird as before.

An hour later, she had the feeling of being watched, and, soon after, Anton walked out of the woods in front of her. Again, Gwaethe pulled her stallion to the side and allowed the convoy to continue. He was no threat and they couldn't afford to lose any time.

She dismounted, looking around for his horse. There was none in sight.

"Well met, Anton," she said. "Were you able to bring the potion?" She held tight to her emotions, reluctant to raise her hopes.

He held out a pouch and a vial, which Gwaethe took. He reached to his neck to remove an amulet, a brilliant amber stone, she had not noticed before.

"You will need this," he said, keeping the necklace in his hand. "It enhances the potion."

Gwaethe didn't understand, but motioned for him to follow her. She caught up with Jacques's wagon and tied her stallion to the back, then she and Anton climbed into the vehicle.

Alique was inside, mixing a liquid over a small brazier. "Who is this?" Her voice was suspicious as Gwaethe hadn't told her of Anton's promise to return with aid.

"This is Anton," she said. "He has a potion which may help."

"Potion?" Alique said, her eyes narrowed. "Where did it come from."

Anton bowed. "Lady, I assure you I mean no harm. This man is at death's door, and I have something which may buy him extra hours. Surely you have nothing to lose?"

"Or so one might think," Alique said. "How can we be sure?"

"Peace, Alique," Gwaethe said. "I am willing to give this a chance."

Alique reached for the medicines. She opened the bag and sniffed long and deep then did the same with the vial. "How are they prepared?"

Anton smiled. "It is simple." He took the herbs and vial off Alique and poured some of the herbs and potion into a small bowl. He stirred the mixture over the heat until the wagon was filled with the pungent smell of thyme, rosemary, sage, and something else Gwaethe could not identify. When the mix had begun to steam, he slipped the amber stone into it, dragging it back and forth through the liquid. The stone began to pulse with a dim orange light.

She met Alique's gaze, but the woman seemed merely curious.

Gwaethe was about to break her silence when Anton removed the amber stone from the mixture and tied it around Jacques's throat. He then strained the herbs from the potion and handed the liquid to Alique.

"Mix in some honey and spoon a little of this into his mouth every hour," he said. Before Gwaethe could ask any questions, Anton left the wagon. She followed him to the flap, but by the time she poked her head out, there was no sign of the enigmatic man.

She pulled her head back in. "He's gone!"

Alique looked up from where she was feeding the potion to Jacques. "A curious man indeed. I wonder where he got this from, and what the stone is?"

Gwaethe shook her head. She was no stranger to magic, but this was still odd. "I will find out who he is, but if this helps Jacques, I will be very thankful." She left the wagon and caught up to the leading soldiers and elves.

Isiloe eyed her curiously. "Where have you been? I thought I saw Anton."

"You did."

Exmund happened to be riding alongside Isiloe, and his ears pricked up. "Who is Anton?"

Isiloe pursed her lips, so Gwaethe explained. "A stranger who happened along yesterday. He returned today with medicine to help Jacques."

Exmund frowned. "You mean a strange man has approached us offering help to the Captain, and you didn't think to mention it to me?"

Gwaethe raised an eyebrow at him. "I admire your devotion, Corporal, but the Captain is my responsibility."

He looked down at his hands on the reins and muttered to himself. "In future, please inform me of anything to do with Captain Vorasava, Princess. He is very important to me."

She studied him, momentarily lost for words. She hadn't expected him to feel so intensely for Jacques. With this young man there did not seem to be anything holding his feelings in check. He wore them outside for all to trample on. "I will inform you from now on, Corporal."

He went red in the face and nodded, failing to meet her eye. "Tell me about this Anton."

Gwaethe considered. "He is mysterious. His hair is long and dark; he is tall and somewhat gaunt; and he said he was drawn to us. I do not know what he meant."

"Anton," Exmund said, as if testing the word. "Is that the only name he gave?"

"It is," Gwaethe said. "Do you think you know him?"

"I wonder if he is Vard Anton. He was the man linked to the kidnapping of Princess Alecia of Brightcastle," he mused. "If so, he was once a respected soldier, entrusted to caring for the Princess."

The story was familiar to Gwaethe, but she had never taken much notice of the details. "You think he might be dangerous?" she asked, her heart kicking up a notch at the thought.

"If it is him," Exmund said, "he would not harm the Captain. They were once colleagues. Many strange events and rumors surround him, but what is truth and what is myth is anyone's guess."

Gwaethe knew a moment of relief. "I am glad to hear you think him no threat to us."

Isiloe laughed. "He is one man, cousin. How could he be a threat?"

Exmund addressed her. "Do not underestimate him, Ramar Isiloe. He can be a formidable ally, but I would not wish to come against him in battle."

"Hah!" Isiloe said. "Just let him try attacking us. I will send him on his way."

Gwaethe didn't share her cousin's bravado. "If he returns, I will ensure you are sent for, Corporal, so you may meet him."

Exmund nodded and turned his attention back to the trail ahead. Gwaethe cast around for the hawk and saw the bird floating high in the sky to the west.

The rest of the day passed uneventfully, but the hawk was never far from the convoy. Gwaethe was sure it meant something, but what she could not say. She climbed into the wagon at hourly intervals to see if there was any change in Jacques's condition, but nothing altered. They faithfully spooned the mixture, including fresh batches, into his mouth on the hour. The stone pulsed amber at his throat.

That night, the camp was subdued, a pall hanging over them, as if they all waited for a sign. Perhaps it was only Gwaethe who waited thus, but she knew she was not the only one who cared for Jacques. This was a mission of mercy. He was known and respected by many of the soldiers and elves who accompanied them. She even caught Isiloe's gaze on the wagon often.

Gwaethe climbed into Jacques's wagon one last time near midnight. As much as she had tried to stay aloof, Anton had injected fresh hope into their mission, and she could not stay away a moment longer. She would sleep by his pallet tonight like a faithful dog. It was not becoming as an elven princess, but Gwaethe knew a desperate urge to be near her lover.

Alique was there, making one last check on her patient.

"Is there any change?" Gwaethe asked, as she settled beside him.

Alique drew a long breath then let it out. "He is no worse which is more than I could have said any other day since we left."

Gwaethe's shoulders dropped. She knew it had been too much to ask that this might have brought him back from the brink. "At least he is no worse..."

Alique reached for her hand. "You care deeply for him."

She gritted her teeth, desperate to prevent tears from falling. Even before her sister-in-law, she would not show such weakness. "I do. But there is nothing for us in the future, even if he recovers."

"I would dearly love to give you hope, but I cannot. You must prepare for the worst."

Gwaethe met her gaze. The pity she saw there infuriated her. "How should I do that? Could you prepare for the loss of your husband? Could you?"

Alique shrugged. "Possibly not, but there is no point having false hope. He hovers on the brink of death. Indeed, I have rarely seen one so ill. The Captain is a very tough man."

"Exactly," Gwaethe snapped. "A lesser man would have perished beneath that mountain. A lesser man would not have lived to lead his men to Amitania. He can come through this, too."

Alique nodded. "Yes, of course."

Gwaethe knew she agreed only to calm her. It was a battle neither of them could win. "I am sorry, Alique," she said. "You are doing your best for him, and I am rude. I am here to spend the night. I hope that will give you a rest."

"Are you sure?"

Gwaethe nodded. "I will tend him and get what rest I can. I will see he gets the medicine hourly. Maybe when you return in the morning, he will have improved."

Alique stared for a moment and then nodded. "I could do with more sleep this night. Farewell until the morning, sister."

Alique left the wagon, and Gwaethe smoothed the covers that lay across Jacques's chest. She settled herself beside him with her head on his shoulder and closed her eyes. Perhaps he might feel her presence and know someone kept him company.

* * *

He wandered alone through a wasteland of mud and dead trees. He couldn't remember how he had come there or where he was going. Not even a bird call disturbed the silence, and the sun seemed to fight to penetrate the gloom. He couldn't tell if it was night or day. He cast his gaze around the horizon and saw only the skeletal limbs of dead trees, smelt only the odor of moist decay. This land had been dead for centuries.

He stopped and looked down at his body. His uniform was rags, many of the brass buttons gone. In this light, he wasn't sure what color it had been. One sleeve of the coat was missing, and his arm, once healthy and well-muscled, was now just skin and bones. He touched his face and felt skin stretched thin over cheekbones, his lower face covered by a straggly beard. His feet were bare and deathly cold.

Where am I? Who am I? He couldn't remember his name. The harder he tried to remember, the further away understanding fled. Perhaps he had always been like this? Maybe this was the total of his existence? But he felt, deep in his core, that life had once been sparkling and full of promise.

If I find light I can walk toward it. But light and life seemed foreign concepts in this world. Something touched his lips, and a name echoed across the land.

"Jacques."

He looked around, hand to his lips, but all was unchanged. A curious taste caressed his tongue: honey, spices and herbs, and something else indefinable.

"Jacques."

Still no one came to claim the voice he heard. Who was Jacques? Could he own that name? Did he know the owner of the voice who so tenderly called?

No remembrance came to increase his awareness, but the voice continued.

"Jacques, you must come back to us. So much depends upon you, not the least myself."

He wanted to know the possessor of the voice; wanted to belong to her. Even though he didn't know how, he realized it was a woman who spoke. His beloved? Did he have one? His past was still blank, a grey nothingness.

"I know you have fought long and hard, but you must fight more. You must fight until death releases its hold on you. Come back, so we can resolve all that stands between us."

The voice cut off abruptly as if torn by a sob. If only he could talk, he might reassure her. He could comfort this woman who believed in him. Long moments drifted past during which he tasted the honeyed mixture. He swallowed, and warmth pooled deep inside him. He held onto it because there was no warmth in this world and he craved it.

"Jacques, it is Gwaethe. You must remember all we have begun and return."

Gwaethe! The name reverberated within him. The warmth in his gut suddenly doubled. *Gwaethe!* But the name was not on his lips, only in his mind. She couldn't hear his thoughts, and she would think he didn't listen. It was *Gwaethe* who spoke, and she meant something to him. She anchored him to a different world where there was a chance of life and joy. But he could not return. He didn't know how to.

Despair blasted through him, and he crashed to his knees. Doomed. He was doomed to roam these lands. He couldn't return to her. Jacques lay on the wet earth and slept.

* * *

Gwaethe wept, her tears wetting the blanket that covered Jacques. All night she had spoken to him and spooned the mixture past his lips. He must hear her! But he was as remote from her as he had ever been since his collapse. Maybe Alique was correct, and she must accept he was gone. But, how could she while he still lived? There had been one moment when she believed he might have heard her. He murmured, and she was sure it was her name. But then he fell into a deep sleep, and she had to admit she was mistaken.

As she stared at his face, Alique pushed through the wagon flap.

"How is he?"

For a moment, Gwaethe didn't speak. She brushed the hair back from his forehead and straightened the covers.

"No change," she said. "He mumbled something earlier, but he has not awoken." She raised her eyes to Alique but flinched away from the pity there. "Perhaps you are right about him."

"Muttering is a good sign, Gwaethe. Keep talking to him and touching him. Have you given him the medicine?"

"I have given both yours and Anton's potion, and it has done no good." She felt utter despair.

Her sister-in-law examined Jacques, listening to his chest through a trumpet-like instrument, looking in his eyes, and touching his skin.

"His color is better, and I believe his breathing to be easier," she said. "Maybe we are winning the fight."

"Are you sure?" Gwaethe placed her hand on his forehead and watched his chest as it rose and fell. "Maybe the sun will be good for him today. Is it fine?"

Alique smiled at her. "The sun is out. I will complete my examination and roll back the canvas. You must have breakfast." Her eyes narrowed. "I prescribe a day off the sick room, Princess. I will keep you updated of any changes."

Gwaethe knew a desperate relief that she would not have to watch over Jacques that day. She was not made for healing but for fighting and leading. She nodded to Alique and left the wagon.

CHAPTER THIRTEEN

Jacques became aware of a light in the foggy gray. He pushed himself to his feet and cast around for the source. Through the dimness, a warm column of light lay ahead, stretching from the ground into the heavens. It was the only change he had noted since he had arrived in this place, so he walked toward it.

As he came closer, the intervening mist thinned, and the light intensified. It became so bright he had to shield his face with his hands. Soon, other columns of light streaked out of the heavens down to the muddy earth. They were all colors of the rainbow. He hesitated, unsure of which one to approach. Even with eyes closed, Jacques saw the colors through his eyelids. What did it mean? The columns were significant, he knew. Were they portals out of this cold, grey, forsaken place? Which was *his* way out?

A man approached. He wore a long grey robe with strange symbols embroidered on the cloth in red. Jacques watched as the man stepped carefully around the columns of light, allowing none to touch any part of him. Would this being help him return to the voice, to Gwaethe?

The robed man stopped four paces from him, and Jacques bowed. It seemed this man was someone who should be respected.

"Well met, my son," he said. "I heard your call."

"I made no call to you or anyone, sir."

"You may call me 'Father', my son. I am here to lead you back to your life. If you should wish to return."

Jacques didn't hesitate. "Of course, I wish to return." Then he thought of his body back in the waking world, wracked with illness, on the verge of death. Could he survive if that was all he had to return to?

"Then you must choose from one of these columns of light. You see they are all shades of the rainbow. The realities they lead to are as varied."

"What do you mean?"

The old man swept his arm across the horizon, encompassing all the light columns. "They all lead back to your life but not to the same one. There is one column which, if you select that one, will take you back directly to the life you had before your arrival here. But the others lead to parallel worlds where your life has taken different courses."

Jacques stared, unable to get his mind around what the man had said. How could he believe such a thing as a parallel world existed?

"How do I choose?" Jacques asked.

The old man smiled. "Only you can know that, my son. Select the wrong column and your life from now will be very different. In one, you will not be a soldier but a farmer with a wife and tribe of children. In others, you may already have achieved your fondest desire. In still more, you may be a pauper, or already dead of a childhood disease or even murder."

"What will become of me if I should choose one of the latter?" he asked.

"Then you shall cease to exist as soon as you arrive in that world. You will simply blink out of being."

A shudder rippled up Jacques's spine. True, he was gravely ill back there, from what he recalled. And the voice had sounded sad, desperate; the voice that had spoken his name and called him back. But there was hope there at least, some sort of life.

"How do I know which one leads where, Father?"

The old man smiled and shook his head. "I cannot say. Only you can choose. Look deep into your heart and choose the column that speaks to you. It is the only way you can be guided."

"Surely you can give me more help than that? What do the colors stand for?"

"It is different for all, my son. I truly cannot guide you more. But do not tarry, for your body needs your spirit back. Without that, the empty vessel will perish. I wish you well, and I hope *not* to see you here for many decades to come." He lifted his hand. "Farewell, my son."

With those words, the old man faded until his essence blew away on a sudden swirl of the breeze.

"Thank you for your help, old man," Jacques said, a bitterness sourer than medicine on his tongue. He cast around at the columns, lost as to which one he should select. But choose he must if he wished to move forward. He focused on the first beam, blue, and looked within.

* * *

Gwaethe stayed away from Jacques that whole day but was drawn back after dinner. She could no longer stand not knowing how he fared. Exmund was spooning the new potion into his mouth when she climbed into the wagon. He nodded at Gwaethe and smiled.

"He is no worse, Princess," he said, placing the bowl and spoon aside. "In four more days we will be in Brightcastle, and he can have the help he needs."

Gwaethe studied their patient. His breathing was slow with good depth and his skin had a faint pink tinge which hadn't been there a day ago.

"You are correct, Exmund," she said, "in fact, he seems a little better." She would not give in to her fears; that four days was still too long to save him. "I will take over here while you get some rest."

Exmund nodded and left the wagon. Gwaethe settled herself for another long night beside her Captain. At least he would know someone waited for him to awake. He tossed his head from side to side and muttered words Gwaethe couldn't catch; something about choosing?

"Jacques," she said, leaning forward to kiss his brow. "Come back to me. We have so much yet to discuss. I need you." Her heart lurched at the admission. She couldn't afford to need anyone, let alone this human, but she had come to realize he was important to her; even vital. If he should die...no, she wouldn't think about that, couldn't entertain it as a possibility no matter what Alique advised.

"You will come back to me, and we will live all the glory of peace in the Kingdom. Come back to me, Jacques." She lay her head on his shoulder and said another prayer to her Gods.

* * *

As Jacques gazed at the blue beam, a sense of calm suffused his mind. He longed for that calm and had experienced it in battle many a time when all was chaos around him. The core of peace within was vital to making good decisions on the run. It was essential when fighting hand to hand. Maybe this beam was the way back to his soldier's life. He took a step toward it, but then red caught his attention from the corner of his eye.

Perhaps red was the way? This column engendered excitement, passion, and boldness within him. Surely these were the essential elements to a soldier? They were qualities he had always admired in his mentors. He faltered and turned toward the red. But did this color resonate as the old man said it should? Did he feel it deep within?

Jacques turned away and found the purple beam in his sight. It filled him with wonder and opened his mind to ideas he had not had since he was a child. He imagined creating all manner of amazing machines, just as his child-self had done. But the responsibilities of an only son had intervened, and he had entered the army to follow his father's wishes. The purple was tempting, but he knew it could not lead to his current reality.

But did he wish to return there? Might there be a better life awaiting him within one of these shards of light? The answer was "yes", but his existence was also threatened should he make the wrong choice. Even returning to his current reality was a huge risk. His body hovered on the brink, the old man had said so. He must get back if he were to salvage any life at all. Was it worth the risk of losing everything to possibly gain a better life? What about the person waiting for him, calling to him, tending to him? Was *she* worth returning to?

These questions were without answer, but he straightened his shoulders and faced the green beam. He brought the light within himself, searching for anything that resonated. He felt healthier for the presence of the color, even though he knew it was not really within his body. If this color could heal him, was this the correct choice? He held onto it, enjoying the sense of peace and well-being it offered. Still he couldn't make the choice.

Beyond the green light was an amber column. If he recalled correctly, it was one of the first to appear. Jacques stared at it, tried to accept the color into his body; and failed. He had never liked orange, so this beam couldn't be the way back. Could it? Had he yet decided if he would return to his current reality? He sought the next light even though something about the amber glow snagged his attention as if to pull him back.

He forced himself to continue to the next column; yellow. This was easier on his mind. He held out his arms to the golden glow, suddenly so happy and optimistic he felt his heart would burst from his chest. He was sure such happiness had rarely been a part of his present life. But did that mean this was the wrong path?

Questions without answers swarmed his mind, and his eyes flicked from color to color, desperate to find something which provided a hint of the correct choice. Did he wish to return?

"Jacques, come back to me. I need you more than I ever realized."

Gwaethe. It was Gwaethe who called him, but the feelings her voice caused were confused - love, desire, frustration, denial, fear - they all battled for supremacy. If he truly loved her, there should be only love and longing, not a bunch of contradictory feelings, and certainly no fear. What was he afraid of? Jacques clutched his skull and closed his eyes against the cascading light bombarding his mind.

Tell me which one! He stumbled forward and fell onto his hands and knees. When he opened his eyes, there before him was the amber light. It beckoned to him, pulsating as though to draw his attention from the others. It might still be the wrong choice, might lead to his destruction. And yet it had snagged his attention more than once.

He stood, took a deep breath, and stepped into the amber glow.

His body was buffeted by winds more savage than any he had felt before. He would be torn to shreds in this tunnel of orange fury. Blinding amber brilliance consumed him, and nothing he did halted his headlong rush.

Where just before he had been cold, now there was heat so strong his skin began to crisp. Jacques screamed as he started to burn. The fire entered his lungs, stole his air, but still he screamed, screamed, screamed…

* * *

Gwaethe held onto Jacques as he shrieked and threw himself from side to side. The amber stone at his throat blasted its rich orange light through the darkened wagon, and outside the sounds of the camp stirring filtered through.

He was too strong for her, but she held on tight lest he hurt himself, and prayed he would quieten soon.

"Jacques," she crooned, "hush, my fierce Captain. All is well…" Tears streamed down her face at the pain in his voice. If this was life, better he should perish.

Exmund joined her and then Alique, and the three of them battled as Jacques struggled and cried, his teeth clenched and every tendon in his body taut.

"It is as though he is being tortured," Alique snapped. "Get the stone off him!"

Exmund moved to do as she advised, but Gwaethe grabbed his shoulder.

"Wait! He has calmed. We don't dare do anything in case we make it worse."

Indeed, Jacques's screams had dwindled to strangled cries, and his movements were less. Slowly he calmed, and his breathing became slow and even. Gwaethe sat back and wiped her tears on her sleeve.

Alique immediately bent to examine him, and Exmund moved to the wagon flap to speak to those outside. He returned and sat at Jacques's head.

"How is he, Lady Alique?" Exmund asked.

She frowned. "His chest has cleared, and his heart is stronger. Whatever crisis he faced, he has returned improved. Perhaps not enough, but it is something."

"Do we keep giving him the medication?" Gwaethe asked.

Exmund added. "And leave the stone around his neck?"

Alique's serious gaze moved from her patient to the two of them. "I think we keep up with all our treatments until we have reason to stop."

Exmund frowned, but Gwaethe was content to leave things as they were. Jacques was improved and may now have the strength to reach Brightcastle. She touched his cheek and stood then left the wagon. Gathered outside were many of their people.

"All is well. You may go about your tasks," she said, dismissing them.

Only Isiloe remained. "You are tired," she said, placing a hand on Gwaethe's shoulder. For Isiloe, this was an unusual display of affection.

Gwaethe closed her eyes and dropped her head lest her cousin saw how afraid she really was. "The crisis is past, and he is a little improved. For that I am thankful. I would go without sleep for a week if only he would come back."

Isiloe frowned. "He means a great deal to you. I pray you are not broken when he dies."

Gwaethe hissed at her cousin. "He will not die if I have any power over it. We will get him to Brightcastle, and this Princess Benae will heal him. Any other possibility will not be considered." She pushed past her cousin and went in search of her horse. When she arrived at the horse lines, Anton was waiting.

"Well met, Anton," she said, wrapping herself in calm. The man was so damned unpredictable, turning up without warning.

"Good morning, Princess. I heard cries and came to see if I could help."

Gwaethe looked him over. His hair was ruffled and the golden flecks in his green eyes were more prominent than usual. He reminded her of a wolf.

"Captain Vorasava had a crisis, but he has settled and seems better."

"You've left the amber stone around his throat?" Anton asked sharply.

"Yes, we have for now. Should it be removed?"

He shook his head. "The healer advised it be left in place until he reaches help. I'm glad he is improved." There appeared to be more he wished to say. Damned man! Why did he have to only tell her part of the truth?

"Who is this healer, Anton? I would know... now."

He considered, his lips working, his usually enigmatic face forming a frown.

"I can take whatever you wish to tell me," Gwaethe said, hands on hips. "I will tell no one else."

"The healer is an old woman called Hetty. She has helped me more than once in the past; she pulled me from the brink of death."

"Is she a witch?"

He nodded. "A powerful witch, but she hides herself in Brightcastle as her life has been threatened in the past."

Gwaethe snorted. "You humans are so afraid of anything you don't understand. Elven lore is full of magic." She turned the ring on her finger; the ring she used to communicate with Kain. "Still, I will keep her secret." She paused, waiting for him to explain why he was there. "Was there something you wished to say?"

Anton took a deep breath. "Apart from enquiring into Vorasava's fate, I wondered if you could answer a question?"

Gwaethe nodded, wondering what he wanted. It seemed to her this man would never need anyone, though he had admitted to seeking help from Hetty in the past.

Again, he hesitated as if his was a difficult request. "I search for someone. This person may be able to help me master a talent I have."

Gwaethe's mind went wild, imagining what talent Anton harbored. Did he have his own magic?

He continued. "Is there one amongst your community who practices magic? Or who keeps to himself and seems somewhat of a mystery? I search for such a person, but my luck has been scant." His voice held an edge of desperation Gwaethe was surprised to hear.

"Many of my people have magic, as I already told you. I cannot vouch for the *Sis Lenweri*, but for my own faction, there are several who keep to themselves. My own uncle is a hermit. I never see him, but Isiloe, my cousin, sometimes visits. She may know more. I doubt he is the one you seek. He is a crazy old man who lives in the forest and is virtually one of the forest creatures."

Anton's eyes glowed, and Gwaethe suppressed a shudder. It was rare for anyone to set her on edge, but this man certainly had the power to do so. In a strange way he reminded her of Kain; hard and unyielding but with an edge of vulnerability, almost desperation.

"I'd like to meet him," he said.

"You should speak to Isiloe, though I caution you to be careful. If she takes a dislike to you, she will not reveal my uncle's location."

Anton nodded, and Gwaethe saddled Rassar and mounted. Anton walked alongside her as she returned to the wagons. The convoy had been organized in her absence, soldiers and elves standing beside their mounts, partaking of a cold breakfast. They all appeared uneasy, as if Jacques's screams had set them on edge. They eyed Anton like he was a viper in a nest of baby birds.

Isiloe ordered the men to prepare for departure and joined Gwaethe and Anton. Exmund handed his reins to a soldier and approached.

He thrust his hand out to Anton. Gwaethe wondered at Exmund's audacity. He was usually shy and retiring.

"Corporal Exmund at your service, sir."

Anton shook his hand. "Well met, Corporal."

"Sir, I believe you were once my commander. Captain Anton is it not?"

Anton stiffened. "I am no longer in the army, so it is merely Anton now."

"Vard Anton, sir."

Why was Exmund making such a point of digging into Anton's name and past?

Anton drew the young man close. "I'd appreciate it if you kept your voice low, Corporal. Some here might wonder if there is still a price on my head."

Exmund had gone pale as if Anton had threatened his life, and yet Gwaethe had heard nothing untoward. She dismounted and joined the two men, as did Isiloe.

"If there is bad blood between the two of you, I must know," Gwaethe said.

Anton stared a little longer at Exmund and then turned his golden gaze on Gwaethe. A chill struck her spine at the blazing orbs of the stranger. Deep in her gut, she knew he was dangerous. And she had followed his advice and help with Jacques...

"There is *no* bad blood between the Corporal and me. The difficulty I had was with Prince Jiseve Zialni, and he is dead. Steward Ramón Zorba of Brightcastle knows of my existence and whereabouts, and he chooses to leave me be; for the moment. I'm sure the Corporal can confirm this."

Gwaethe looked at Exmund. "Corporal?"

"Everything he says is true, Princess. The bounty on Anton's head has been withdrawn. However, I believe there would be hostility should he return to Brightcastle without Princess Alecia."

Gwaethe shook her head. "I don't understand any of this. Are you saying Anton and the Princess are linked?"

Isiloe hissed. "They disappeared together from Brightcastle around a year ago, cousin. The Princess is still missing, and this is the man who was last seen with her. I say we take him back just to be sure he is no longer wanted."

Anton turned his powerful gaze on Isiloe. "This is not your fight, *Ramar*. It's a matter between me and the Steward of Brightcastle; and possibly the King himself. I have another task for *you*."

Isiloe drew herself up, her pale blue eyes striking sparks. Anton appeared not to notice.

"No man orders me where to go, human," she said.

Gwaethe groaned inwardly and stepped between Isiloe and Anton. "He is right, cousin. This matter of the Princess has nothing to do with you or our people. All I care about for the moment is that no harm should come to Jacques." She turned back to Anton. "And this man has declared he wishes to help Captain Vorasava, that there is a connection between them."

Anton nodded. "He's a good man."

"He would vouch for you?" Isiloe snapped.

Anton's gaze wavered for a moment, but he stilled his body and nodded. "I believe he would. At least I hope so."

"Hardly a ringing endorsement, Anton," Gwaethe said. "However, it is too late to question your motives. Jacques is improved, and it appears your help has indeed been valuable. Will you travel with us?"

Anton appeared to consider. "I fear I must decline, Princess. I will check on you again before you arrive in Brightcastle, if I am able. I wish you well." He nodded to Isiloe and Exmund, turned and stalked off toward the trees.

"He is an odd man." Isiloe's hostile gaze followed Anton until he disappeared.

"Very much so." Exmund said. "Almost a year ago, there were all kinds of rumors about him. Princess Alecia fell under his spell and left

Brightcastle. She is still absent from her family home. But Steward Zorba returned from his latest trip just as we left Brightcastle on this mission. He said he had found the Princess safe and well, and she would return within a season. He also removed the bounty on Anton's head."

"And what of his relationship with Captain Vorasava?" Gwaethe asked.

Exmund frowned. "They were rivals, but respected each other, or so I believe. Captain Vorasava once said Anton was the most gifted swordsman he had ever seen. But, still the rumors of assassins and strange happenings surround him. Once, I heard a tale he was originally sent to Brightcastle to kill Prince Zialni, but the Prince was still alive when Anton fled with the Princess." He paused, his gaze troubled. "To be honest, I don't know what to believe about him; whether he is the greatest hero of our time or a demon dressed as a man."

Isiloe huffed. "He appears perfectly human to me. Though his eyes are ...unsettling...like a wolf." She drew herself up. "Not that I found him frightening. I merely imagine he has that effect."

Gwaethe clapped her hands. "We have wasted enough time discussing Anton. Let us be on the road."

At her words, the convoy mounted and rolled out of the clearing. Gwaethe glanced skywards in time to see the beautiful hawk gliding above them.

The remainder of their trip to Brightcastle passed without incident, though Gwaethe was plagued by dark dreams. Something threatening loomed over them, and she spent her sleeping hours looking skyward trying to discover the threat. But the weather stayed fine and mostly sunny, and they were able to pull back the canvas each day to allow their sick and injured to warm themselves.

Jacques gained color but never awoke. He took in liquid sustenance, but it wasn't enough to wipe the frown from Alique's brow. Each time Exmund rolled Jacques onto his side to beat his back, foul grey matter with red streaks of blood oozed from his mouth. Gwaethe had witnessed it herself twice and now made sure she was nowhere near when the Corporal attended to his duty. She couldn't bear to see evidence of Jacques's illness. How could he survive with that poison in his chest?

Of course, Alique did not believe for one moment Jacques would survive his illness, so Gwaethe had taken to avoiding her. She did not need to hear Alique's dire predictions of Jacques's future again. There was no preparing for his loss, no matter what Alique said. Better to dwell in the moment. Jacques was alive, and they crept closer to Brightcastle with each hour. She would not believe his life could be lost. If sheer strength of will could save him then that was what Gwaethe would provide.

And so she sat with him in the evenings and slept by his side every night. She spooned the potion past his lips and spoke to him of all they would share when he was well. She told him of her hopes and fears, even those so deep in her heart she had never told them to any other being. From him she received nothing; not a murmur, a word, or a smile.

On the morning of the tenth day out of Amitania, the towers of Brightcastle Keep appeared above the treetops. Gwaethe paused, her heart swelling as she realized she had succeeded in bringing Jacques home.

CHAPTER FOURTEEN

Gwaethe closed her eyes as emotions stronger than the stiffest gale roared through her. She had not realized how much fear, hope, and determination she had been holding in, until she achieved her goal. It was as if the wall of a dam had burst within, and a torrent swept all her composure along with it. But she did not show any of it to those around her. She had to be strong.

She took deep breaths, only opening her eyes when she had her feelings under control. The first person she saw was Isiloe and it almost undid all her work. Her cousin gazed at her, eyes soft, and appeared on the verge of approaching. It could not happen!

Gwaethe gave her head a small shake, and Isiloe turned and stalked off, whipping those around her into movement once again. Gwaethe allowed all the men and wagons to pass and only continued when Jacques's wagon pulled alongside her. She pushed thoughts of him aside and turned her mind to how she would handle their arrival in Brightcastle.

The hostile eyes of townsfolk followed them as they entered the town. Already they had been challenged at the gate. Having no Brightcastle soldier of enough rank, a message had been sent to the barracks for an escort to the keep. Gwaethe ground her teeth at the delay, but, if she wished for help, she must fall in with their host's conditions. Besides, an escort ensured their safety as it was clear her elves were not welcome within the town.

As they entered, she scanned the roofs and passages for danger but discerned none. Isiloe rode behind, also vigilant for any threats. It would be too easy for an assassin to shoot an arrow; an assassin sent by Faenwelar or even the King himself, though Gwaethe doubted King Benial Zialni would try to take her life. The King himself had assassins attack him at the funeral of his brother in the center of this keep. Ramón Zorba had stepped in and taken the crossbow bolt into his own body. He had almost died, but his valiant deed had led to him being declared Steward of Brightcastle. Nonetheless, if assassins could penetrate the keep, how much easier would it be to infiltrate the town itself?

She continued to scour the rooftops as she mused on what her reception would be at the castle. The leader of their escort had been coldly polite. He had detailed his own soldiers amongst Gwaethe's convoy to bring up the rear while he and his squad of twenty men led them to the castle. Surely bringing one of their own leaders home would engender respect? She did not care for herself, but Jacques must receive the best of care.

Isiloe rode forward. "How should we play this, cousin? I fear hostility once we reach the castle."

Gwaethe shook her head. "You will hold your tongue and be respectful even if it kills you." She bent her stare at Isiloe and was gratified to see her drop her gaze. "It is likely to be tense, and you will *not* make it worse."

Isiloe pulled her horse away, muttering under her breath. Hopefully she would hold her tongue as ordered. Lady Alique was the next to approach.

"We are here not a moment too soon," she said. "I've done all I can for Captain Vorasava. I hope Princess Benae can achieve what I cannot."

"Will she agree to help? I have heard she has shied away from illness now that she is expecting."

Alique squared her shoulders. "That's true, but she is married to my brother. She will help."

"Oh, yes! Now I remember the connection," Gwaethe said. "It is a weight off my mind. The Steward can hardly turn his own sister away."

"He could, but he will not. We are on good terms now. Almost losing your life tends to make you appreciate your siblings all the more."

Gwaethe wondered what had happened between the two Zorba children, but she didn't yet know Alique well enough to ask. "It will not be easy hosting elven soldiers in the midst of a civil war," she said. "I must advise the Steward he will soon have prisoners of war to deal with."

Alique snorted. "I can't imagine my cousin will stay long in Brightcastle. He will take the *Sis Lenweri* prisoners with him."

Gwaethe frowned. "Ah, yes the General is your cousin. There is a family resemblance."

"And that is where the similarities end. He is a pompous idiot. When I think of him replacing Kain as Army general and why it occurred, I want to scream."

"Kain's relationship to me has been damaging. I can understand the King not wishing to trust him with the top position, but to replace him with Formosa... I have never met anyone so hot headed."

"Pig headed, you mean," Alique snapped. "Listen Gwaethe, when Josef arrives I fear he will cause trouble for you. It may be best if you leave before that happens."

"I will not leave Jacques while his life hangs in the balance."

"Even if yours is at risk? He wouldn't wish for any harm to come to you."

"There is nothing you can say that will alter my stand on this," Gwaethe said. "I will see him well."

Alique frowned and looked down at her hands on the reins. "He is lucky to have such a loyal friend. You know that is all you can ever be? Neither his side or yours will ever accept you as a couple."

"I am not thinking of that. I merely wish him to be healthy. Thorius needs good men like Jacques." Gwaethe hoped she had convinced Alique she had no interest in Jacques beyond saving his life. A pity she couldn't convince her traitorous heart of the same thing. Alique was right. The Kingdom was not ready to accept a union between an elven princess and a human soldier.

On that dismal note, Gwaethe approached the imposing gates of Brightcastle Keep. A small force of soldiers was arranged before the outer wall. To the right stood a large barracks with men coming and going. A stable lay alongside it. The outer shell of the keep shone in the midday sun. Gwaethe recalled it was clad in quartz and that witchcraft had been used in its creation. She stole a moment to admire its beauty.

The leader of their escort spoke to the soldier on duty at the gate and then approached Gwaethe.

"You are to come with me and report to Steward Zorba, Princess," he said, bowing. "He is most keen to hear what has transpired at Amitania."

"I appreciate that, Sergeant, but your Captain Vorasava lies in the last wagon, gravely ill. He requires urgent care, or I fear he won't survive."

The Sergeant frowned. "Captain Vorasava, you say? I will have him transported to the barracks and the doctor fetched."

"No!" The sharp retort was out before Gwaethe could school her voice. "I wish for Princess Benae to see him. I hear she is very skilled."

The Sergeant frowned even deeper. "The Princess is not a common healer. She will not be called to tend to the Captain. It is not fitting."

Gwaethe had been afraid of this hurdle, and Jacques's life drained away with each minute. But, equally, she was in no position to argue. This man wouldn't listen to her. Yet she couldn't abandon Jacques after bringing him all this way.

Exmund stepped forward. "I will stay with him, Princess. I'll see no harm comes to him."

Gwaethe smiled. "Do not leave his side, Exmund, no matter what anyone says."

He nodded and rode back to the wagon. Gwaethe faced the Sergeant.

"Take me to the Steward," she said. "I trust I am allowed two aides to accompany me?" She ushered forward Isiloe and Alique. "These are Ramar Isiloe, my second in command, and Lady Alique Jazara, the Steward's sister."

"As you wish, Princess," he said, and they approached the grand entrance of the castle.

Another soldier took their knives, before a footman ushered the three women into a small reception room. Gwaethe studied the furnishings while Isiloe prowled the room, no doubt looking for hidden dangers or possibly escape routes. Alique walked over to an ornate chair with golden upholstery and gilded wood, and sat, a picture of tranquility. Gwaethe wondered if she really was as calm as she appeared.

A large tapestry sporting a golden-haired queen at the head of a formation of soldiers caught Gwaethe's attention. She remembered hearing Thorius once had warrior queens where now only kings reigned. Perhaps this was one of them?

Alique's voice carried to her. "Queen Izebel," she said. "The last of the Kingdom queens to reign in her own right."

"It seems hard to imagine a queen leading an army," Gwaethe said. "In either of our cultures." It should not be so, in her opinion, and she would see it changed one day, somehow.

"I wonder if it was ever the case," Alique said. "Perhaps it's just a fairy story."

A striking blond-haired man strode into the room, his blue tunic matching his eyes. Gwaethe found herself unable to look away. This man had such presence! Was this Alique's brother, Ramón Zorba?

His vibrant blue gaze caught hers, and all words left her head.

"Princess Gwaethe Arenil, I presume," he said, sweeping a deep bow.

The gesture startled her as she was accustomed to disrespect from humans.

"Ah, yes," she said, inclining her head. "Steward Zorba?"

He smiled. "For all my sins, yes, I have that title." A fleeting frown settled on his brow but was gone in seconds. He turned to Alique who stood and dipped into a curtsey. When she stood, the steward drew her into his arms. "I am so very relieved to see you well, sister. It appears we are both adept at getting ourselves into dire situations. How is your husband?"

"Kain is well. He will be here presently with prisoners."

"So I hear. The small intelligence mission turned into a full-blown battle."

Isiloe cleared her throat, and Alique introduced her.

Zorba took Isiloe's hands in his and kissed them. "Well met, Ramar Isiloe. I have heard great things about your courage."

Even Isiloe appeared to be awed by the beauty of the man before her. "You are kind to say so, Steward, but all elves are very courageous."

Gwaethe had no desire for their host to continue a conversation with her cousin. It would only be a matter of time before she said something to insult the man, and they had not even mentioned Jacques yet.

"Steward, I have a matter of great urgency which I need you to help with."

"Of course, Princess. When the elven prisoners arrive, I will be only too happy to accommodate them. I believe the High Prince Faenwelar's son is among them."

Gwaethe shook her head as a bad feeling entered her gut. "That is not the matter I had in mind." She folded her hands in front of her lest she appear to be begging for help. "It is Captain Vorasava. He is gravely ill and needs special care. He needs Princess Benae."

The Steward's tanned face paled. "The Princess is close to her time. I'm afraid it is out of the question."

Isiloe hissed and Gwaethe took a step forward. "You don't understand, sir. He will die. I've managed to get him this far, but he needs the special care of your lady. Please do not allow him to die."

A wild look had entered his eye, and he turned to Alique. "What of this, sister? Have you tended Vorasava? Can he be saved? I hear a mountain fell on him."

Alique flicked a glance at Gwaethe before answering. "I truly don't know, Ramón, but we have tried everything there is to try. I beg you to speak to Benae on his behalf."

He walked back and forth across the chamber, his teeth snagged in his lower lip. "I will broach the subject with her, but I urge you not to raise your hopes. Benae's pregnancy has not been easy, and she will not risk her unborn child."

"A potion then?" Gwaethe asked, detesting the desperation in her voice.

"Possibly," he said, "but Benae will still need to examine him to judge what he needs. I will speak to her. In the meantime, the footman will show you to your rooms."

He bowed to all and left without another word.

Gwaethe crossed to Alique. "You must convince him. Otherwise Jacques will perish. Princess Benae has a special talent. I know she can help."

Alique's eyes widened. "You mean witchcraft?"

"I did not say that!"

"No wonder Ramón is reluctant to involve her. Think of the rumors if she should be successful."

"She must help him. I will not lose him!"

Alique grasped her by the upper arms and gave her a small shake. "Gwaethe, bring your feelings under control. Take a deep breath."

Gwaethe did as she asked, closing her eyes and filling her chest, holding and then allowing the breath to slowly escape. She repeated the exercise and felt better, more in control.

"Nothing will be helped by being hysterical," Alique said. "Calmness will get us further; and a sensible argument. If you believe Benae can help, then we shall make it so. After we are shown to our rooms, I will bathe, dress, and request an audience with her."

Tears threatened, but Gwaethe would not succumb to her emotions again, not until Jacques was saved. "Thank you." She dared not say more.

Isiloe snorted. "You humans are stupid. You worry so over illness when all you need do to avoid it is eating the fruit of the forest and the herbs. The Captain cannot harm the unborn babe, and someone should tell the Steward's wife that."

Further discussion was cut short when a footman came to show them to their rooms.

Alique had a room to herself while Gwaethe and Isiloe shared theirs. Isiloe paced the floor of their sitting room, grumbling about disrespect, but Gwaethe was secretly relieved to have company even if it was her irritable cousin. She had always been there, ready to support Gwaethe in all things, whether physically in battle, or to back her up when devising a plan; or even cheering her up when all seemed very black.

She sighed and wandered into the dressing room where there was a small assortment of gowns. The footman had said they could avail themselves of the clothing, so she pulled out one after the other, finally choosing a pale-yellow sheath that hugged her body and finished in a small train. It would be difficult to walk in, but she enjoyed wearing pretty Kingdom clothes.

Isiloe entered, and Gwaethe spun around to show off her new attire.

"You look very human, but not enough that they will forget who they are dealing with. Add to that, you will be unable to move. I must stick close to you to rescue you when you are attacked."

Gwaethe scowled at her cousin. "Must you always see the darkness when I wish to enjoy a little light?"

"And they dare to house you, an elven princess, in a shared room, when Lady Alique has one of her own!" Isiloe paced again, her frame quivering with indignity. "You should have demanded a room worthy of you."

"Might I remind you Alique is family?" Gwaethe drew herself up and gave Isiloe her sternest look. Honestly, she pushed her role of protector too far sometimes. "There is a time for asserting oneself and a time for humility, Isiloe. This is certainly the time to be humble. Moreover, this room is a very fine one and comfortable. I enjoy having you with me."

Isiloe's face turned a charming shade of crimson, and Gwaethe had to battle to keep a smile from her face.

"You are right, Gwaethe," she said. "As usual you see to the core of what is important. But I burn to put these humans in their place. You realize they think themselves far above us?"

"Not all of them," Gwaethe said. "There are many who are fair and equitable, many who would welcome us into a larger role within their culture."

Isiloe hissed. "You are deluding yourself if you believe that. No human wants to see more of us than they already do. And, now Faenwelar is making his mischief, we will be very lucky if we are not forced from Thorius. You had better give some thought to where we will flee."

Gwaethe's mouth fell open. For a moment she was lost for words. "I never thought to hear such defeatist words from your mouth, cousin. Perhaps I should rethink your position if you cannot provide better council than that!"

"But, Gwaethe—"

"I've heard enough!" she snapped. "We will prevail over Faenwelar and over the humans. I never wish to hear you utter such words again. If they pop into your head, you will sweep them out immediately. Do you understand?"

Isiloe's gaze dropped to the carpet. "I hear and understand." She turned and stalked off into their bed chamber, and Gwaethe sank into a chair before the fireplace. Despite her words to Isiloe, she worried they might indeed be pushed from the Kingdom; a disaster which could lead to the end of their race.

There was a knock at their door, and Alique entered. She had changed into a pale green and silver gown that would not have looked out of place at a ball. Gwaethe knew a pang of jealousy at the fates that had placed Alique in this privileged position while Gwaethe's status as a princess didn't even appear important to her own race. Indeed, she had been whipped because of her title!

She swallowed her anger and stood, turning to face her beautiful sister-in-law. No wonder Kain had fallen for her. How could she, Gwaethe, hope to attract Jacques when there were beautiful women of his own kind as competition?

Alique smiled. "That gown suits you perfectly. You could slide into a Kingdom ball, and no one would be any the wiser."

Gwaethe couldn't help the bitter laughter that followed the comment. "You are kind, sister-in-law, but no one would mistake me for anything other than a dark elf. Where in the cities of Thorius have you ever seen skin this color?"

Alique crossed to her and raised her fingers to Gwaethe's face. "You sell yourself short, Gwaethe. Please don't waste time wishing you were someone other than who you are; an intelligent, beautiful, caring, brave woman who can be anything she wishes. I should not have to tell you this."

Tears filled Gwaethe's eyes. "It is good to hear you say those words. I know you truly believe them."

She gripped Gwaethe's hands. "I do, and you must believe it too."

"I would have said I did before my father died. How naïve I was then, thinking I was the ruler of my world; oblivious to the evil forces who would bring about my downfall."

Alique smiled, but her eyes were sad. "I was just like that naïve elven girl before I met Kain. I thought I could snap my fingers and everyone would leap to do my bidding. I was a Lady-in-Waiting to the Queen and from a respected family. My entire world was the Royal Court. I indulged in gossip and meaningless flirtations, and thought I was the cleverest person in the world." She dropped Gwaethe's hands and walked past her to stare into the fire.

Gwaethe said nothing, fascinated to be given this insight into the woman her brother had given his heart to.

"And then I almost lost Ramón. It was the beginning of my growing up. Soon after, my family was taken hostage by Faenwelar's elves, and then I was captured. When all power was stripped away, I saw how fragile my world had been. I also saw how meaningless it was without those I loved." She turned to Gwaethe. "I know that's not exactly your story, but I also know what it is to confront one's long held beliefs and be forced to change. It was difficult, and I almost died, but I'm a better person for all that. You will be as well."

Gwaethe let out a long breath. "I hope you are right, and this struggle is all worth it."

"As do I," Isiloe said from the bedroom door. She had changed into a pair of soft grey breeches and a grey tunic with a white shirt underneath. On her feet were slippers made of black suede. She looked stunning even though the bottoms of the breeches' legs were rolled up, since they were made for a taller woman. "Now let us meet with the Steward and see what the Princess's reply was."

"I think I should go alone," Alique said.

"And *I* believe there is none better qualified to speak on behalf of Jacques than I," Gwaethe said. "I have been there from the start of his illness, and I…care…for him."

Isiloe snorted. "She is in love with the Captain, though little good it will do her. He will go running home to his parents and his arranged marriage as soon as he awakes."

Gwaethe cast her cousin a look which she hoped would shut her down. "It does not matter what my feelings for Jacques are. I will be there to argue on his behalf."

Alique sighed. "Very well. Let us find Rámon. But Isiloe must stay silent. Brightcastle is not ready for her."

Isiloe smirked as if she thrived on being known for her sharp tongue.

The three ladies were shown into an intimate anteroom Alique said was Ramón's private province. Gwaethe roamed around the room, trying to keep her mind from the discussion ahead, and examined the tapestries on the wall. Most were forest scenes, some including deer, bears, and mountain lions. She assumed from this that the Steward was an animal lover and not a fighting man; though he moved like a swordsman and was built like a fighter. All together, he was a puzzle she would like to solve. Perhaps Alique would have more insight into her brother?

She glanced across at Isiloe who leaned against the wall in a shadowy corner, seemingly relaxed, but ready for action as all fighters were. She hoped she would not need her fighting skills; indeed, if she did, it would foretell disaster for Jacques and their cause of peace. A large part of her wished Isiloe had remained behind.

The door opened, and Ramón Zorba strode into the room. Three sets of feminine eyes were immediately upon him, and Gwaethe noticed his body stiffen, his hand going to his left hip where a sword might usually hang. After a short pause, he smiled and appeared to relax.

"Good evening, ladies," he said. "To what do I owe this visit? I had thought to speak to you at dinner."

"You know full well the reason for our meeting, Ramón," Alique said. "There is a man dying in your barracks, and something must be done to save him. Have you spoken with Benae?"

His eyes shifted again and then settled on his sister. "I'm afraid Benae has declined to see Captain Vorasava. She will send him potions and wishes him well."

Gwaethe was across the room before she realized she had moved. She stood before Ramón. His eyes widened, and he drew himself up, shoulders back, and stared down at her.

"I must speak with the Princess," Gwaethe said, her hands before her, palms up. She tried to keep the pleading from her voice but feared she had not succeeded. "He is your countryman. Does that not mean anything to you?"

"Of course it does, but stacked against the health of the heir to the throne, even Vorasava would not want Benae and the babe put at risk." Ramón studied her, his eyes narrowing, their intense blue boring into her. "If I might ask, why does this mean so much to you? If seems rather strange that an elven princess would take even a moment to care what happened to a human commander."

Gwaethe was lost for words. Should she tell him how she felt, how close the two of them had come? Would Jacques agree on the matter? He had been so sick recently, and they had been fighting for survival; they had not had the time to properly discuss their relationship. Would it mean anything when this conflict was over? Or would they both return to their respective communities and forget all about their troubled relationship?

"We have become close during this latest conflict." No need to tell him just how close.

"And, because of this, you expect Princess Benae to expose herself and her child to the Goddess knows what disease, so she can tell you she can do nothing?"

"I don't believe that to be true," Gwaethe said. "Neither the risk or your assertion your wife cannot help." She squared her shoulders and again met his eye. "I do not believe there is danger of this illness spreading to the child you protect. Jacques has a chest full of mud and slime, and he needs help. I know your wife can provide healing."

"I have asked her, and that is all I can do," he said. "Our court physician will do his best."

Alique gave a ladylike snort. "Forgive me, Ramón, but I do not have much faith in doctors. I myself have treated Captain Vorasava and know of nothing else a doctor can do that I have not already tried."

"There you go, then," he said. "How can you think Benae can succeed where you have failed?"

"There are rumors," Gwaethe snapped.

Ramón's wild eyes slammed into hers. "What rumors?"

"Tales of miraculous healing by your good wife," Gwaethe said. "I have heard it from more than one source. If there is even a small hope, I have to try."

The Steward closed his eyes, but not before Gwaethe saw terror in his gaze. "I cannot allow her to expose herself so. If there are already rumors of her gift, the healing of Jacques Vorasava would only start more."

"Then you know she can help?" Gwaethe almost grabbed his hands but stopped herself at the last moment.

"I don't know anything." Ramón walked across to the window and peered out. "She was unable to save her parents; perhaps this will be another of those cases."

"And perhaps not." Alique moved to stand behind her brother, one hand on his shoulder. "You must try, Ramón. Talk to Benae again."

"What must Ramón talk to me about?" a musical voice sounded from the door.

They all turned to find a petite, dark-haired woman, great with child.

"Alique," she said, crossing to her sister-in-law and kissing her cheek. "I heard you had arrived. How lovely to see you. Who are these other ladies?"

Gwaethe thought it most curious Benae did not appear to know of their presence in the castle when her husband had supposedly discussed the possibility of her helping Jacques. Unless he had not mentioned them, had only spoken to her of helping Jacques. Yes, that must be it.

"This is Princess Gwaethe Arenil of the *Lenweri* and her cousin, *Ramar* Isiloe." Alique said, drawing Gwaethe forward.

Benae's eyes grew large and she wrapped her arms protectively over her stomach. "Welcome to you. I trust you are comfortably housed within our home?" Her vibrant green eyes swept across the room to bore into her husband. His feet shifted before he straightened and met her gaze.

Alique answered. "We are most comfortable, thank you Princess, but I'm afraid we have a matter we must discuss with you. It cannot wait."

"Oh? And what would that be?" Benae asked.

"It is Captain Vorasava, Benae," Ramón said, "I expressed to these ladies that you were unable to attend him as his physician; it would pose a grave risk to your pregnancy. They have asked to speak on his behalf, once more." Something unspoken passed between them and Benae frowned. It was all most awkward. Gwaethe decided to take matters into her own hands.

"You see, Princess," she said, "Jacques - Captain Vorasava - lies gravely ill in the barracks. He was trapped under an avalanche and almost died. Since then he has had a problem with his chest and been very ill. He has fallen unconscious, and there seems nothing any of us can do to help him. We hoped you would agree to attend him."

Gwaethe held her breath as Benae looked at her hands resting on her belly. When she looked back up, her gaze revealed a bleak terror.

"I've deliberately held myself aloof to avoid exposing myself to any dangers. I'm very sorry for Captain Vorasava, but I cannot help."

Gwaethe's heart sank, but she would not give up.

"I don't believe the Captain can pass any illness on to you. All of us who have cared for him are hale. Please, I will do anything to help him."

Ramón cleared his throat. "You heard Benae. She will not risk the babe. I'm afraid Vorasava will have to live or die without her help."

Gwaethe was watching Benae when he said the words, and she flinched as though she had been hit. This woman cared deeply for people and would not willingly withhold aid for Jacques. She just had to find a way to make it happen.

"I will have him brought here," Gwaethe said. "We could house him in the servant's quarters. Alique and I can tend him."

Benae stiffened. "No, if I decided to attend him, I will go to the barracks. I think that would be safer."

"Benae!" Ramón said. "There are enough rumors about your special skills in healing. This will only start more! I forbid you to attend the barracks."

Benae's green eyes grew cold. She opened her mouth, and Gwaethe expected harsh words, but instead she clamped her mouth shut and crossed to the fire, her forehead resting on the mantle. Ramón joined her, speaking in low, soothing tones.

"It's too much to ask of her," Alique whispered. "You see how fearful she is for the child. I cannot blame her." Again, she had tears in her eyes. Gwaethe wondered what had touched her sister-in-law so profoundly. Was she longing for a child of her own?

Gwaethe watched as Benae and her husband talked. Ramón appeared most protective of his wife. She wondered how it would change their relationship when the Steward was tasked with raising another man's child. Prince Zialni had died in the act of coupling with Benae in the early days of their doomed marriage. So far, Ramón Zorba had made an excellent job of stepping into the Prince's shoes.

The two turned to face Gwaethe and Alique.

"Benae has agreed to see Vorasava," Ramón said. "But he will be brought here and housed in the servants' quarters. I will have two rooms set aside for him; one for his chamber and the other for Benae to disrobe and wash before and after seeing him. The Goddess protect her and her unborn child."

Benae's teeth were pressed into her lower lip, and her eyes were huge. "I'll do all I can for him, Princess." She turned to her husband. "Bring him with all speed. I'll have the necessary arrangements made."

Ramón left his rooms after kissing his wife on the forehead.

"Now I must collect my maid and make preparations," Benae said. "It may be a long night."

Gwaethe clutched her elbow as she moved past. "Please accept any help I can give, Princess. Jacques is precious to me."

Benae nodded, and Gwaethe released her hold.

CHAPTER FIFTEEN

They all gathered in a stone chamber deep beneath Brightcastle Keep. The walls were roughhewn, but the large fireplace provided enough warmth if it was regularly fed with logs. According to Ramón, this room had once been the guardhouse for the dungeons. The room next door, that Benae would use to change and prepare her potions, had been the weapons store.

Jacques lay unmoving on the small bed, Alique in attendance. The amber stone still lay at his throat, and Gwaethe briefly wondered where Anton was. She had to steel herself not to display affection toward her love. She walked a knife edge between hope and despair, but could not express it openly. Isiloe stood behind her, one hand on her shoulder, as if she knew how close to breaking Gwaethe was.

The door across the room opened, and Benae, clothed in a rough gown and apron, entered the room. Her maid, a stocky blonde girl named Tyra, carried a bowl and goblet. As Alique moved to the side, Benae got her first glimpse of her patient and gasped. Her face went instantly pale. She hurried to the bedside and placed her hand on Jacques's forehead. Her eyes sought Gwaethe's, but she said not a word. Isiloe's hand squeezed harder.

Benae unbuttoned Jacques's shirt and laid her right palm on his breastbone. She closed her eyes for a long moment. There was no sound but the harsh breaths of all in the room. Then Jacques heaved a great lungful of air and coughed. The first cough was followed by more, until Gwaethe feared he would cough his lungs up. Alique helped Benae to roll him onto his side and a trickle of foul-smelling red soupy material drained from his mouth.

Gwaethe watched, heart pounding, as Benae's maid collected the horrid material in a bowl. The process went on and on, the two women pounding on Jacques's chest, this side then that, while he lay on one side then the other, the ever-present red material leaking from his mouth. He was not awake, Gwaethe could tell that much. She idly wondered how much pounding his body could bear.

Eventually the flow stopped. Again, Benae laid her palm over his chest and closed her eyes, and again the room grew still. Finally, she stepped back.

"You may give him the medicine now," she said to her maid, "and then he must rest."

Gwaethe hurried to her side. "Thank you for seeing him. What should we do now?"

Benae's gaze had lost much of its sparkle and her shoulders sagged

"I'll leave this medicine for him and return tomorrow morning for another treatment." She paused, studying Gwaethe as if she wished to take her measure. "He is gravely ill, but my treatment has helped. If only I could flush the mud and muck from his lungs …but that would drown him. In a way, he is drowning already. However, he is now getting more air. His color is better." She looked back at her patient.

Indeed, Gwaethe saw Jacques's skin was pink where before it had been grey.

"What is the stone around his neck?" Benae asked, fingering the amber talisman.

Gwaethe debated how much to tell her. "It was given to us by a wise woman, along with a potion which seems to have helped extend his life."

Benae's eyes narrowed. "What wise woman?"

"The friend of a man called Anton."

"Anton!" Ramón's voice sliced through their discussion. "Do you mean Vard Anton?"

Gwaethe recalled the Steward had recently found Anton and Princess Alecia. "Yes…I believe that was his name."

Ramón swore under his breath. "I thought the stone looked familiar. If that's his, there's a good chance he has left Alecia once again."

Benae looked up at her husband, and again unspoken communication passed between them. She did not appear happy at the turn of events and neither did the steward. He crossed to his wife, whispered in her ear and stalked from the room. Gwaethe watched him go. Maybe Alique would have an explanation for the strange behavior later.

"Should we leave the stone against his skin, Princess?" Gwaethe asked. "Anton said he would see us again before we arrived in Brightcastle, but we have not seen him."

Benae fingered the talisman, then removed it from around Jacques's neck. "I think not." She handed the amulet to Gwaethe. "Return it to its owner if you can. If it ever was any use, then it's no longer required. I will see to his needs now. We need no potions and spells." With those words, she beckoned to her maid. The two of them left through the door to the adjacent room.

Gwaethe met Alique's gaze across the sleeping Jacques. "She is an intense woman, is she not?"

Alique appeared troubled. "Benae sets very high standards for herself and has a long memory. She never forgives others or herself. Anton is associated with Princess Alecia's disappearance from Brightcastle a year ago. My brother hates him. If he has left the Princess a second time, I hate to think what Ramón will do. And any reminder of Alecia hurts Benae as Ramón was in love with her before she ran off with Anton."

Gwaethe had heard enough. "It is a complicated situation indeed, one I do not wish to become entangled in." She glanced at Jacques and placed her palm on his forehead. "He rests easier. I will find Exmund and tell him what has happened to his captain."

She took a long last look at Jacques, willing him to awake so she could tell him all she had so far failed to express, then left the room.

The next two days proceeded in a blur for Gwaethe. She played the part of Kingdom lady, dressing in the beautiful gowns which hung in her wardrobe. She spent long hours reading to Jacques, while Benae worked more of her healing, and she and Alique pounded the foul humors from his chest. Each treatment brought less of the stuff, and the material began to clear, but Benae was never content. Gwaethe began to understand what Alique meant when she said Benae was hard on herself. She was doing her best and still it did not seem enough.

Jacques had not awoken, but his skin glowed a healthy pink, and he could now swallow water and broth readily. Alique had given a guarded opinion he might make a full recovery in time.

Even so, Gwaethe did not allow herself to hope. She went through the motions of caring for him in a daze, trying not to imagine the future either with or without Jacques. She supposed she must have been difficult to bear, for Isiloe, usually such a rock, had taken to avoiding her. Her cousin could usually be found practicing weapons with the elves who had accompanied them. She even took most of her meals with them.

Gwaethe sighed as she straightened Jacques's cover across his chest. Benae had said it would be another three days before he would awake, but Gwaethe had noticed little things, such as eye flutters and changes in breathing which gave her hope it would be sooner. But not today. Which meant she must report to Exmund, who was going slowly insane with worry.

When she found the Corporal, he was teaching Isiloe the sword with practice blades. The bundled wooden weapons made a sharp thwacking sound as they landed blows. They could injure, but not seriously. As she watched, she realized Isiloe had a lot to learn.

Gwaethe clapped as their lesson came to an end. Exmund, who had not heard her approach, blushed.

"*Ramar* Isiloe learns quickly, Princess. Soon she will have to find a more gifted swordsman than me to teach her. How is the Captain?"

Gwaethe smiled. "Captain Vorasava improves every session. I expect him to awake very soon."

"Begging your pardon, Princess," Exmund said, "but you said that yesterday."

"It is difficult to know when he will stir, but I assure you he is improving. There is less muck coming from his chest every day, his color is better, and he is drinking on his own."

He smiled. "That's good news. Do you think I might see him?"

"Give me a day to arrange it," she said, but Exmund's attention had been snagged by a commotion at the gate.

"What the devil?" he said, striding off, leaving Gwaethe and Isiloe to follow.

She kept her eyes on the soldiers and horses at the gate, Isiloe at her side. She soon spied General Formosa and bit back a curse.

Isiloe was not so controlled. "What is he doing here so soon?" she asked.

Gwaethe hushed her. "He is the supreme controller of the King's forces and can go wherever and whenever he pleases. However, it would have been nice for Jacques to be hale. I need someone on my side."

Captured *Sis Lenweri* were being herded toward the prison, surrounded by Kingdom soldiers, who carried torches to dispel the gathering gloom of dusk. Gwaethe wondered where Prince Gorin was.

She shuddered as she recalled how he had hurt her, pulled her down to the lowest level. But, beside the hurt and shame, was anger so hot she could have boiled her blood with it. *He will pay!* She would see to it personally. Isiloe's hand grasped her shoulder as if she knew what Gwaethe was thinking. As quickly as it landed there, Isiloe's comfort was gone.

Gwaethe halted to await her chance to speak with Kain. Maybe she should alert him to her presence. She grasped her ring and sent out the thought.

I am here, brother. Jacques still lies abed but is improving. Alique tends him within the keep. Please join me in my chamber as soon as you can.

A halting reply came back. *Gwaethe! It's good to hear your voice, even in my head! I'll meet you soon. We have much to discuss.*

Gwaethe bit her lip as she spied Gorin. His gaze burned her from across the castle forecourt as he was reefed around and ushered to the prison.

Let his filthy traitorous bones rot in there!

The General dismounted from his white charger, and his attendants surrounded him. Their attention was on the castle turrets and other high structures. A well-placed arrow might easily take their leader, and assassins were never far away. Gwaethe shivered again and moved to the shelter of the keep where she was more protected.

Isiloe stood in front of her, scanning for any sign of a threat. If she were a cat her tail would have been a stiff brush. She balanced on the balls of her feet, and a knife had appeared in her fist.

"Isiloe!" Gwaethe hissed. "Put the knife away. You will have an arrow in your back if anyone sees you!"

She grumbled as she replaced the blade in her boot. "You are too relaxed, cousin. There are enemies everywhere and none more so than in this keep."

"Do you not think I know that? I cannot be a scared mouse everywhere I go. And you cannot provoke the humans so. They will take any excuse to kill you, especially the General."

"Speaking of Formosa," Isiloe said, "here he comes."

Gwaethe squared her shoulders and held her head high as Formosa approached. He wasn't a large man, but his blond good looks and classic blue eyes made an impression. A pity his eyes held such coldness.

"Princess," he said, dipping his head slightly. "I hope your journey was safe and uneventful."

"We arrived in time to get the Captain the help he needs, General," Gwaethe said. "He remains, however, gravely ill."

"That is a pity," Formosa said, though his eyes had brightened at Gwaethe's words.

Her lip almost curled at the thought that this man might wish to eradicate Jacques from a position of competition. Was that all he cared about? His standing with the King? She took a deep breath, reminding herself Jacques was on her side and would not place his career before his people, or even hers. Would he? She briefly wondered what really motivated Jacques. She knew so little about him.

Formosa continued. "I will not disturb him. Please convey my regards to the Captain when you see him. I'll be far too busy with Gorin's trial for the next few days. Good day."

He strode away toward the senior attendant who ushered him into the keep. As a relative of the Steward, Formosa would be given one of the best guest rooms. Gwaethe wished she did not have to confront him again. She wondered where Kain was to be housed.

"We should return to our rooms, Isiloe," she said. "Kain will meet me there. Please fetch Alique from the sick room."

She continued to her chamber, ignoring the glare Isiloe shot her. Her prickly cousin would not like being ordered about like a palace servant, but if she insisted on being at Gwaethe's beck and call, she could not complain when sent on a task. Gwaethe smiled at Isiloe's loyalty as she opened the door to her chamber. Kain stood before her fire.

"You were quick getting here, brother," she said, crossing to him and embracing him. He stiffened momentarily before retuning her hug. Her heart ached that he was not more natural with her. She reminded herself he did care about her and about the elven cause.

"How are you, Gwaethe?"

"I am well, and so is Alique. We convinced Princess Benae to help Jacques, and he is getting better with each day. I hope he will awake soon."

Kain frowned. "You're sure he is on the mend? It sounds as though not much has changed. I had hoped to be able to speak with him and enlist his help against Formosa."

"What help?

"The man is out of control. He intends to have a trial here and now, and execute all the elven prisoners, if he can get the support of the ranking officers. I can't convince him to take them to the King in Wildecoast."

"What of the women who are with child? Will he turn them over to me?"

Kain paled at the mention of the elven women. He took a deep breath and met Gwaethe's gaze. "There was an ugly incident on the trip here. One of the heavily pregnant women was raped by several soldiers. She and the babe died as a result. When the other women discovered her fate, they went mad and attacked the soldiers who guarded them."

Gwaethe clenched her fists at her sides, steeling herself for more bad news. "What happened then?"

"A dozen women were killed and six soldiers. But for a few of us stepping forward to stop the carnage, it would have been much worse. Some of the pregnant elven women are to go on trial, and many of those who were injured miscarried their babies." His voice broke as he spoke the last news. Gwaethe clutched his shoulder.

"It has been difficult for you, brother." She shuddered at such loss of innocent life, imagining what Kain had dealt with on the march with limited medical help. "Where are the injured elven females? Are any of them still with child?"

"A few injured have retained their babes. They are housed in two wagons. I don't know what to do with them. They can hardly enter the keep, but neither can they go to the barracks or the prison."

Gwaethe agreed. "I must see them and then I can decide the best action. Perhaps a nearby public house can help?"

Kain ran his hand through his hair, making it spike at crazy angles. "Perhaps."

Alique entered, her shoulders slumped, until she spied Kain. She squealed and threw herself into his arms. The two held each other, eyes closed, hands running over each other as if taking inventory. Gwaethe should have averted her eyes, but she couldn't. She found it fascinating to watch the relationships of others and lately yearned to experience the real thing.

Alique stepped back, her hands linked with Kain's and studied him. "What's wrong? You look sad."

"I'm merely tired, my love."

"I have seen you tired, Kain, and this is not just exhaustion. Tell me."

He sighed. "There has been trouble between the elven women and our soldiers. Lives have been lost on both sides, and I have injured pregnant females to attend to."

Alique gasped and covered her mouth with her hands. "Can I help? Where are they?"

Gwaethe touched her shoulder. "We were about to check on them. But where can they be housed? At present they are in two wagons."

"I will fetch my cloak and bag, and meet you in the entry," she said as she marched from the room.

Gwaethe smiled at her brother. "Go, follow her and say a proper 'hello'. I will meet you in the forecourt."

Kain didn't hesitate before following his wife from the room.

Gwaethe couldn't comprehend what she had experienced over the last three hours. She now sat in the common room of the Brightcastle Arms, her hands around a mulled wine and her thoughts with the women upstairs. Alique was still with one poor young thing who was miscarrying her baby. Her admiration for her sister-in-law had soared while watching her deal with the unfortunate elven women. She had so much compassion and appeared to know just the right thing to say to the grieving mothers.

Gwaethe, on the other hand, knew little of motherhood, even if she was well acquainted with loss. On the battle field, if you lost a comrade, you bundled the emotion up and locked it away to deal with at another time. There was no talking through it; there was simply no time for it. Eventually you just got used to losing friends, it was part of the life of a warrior. But that was not the case for the elven mothers. They were losing a part of themselves, and Gwaethe had no idea what to say to get through to them. When she tried, she had made them feel worse. Alique, on the other hand, held them and soothed them and promised these lost children would never be forgotten. She encouraged them to name their children and was planning burials for the ones she had delivered stillborn.

Kain sat opposite Gwaethe, along with one of his men, a sergeant called Jer Blas. The Sergeant had been polite to her, if aloof. At least he was not outright hostile. Kain seemed to depend on the man for support. Her brother certainly needed someone in his corner. Most of the Kingdom soldiers hated him after finding out his father was an elven king. Gwaethe still hoped Kain would one day step into his father's shoes and rule her people, but whether the *Lenweri* would accept Kain as leader, she couldn't predict.

"I should return to the castle and check on Jacques," she said, seized with a frantic desire to escape the misery she had dealt with for the past three hours. She felt guilty at the thought, knowing Kain had endured far more misery lately than she had.

You have had your own battle with sadness! It was so like her to blame herself and not acknowledge her struggles. It was not healthy.

Kain raised tired eyes. "Yes, you go, and thanks for helping to organize these rooms. The General won't approve, but at least the women are comfortable. I will escort Alique back when she has completed her tasks."

"She will not wish to leave them," Gwaethe said, "but see she does. I worry she doesn't look after herself."

"You and me both," he said. "I will carry her home bodily if she refuses."

Gwaethe grinned at the mental picture of Alique over Kain's shoulder, being carried kicking and screaming back to the keep. Kain smiled back, and it warmed Gwaethe's heart to share a private moment with him. She patted his shoulder and left. Isiloe fell into step with her as she exited the inn.

"You should not walk alone," she said, eyes darting all around. The dark alleys and nearby roofs could hide all manner of threats. "You are certainly a target."

"So are you, cousin." Gwaethe would not fight with Isiloe tonight. She was too heartsick. "I do not stand out as much in a Kingdom gown. Hardly anyone will see me as elven."

"Oh, that is good news. A woman on her own out at night would be most safe." Sarcasm dripped from her words. "Sometimes I wonder how you have stayed alive this long. You put yourself at risk. What do you think would happen to the *Lenweri* if you died?"

"Kain would be forced to step up," she said as they walked briskly along the broad cobbled street.

Isiloe snorted and none too delicately. "The best chance of Kain stepping into the role of king is if you are alive; in my opinion."

Gwaethe considered Isiloe's statement. Was she correct? If she died, would Kain walk away, guilt-free? And even if he tried to take the elven throne, would her people accept him without her to support him?

"These are problems too difficult to tackle tonight," Gwaethe said. "We have more immediate matters to attend to; such as General Formosa and the debacle of our elven women."

Isiloe hissed. "There will be hell to pay on both sides. The soldiers behaved like animals, but the women made it much worse. How can it ever be fixed?"

"Let us discuss this in the morning when we have both had a night's rest," Gwaethe said as they walked through the gates.

She left Isiloe at the base of the staircase and went to check Jacques. It was the longest she had spent away from him since arriving in Brightcastle, and she knew a burning urge to see his face, touch his hand and hear his regular breaths.

An elderly woman sat by his bed, but she rose as Gwaethe entered, curtsied and left the chamber. Gwaethe watched her go and sat in the chair she had vacated. Jacques looked just as he had when she left him. His chest rose and fell with the even breaths of deep sleep, and his cheeks had a healthy glow, even if they were sunken.

"Oh Jacques, please wake up! I have so much need of you." She was ashamed of the words, but, after dealing with all the sadness of the women, she was depleted, a mere shadow of her usual self. "Everything has gone wrong, and I don't know the right thing to do."

She brushed the hair off his forehead and rose to kiss his brow, then his nose and finally his lips.

"I've died and gone to heaven," he croaked.

Gwaethe leaped back in fright, her breath hard and fast. Then she flung herself at him and hugged him as best she could with him lying on the pillows.

"You are *not* dead, Jacques," she said, planting a last kiss on his forehead. Tears filled her eyes, and she blinked hard to disperse them. That only resulted in them splashing onto her cheeks.

His thin fingers brushed them away. "I've never seen you cry. Must be something very good or very bad to move you so."

"Both," she said, her voice breaking. "Mostly very good. I have hoped against hope for weeks you would come back to us. Now you are here."

He tried to sit but collapsed against the pillows. "I'm so weak." His breathing rasped in and out of his chest, and he closed his eyes until it slowed. "Where am I?"

"Brightcastle Keep. You've been here several days. It's been two weeks since the battle in Amitania. You collapsed, and we brought you here to be tended by Princess Benae."

"*She* helped me?"

"She did, and it has worked. But you were so close to death on the road, I had to get help."

"What sort of help?"

"Never mind that now," she said. "You must regain your strength. Kain needs you against the General. The rest of the army is here and …things are tense."

Why had she blurted all that out? Jacques needed his rest, now more than ever. He needed to recover without relapses, and here she was putting him under pressure to help. Damn her loose tongue!

He pushed himself up, but collapsed back on the pillows. "Can you have a meal brought to me? Just broth and bread. I'm starving."

Still berating herself, Gwaethe hurried to the nearby kitchen where the cook warmed some broth and cut a slab of bread. All the while the woman worked, Gwaethe paced the kitchen, desperate to return to Jacques. When she accepted the tray from the cook, there were two bowls and two slabs of bread.

"Feed yourself too, Princess." The woman smiled, and Gwaethe felt warm for the first time since she had learned of the fate of the elven women. There was still kindness in this world for her people.

"My thanks, cook. You are kind." Gwaethe smiled and returned to Jacques. She enjoyed feeding him, there in that sickroom in the depths of the keep with all quiet around them. The delicious broth and doughy bread filled a hole in her stomach she hadn't known was there. She did feel more optimistic for it. Jacques managed to eat all his broth and half the bread before reclining on his pillows and promptly falling asleep.

She let out a long sigh and leaned forward against the bed, her head in her hands. The next she was aware, Isiloe was there, ushering her up from the chair and out of the room. As Gwaethe looked back, she saw the old servant settle back in the chair beside his bed.

"He is in good hands, cousin," Isiloe said. "You need your rest."

CHAPTER SIXTEEN

Whated of Gwaethe and her large, dark, tortured eyes.
He couldn't remember her appearing as hopeless as she
had last night. What caused it? Was it merely his illness or was it
this mysterious situation that required his help? He could certainly
imagine Formosa was causing trouble for the *Lenweri*. Had he also
dreamt of her kissing him?

No, that had been real, but here in this place it was hardly appropriate.
He had his reputation to think of. If the servants began speaking of
the love between the Thorian captain and the elven princess, his career
would be as dead as Kain's.

He turned his head and saw a blanket flung over a chair. That would
do for now to cover his nakedness. It took several tries, but he managed
to swing his feet over the side of the bed and stand. The movement set
off a coughing fit that had him sitting back on the bed. Eventually the
cough subsided, and Jacques hauled the blanket around his shoulders
and stood once again.

"Just what do you think you're doing, Captain?"

Before he turned, Jacques knew the voice belonged to Princess
Benae. She was dressed in a brown smock which accentuated her
pregnant belly. Dark smudges lay beneath her eyes. Even in such
circumstances, Jacques couldn't deny her beauty and magnetism. There
was a time when Jacques had lusted after the Princess, before she
turned her eye first on Prince Zialni and then Ramón Zorba. She

cast her gaze over him, but it lacked any real warmth. He was not her favorite person.

"It appears you're feeling better," she said.

"Yes. I hear you are responsible for my recovery. Thank you from the bottom of my heart, Highness. I would bow, but I would likely fall over."

A tiny twitch of her lips was all he got. "Then you had better sit back down. I have your medicine, and then you may have breakfast." She helped him back into bed, her touch firm, her movements brisk and economical.

The Princess completed her tasks in short order and sent her maid for a breakfast tray. She stood at the end of the bed, seemingly waiting for him to speak.

"Can you tell me how ill I was when I arrived, Highness?"

She frowned. "As ill as you can get without dying. Any longer and I doubt anything could have been done for you. But don't be complacent. Your chest has been damaged by your illness. You must be very careful. I believe it would be wise for you to leave the army. You would be at risk in that environment."

Jacques mouth dropped open. "Highness, that's out of the question. My career is everything to me. Besides, a soldier accepts risk. Each time we take to the road or approach a battle, we know it might be the end for us. I will not retire."

"You may have no choice. You must show you are still fit for command."

How she had changed since arriving in Brightcastle to offer herself in marriage to Prince Zialni! As mother of the heir to Thorius, she was also responsible for the day to day running of the principality of Brightcastle. Along with her husband, Ramón Zorba, she made the decisions regarding security. If he didn't convince her he was fit for duty, he could kiss his career goodbye. More reason to recover as quickly as possible and show her and the Steward he was as fit as ever.

"I assure you, Princess, I will recover my fitness and resume my previous position, as long as you wish it. I would also like to help the General while he is in Brightcastle. What can I do?"

Benae frowned. "I don't intend to speak of those matters while you are unwell. Possibly in a day or two, you will be well enough to leave your bed, and then I'll see you are briefed. Not before." She fixed him with a stern look, and Jacques heard a bell tolling from high in the keep.

"What's that?"

"Nothing to concern you, Captain. Ah, here is your breakfast." Benae's maid handed him a tray with gruel and fresh bread, along with goat's milk in a pitcher and a large pot of honey. His stomach grumbled loudly.

"Please concentrate on your recovery and leave the rest to others for the moment." With those words, she left the room, followed by her maid.

Jacques was adding milk and honey to his gruel when Gwaethe popped her head through the door. "Can I join you for breakfast?"

If he was going to distance himself from her, now was a good time. The trouble was she looked damned fetching in her Kingdom gown of green and gold. And he couldn't bear to upset her, not yet. "Go ahead."

She smiled and entered with a tray piled high with toast and marmalade. A teapot with two cups sat beside it. "I thought you might like company. At least, I hoped you would."

"Are you well?" he asked. "You appeared tired last night."

"I was exhausted and didn't know it." She sat and placed her tray across her knees. "Yesterday was a trying day, not to mention all the fear over your recovery I've been trying to ignore. But here you are, ready to rejoin the land of the living."

"Not for a couple of days if Princess Benae has any say about it."

"Oh?"

"She has been most clear I am not to turn my mind to matters of war or politics until she gives me the word." He shoveled a spoon of porridge into his mouth, and the taste was ecstasy after his long fast. "Never thought I would welcome such simple fare, but this is glorious."

He proceeded to down the entire bowl while Gwaethe munched on her toast. When he was done, she poured them both a cup of tea, and they sat in companionable silence as they sipped. Well, perhaps there was some tension, come to think of it. Gwaethe appeared edgy this morning, and there were persistent dark circles beneath her eyes.

He cleared his throat. "Tell me of what transpired after I collapsed. You say it was two weeks ago?"

Gwaethe nodded, her fingers gripping the delicate china cup as though it was a lifeline.

"We left Amitania ahead of the main force as we could travel quickly that way. Still, I was told you would not survive. Lady Alique has been marvelous, but nothing seemed to work." She told him of the battle to keep him alive long enough to reach help. "A few days out of Amitania, a man approached us. He was tall, almost gaunt, had dark hair, and the most astonishing gold flecks in his eyes."

Jacques stiffened at the description. "Are you telling me Vard Anton approached you?"

She retrieved the amber amulet from her belt pouch and held it up. "He gave me this to place around your neck. And a potion and powder you had to take on the hour."

Jacques stared at the orange stone, which seemed to wink at him. He clutched his throat, sure that magic had been involved in his treatment. "I don't want that thing near me."

Gwaethe frowned but stowed it back in her belt pouch. "He told us the amulet and medicine had been provided by a wise woman and would buy you time."

"If it's from Anton, it will involve witchcraft. You wouldn't be so ready to trust him if you had heard and seen the things I have."

Gwaethe frowned. "We were ready to try anything."

Jacques pushed himself forward. "Even with the risk that the man might be trying to do away with me? He and I were never friends; indeed, he was raised over me for no reason I could see. It was when he first came to Brightcastle. He was made guardian of Princess Alecia, and you saw how well that turned out."

"He appeared genuine. I had no better options. Even Exmund agreed we had to try it."

"Would you drink a potion if a madman walked out of the forest and gave it to you?" He knew he was being somewhat unfair but - by the Goddess! Gwaethe should have had shown more caution!

Gwaethe stood and placed the breakfast tray on a nearby table, her movements precise, deliberate. "When you are ready to speak with civility, I will finish the story," she said and turned to leave.

"Wait," he called out, "I didn't mean to sound ungrateful."

"You are ungrateful. I didn't lose sleep the last two weeks to have you take me to task over decisions I took with your wellbeing always in the front of my mind." She turned to face him. "Perhaps you should consider that the next time we speak."

With those words, she walked out, and no amount of calling her back so much as slowed her strides. The door to the corridor closed behind her with a sharp click.

Hell, she had class! Even furious, Gwaethe maintained the poise of a princess; more poise than most spoiled princesses showed. Most would have thrown something at him and stormed out.

He reflected on the issue that had caused the harsh words. Vard Anton! The man was an enigma and caused trouble even when he wasn't there. The thought Gwaethe had met with him sent chills up his spine. His disappearance with Princess Alecia was still the talk of Thorius, even though Ramón Zorba had found the pair and declared all was well. Neither Princess Alecia nor Vard Anton had returned to Brightcastle, though the Steward had said the Princess had promised she would be back before winter set in. If she didn't return soon, she might be stranded in whatever outpost she had made her home over the last year.

Could he trust that Ramón Zorba told the truth about finding the Princess? Jacques recalled the unpleasantness over Prince Zialni's death and the fact Zorba had always been one step away at that time. So many questions remained, even though the physician had declared natural causes. The fit prince had apparently died of a weak heart and been taking potions to enhance his virility; all in the hope of getting Princess Benae, his then wife, with child. All through the courtship and early days of the ill-fated union, Ramón Zorba had been close to Benae; too close in Jacques's view. And now Zorba was Steward of Brightcastle and *married* to Benae. It was all very convenient; and somewhat distasteful.

Jacques longed for the day when their principality lifted itself above the rumors and tragedies of the recent past and enjoyed a new era of wealth and happiness. He did not believe that would happen with Princess Benae and her husband in control. Personally, he wished for the return of Princess Alecia. Even though women didn't rule in Thorius, that might be changed. It was no secret Alecia loved her citizens and would make a flawless leader. She deserved the chance to rule in her own right as daughter of the previous prince, who had been heir to the Kingdom.

Jacques imagined her standing upon the battlements of Wildecoast, queen of all she surveyed. Her uncle, the King, would never agree to it, but he wouldn't live forever. As soon as Alecia returned, Jacques would find a way to get close to her and make it known she could depend upon him.

His speculation had taken him on a path he had never fully contemplated before. However, Princess Benae's assertion he should retire from the army had made him rethink his goals. Could he make his way forward by stepping up for Princess Alecia? Clearly his time was limited in Benae's army. Better to hedge his bets and make allies across a range of powerful leaders.

At the thought, Gwaethe's face popped into his mind. She was powerful amongst the *Lenweri*, but she wielded very little power in the Kingdom. He knew without a doubt his association with her would do him no favors, no matter his strong feelings for her. She was important to him, and he would do all he could to ensure her safety and success. But more than that was unwise. No one must know the depth of their connection. Yes, as soon as he could, he had to let her know their association must from now on be a friendship only; better still, purely professional.

* * *

Gwaethe sat at a small table by one of the tall windows in her sitting room, sipping another cup of tea and staring at Kingdom soldiers performing drills in the castle forecourt. But her thoughts were not on the soldiers. Light from the window struck Anton's amber talisman that lay before her. She had seen others like it. Indeed, it might be elven in origin. Pieces like this held magical power of their own and could be enhanced by external spells.

But Jacques had rejected it and revealed deep hostility toward Anton. Not only that, but he seemed to blame Gwaethe for accepting Anton's help. She would never apologize for the decisions she had taken on the trip back to Brightcastle. Indeed, he was alive, wasn't he? She had done nothing wrong, and Anton had proven to be a valuable ally. Jacques was an ungrateful cur, and she would be better off if she cut all association with him. She had thought they shared something deep, but, clearly, she was mistaken. A crack opened in her heart at the thought she must carve Jacques out of her life; before she lost a piece of herself and destroyed her nation in the process. She would marry an elven man who would likely assume Gwaethe's power. And Kain might one day rule in her father's place. She sighed heavily and wiped a tear from the corner of her eye.

Isiloe's voice brought her out of her reverie. "You are thinking of the Captain again, cousin."

Gwaethe sighed again. "You would approve this time, Isiloe."

The diminutive elven woman sat opposite her. "Then you must have finally seen your association with him is a mistake. What happened?"

Gwaethe found it difficult to take her eyes from the talisman. "He discovered Anton's involvement in fighting his illness and took me to task. Seems he doesn't trust the man." She lifted her gaze to her kinswoman. "I thought we were building a relationship, but if Jacques can accuse me of hurting him, I'm not sure what sort of future we could have had."

"It is merely a passing thing, cousin," Isiloe said, reaching for her hand. "I know it hurts now, but in time you will forget."

"That's just it. I have never felt for anyone the way I feel…the way I felt for Jacques. But if he does not return my regard…"

Isiloe stood. "When do we leave for home? When do we resume the search for Faenwelar on our own and forget the humans?"

Gwaethe met her eye. "I think you are correct. Our association with the humans has done us no favors. The High Prince has been one step ahead of us from the very beginning; from the day he killed my father. It is time to return to our home and organize our own assault. If that puts us against the Kingdom men, so be it."

Isiloe's eyes gleamed, and her lips curved in the broadest smile Gwaethe had ever seen from her. "Just give the word, and I will see it is carried out." She took a step toward the door, willing to leap into action for her leader.

Gwaethe grabbed her wrist to keep her close. "But we do not leave without those women or without Prince Gorin."

Isiloe gasped, her pale eyes wide. "You have traveled beyond even my ambitious plans!"

"We need Gorin as a bargaining tool, and I won't leave all those women to the General. I know what their fate will be if I do."

"True," Isiloe said, "but how can you accomplish all of that? You will not be able to tell even Kain, and certainly not Vorasava. Are you ready to accept the anger both will send your way?"

Gwaethe stood and turned her back to Isiloe. "Unbutton this gown. I have spent long enough in Kingdom raiment. It is time to remember I am elven and a princess. If my *Lenweri* are to survive, I must take the reins, not wait for the Kingdom, or Kain, or Jacques to help. They all have their own agendas."

Isiloe's fingers worked furiously on the small buttons, and soon Gwaethe stepped from the pretty green and gold fabric. "Finally, you see what I have long known to be the case, cousin. I am proud to serve." Isiloe stepped back and slapped her fist against her chest. "I await your orders."

In minutes, Gwaethe had stripped off all her gown and undergarments and was dressed in the familiar green and brown of her forest tunic and breeches. She didn't examine the sadness in her heart.

"First I need you to find out where Gorin is held and speak to the *Lenweri* in Brightcastle. They must all come with us. I will leave no one behind who is fit to travel. Then you will track down all the females and report where each of them is staying. See horses are found for everyone and have them housed close to the palace. I will move Rassar from the palace stable to the new location.

"What will you do?"

Gwaethe smiled. "I will discover what the General intends for Gorin and the females, so I can wrest them out from under his nose."

"And what of Kain? Will he be against us or for us?"

"I cannot risk telling him. Allow him to believe we follow Formosa's plan."

"You will require great cunning to pull that off. Kain and his wife are your family, and you will be deceiving them." Isiloe narrowed her gaze, her forehead wrinkled.

"I will do what must be done. You are right and always were, Isiloe. We must depend on our own kind. What will be will be, but I no longer wait for the Kingdom to take action against Faenwelar." She looked at her cousin. "Now go and be careful."

Isiloe left the room without another word.

CHAPTER SEVENTEEN

Gwaethe stood at the front of the large audience chamber, in the shadow of a great column. She had been one of the first to arrive and that was the way she liked it; able to observe those who arrived without being seen herself. Her elven attire helped her blend into the darkness beside the column. It was not that she wasn't permitted to be there, just that she wished to remain inconspicuous.

Kain sat on the far side of the hall at the front, arms crossed and a scowl on his face. He fingered the bracelet at his wrist. His words echoed in Gwaethe's mind, but she ignored them. It hurt her to shut him out, but he was not with her and so that meant he was against her. Alique entered, resplendent in a sky-blue overdress that exposed her cream lace bodice. Her hair was piled in an elaborate creation of loops and pearls. She spoke to her husband, and he reached for her hand.

Nobles drifted in and took position in the first three rows of the hall according to their rank. A handsome blonde woman in black caught Gwaethe's eye. As she seated herself, a low murmur ran through those assembled. A prickle ran up Gwaethe's spine. There were so many undercurrents here. Everyone appeared to have their own agenda. She was suddenly very grateful she had made the decision to leave. Her heart pitched at the thought of abandoning Jacques, but she must adapt to being without him. He was of this world, and she was not.

Two soldiers brought Prince Gorin in and fixed his chains to a ring on the floor facing the two thrones, which sat on a raised dais. The elven prince did not look around but kept his eyes fixed on the large tapestry of a king mounted on a white charger, which adorned the back wall of the hall. Gwaethe felt nothing but hate toward the prisoner, and her fingers twitched. How she would love to thrash him the way he had hit her. Shame swept through her at the memory, and she ground her teeth on the snarl that fought its way up from her gut. She would not allow the humans to keep this creature. He was needed to flush his father out, then both would regret the day they had ever been born. Once upon a time, her mother and father had proposed a union between Gwaethe and Gorin, but she knew now that would never have come to pass. She shuddered at the thought of living the rest of her life with such a husband. He would learn his lessons at her hands.

General Formosa entered and strode to the front of the hall, his eye on the dais and thrones as if he wondered if he should be seated there. He walked across the hall, below the step, staring at Gorin as he passed. The elf ignored him like he wasn't there. Formosa certainly had more than enough arrogance for six men! He stood, staring down his nose at the assembled nobles and dignitaries.

Last of all, Princess Benae and Steward Ramón entered and seated themselves on the thrones, Benae on the larger and Ramón on the smaller seat. The Steward was a handsome man and his lady one of the most beautiful and composed women Gwaethe had ever met. They appeared to have it all, but she did not envy them the position they found themselves in; at the center of a power play within Thorius. How could they know who was loyal and who was merely currying favor for their own gain?

At least Gwaethe knew who her enemies were; mostly.

As the Princess and Steward settled back in their seats, the hall hushed. Gorin fixed his hostile glare on his hosts.

Benae stood, and the assembled guests followed her lead.

"I would like to welcome General Joseph Formosa and his aides to this court," she said, her voice carrying to the farthest reaches of the space. "Welcome, too, are my husband's sister, Alique, and her husband, Kain Jazara." She paused, scanning the hall, and Gwaethe stepped forward.

Benae continued. "We are also honored to host Princess Gwaethe Arenil of the *Lenweri*." Mutters and hissing sounded throughout the crowd. Benae clapped her hands until there was silence once more. "I will not have our elven guest treated to this show of disrespect." Her voice, though low, held enough scorn to shame most of the nobility assembled. The General, however, frowned deeply, and the prisoner hissed at Gwaethe.

She held her head high and stared Gorin down, promising herself he would pay for the ill he had already done her, not to mention her people. She thought she witnessed a flicker of uncertainty before he dropped his gaze. She nodded her acknowledgement to Benae and stepped back into the shadows. Isiloe appeared at her side.

"I thought you might need me, cousin," Isiloe said.

Gwaethe did feel better knowing she had someone she trusted at her back. She nodded and turned her attention to the proceedings.

"General Formosa, who is this you bring before us?" Benae asked, her hands outstretched.

"Highness, this is Prince Gorin of the *Sis Lenweri*," the General said, hands behind his back. "I captured him at the battle of Amitania. He is accused of war crimes against his own people and of invading the lands of men within Thorius."

Benae nodded. "Do you have any who can confirm your charges?"

Kain stood. "I can, Your Highness."

Formosa sneered at Kain. "Not only this man here, Princess, but all my aides and officers will attest to Gorin's guilt."

"Are there any who will stand for him?" Benae continued.

"Only those who are also prisoners," the General said. "I have asked them to appear, but they have declined."

"You have asked *Lenweri*!" Gorin snapped. "I am at war with them."

"*Lenweri, Sis Lenweri*," Formosa said. "I see no real difference. Although how you can torture your own is a mystery to me."

Benae clapped her hands. "Enough! What do you seek, General?"

"I request a trial for this elf here and, if he is found guilty, immediate execution."

Formosa's words sent a ripple through the hall, and Kain jumped to his feet. "If I might speak, Princess," he said, stepping up beside Gorin.

Benae nodded.

Kain cleared his throat. "While I agree with the charges against this elf, I can't support execution. Even this trial should not be taking place. Gorin should be conveyed to Wildecoast where the King can oversee proceedings."

"Lucky you have no power any longer, Jazara," the General growled, hand on his sword. "The sooner this elven scum is wiped from the face of Thorius, the sooner we can rest easy."

"Princess," Kain said, taking another step forward. "Killing Gorin achieves no real advantage. We still must deal with his father, High Prince Faenwelar. Indeed, keeping Gorin alive may give us more of a bargaining tool."

Benae held her silence, considering both the requests. She turned to her husband, and they spoke in hushed voices. Gwaethe tried to relax but, with everything riding on this decision, it was a difficult task. In the end, she could not stay quiet.

She stepped from the shadows. "Princess Benae."

The General sent her a furious scowl. "*Your* opinion does not matter, *Princess*." He said the last with such a sneer Gwaethe was left in no doubt about his level of respect for her.

Benae hushed the court. "On the contrary, General, Princess Gwaethe should have her say. She has been grievously harmed by Gorin; indeed, from what I hear, she almost died at his hands. Go ahead, Princess."

"I would dearly love to see the end of this elf before us," she said, "but I cannot agree with his execution if found guilty. He is more valuable to us alive than dead. I believe it will be a grievous mistake to kill him now." She bit back words that would have sounded more emotional than they should. It could not appear she cared too much about the outcome of this trial.

"Of course, you agree with Jazara!" The General's blue eyes blazed with a kind of mad intensity. "I hear you share a common father."

The crowd shouted, and cat calls bounced from the walls. Gwaethe looked to Isiloe who stood balanced on the balls of her feet. She shook her head until her cousin relaxed. That was just the effect the General was after; enrage the elves and incite a bloodbath in which he could kill as he wished. He would not win!

Ramón stood beside Benae, his hand on his sword, and the General stood amidst his aides.

Benae shook her head at something her husband said and raised her arm. Palace guards, including Benae's own female protectors, filed down both sides of the hall.

"I call for calm," she said, her voice steady and her emerald eyes flashing fire. "How dare you bring anger and threats into my hall! I will now make my ruling, and, remember, I stand in the King's place. I declare Prince Gorin of the *Sis Lenweri* is guilty of the crimes stated. I also declare he should be conveyed to Wildecoast – to the King – for sentencing. Any appeal he wishes to make can take place at that time."

Gwaethe let out her breath, her head dizzy with relief. They would have their chance to steal him away and make Faenwelar pay. She exchanged a glance with Isiloe who left immediately.

"I protest, Princess!" Formosa stepped out from amongst his bodyguards. "Conveying the prisoner to Wildecoast opens up the very real risk he will escape. At least dead, we cannot lose him."

Benae drew herself up, and when she spoke her voice was tinged with ice. "Then you shall have to be very careful on the trip to the coast, General. I will immediately notify the King, by pigeon, of what has transpired here, so he can be prepared before your arrival. You may leave first thing on the morrow."

Gwaethe settled herself back in the shadows of the column, where she could observe as the hall emptied. Benae and Ramón were first to leave, the General almost forgetting to bow as she passed, so upset was he. Guards surrounded the two as they left the space. General Formosa frowned at Gwaethe before gathering his cronies and storming from the hall. Gorin was handed over to the duty sergeant who escorted him out, but not before the elven prince glared at Gwaethe with eyes as black as his heart.

She lost interest as the nobles and master craftsmen and women left, buzzing with the drama they had witnessed. She was suddenly drained of energy and wanted nothing more than the relative safety of her mountain home. She had been away too long and too much of late. But first she had a task to complete. She must find Isiloe and ensure their scheme was set. Then she would pack quietly and move out of the castle.

Gwaethe stepped out from the protection of the column and straight into the arms of Jacques Vorasava.

"Oh! You startled me, Jacques," she said, stepping back out of reach. "What are you doing here? Benae said you were to rest another day at least."

He stared at her as if impressing each feature to memory. Or perhaps that was merely how she felt.

"I had to escape that dungeon, Princess." He stopped, frowned, and began his leisurely examination of her again. "I needed to see the sun and feel fresh air on my face. And apologize."

"Well, you should be in bed." She had to get away from him before he guessed her intention. She had intended to leave without seeing him again, knowing how difficult it would be to say farewell, even without saying it. Better just to cut and run. Her gut clenched at the cowardly action, but that was what he had reduced her to. "I should go. Someone will see us and wonder what we are discussing."

"They will assume we discuss Benae's decision, surely?"

"I'm surprised you can be so unconcerned."

"What has happened to you, Gwaethe? You seem so cold, so edgy."

She looked up at him. Her heart skipped in remembrance of his kisses and his hands on her body. "Your accusations wounded me, Jacques. I thought we had moved beyond that, but I was mistaken."

"I'm sorry," he said, reaching for her hands. She held them behind her back. "I was shocked Anton had returned, that my recovery could be in any part due to him. I don't trust him, but I should have trusted *you*. At least not blamed you. I know you would never deliberately hurt me."

But I am going to anyway, my love. "I forgive you, so let that be the end of it." She tried to sidestep and get past him, but he moved so he was still in front of her.

"Gwaethe…You are important to me…After what we've shared…I need to know we are still friends."

His words drove a knife into her heart. *Friends. Friends!* It seemed she wasn't the only one wanting to distance themselves. But Jacques had stepped back first with his mistrust of her.

"So, Jacques, this is it? This is you cutting free of me? When did you decide I was not the one for you?"

"I never decided…at least…" His gaze dropped to the marble floor. "It would never have worked between us. Don't taint what we shared by getting angry. I will always remember you with fondness." He seized her hand and pressed his lips to her skin.

Gwaethe battled harder than she ever had to keep the tears inside. She loved him, but he was right. Their world was not ready. She bottled up all the words of love that tried to tumble out at Jacques's tender gesture and strode away. The next thing she was aware of was being in her chambers, the door closed and hot tears running in a torrent down her face.

Under the cover of darkness, Gwaethe met Isiloe in the stable yard at one of the inns where the elven women were housed. Her horse was tied to the hitching rail out front. She handed Isiloe her pack.

"You weren't seen leaving?" Isiloe asked.

Gwaethe shook her head. She didn't trust her voice. All she could think of was Jacques's face when he learned she had left. It was better this way; a clean break for them both. She had been unwise to hope for more than friendship.

"Are you well, cousin?" Isiloe had returned to their room to report and seen the devastation Gwaethe had suffered after she spoke to Jacques. For once, she had been gentle and just sat beside Gwaethe and hugged her until there were no more tears.

"I will be."

"I will fetch the women." It was the last inn. They had twenty-five willing elven women with them. Some had babes, some were pregnant, and others had lost their babies. Gwaethe forced the losses from her mind. Once the women were freed, they would find Gorin.

Isiloe returned with the elven soldiers and women, and all moved silently out of the stable yard and into the street. Gwaethe collected Rassar, and they took the shortest route out of the city and into the northern forests, while Isiloe disappeared back toward the prison where Gorin was held. She had convinced Gwaethe not to be involved with the mission to free the High Prince's son. If anything happened, Isiloe insisted it was best she risked her freedom rather than Gwaethe's. Gwaethe shook her head and hoped her cousin would return.

They moved silently, even the women. Gwaethe wondered how they were feeling about their fate. She had secured agreement back in Amitania that the women would stay with her until their babies were born, but so much had happened on the trip back to Brightcastle. Some of these women had the blood of Kingdom soldiers on their hands. Would they settle happily with her *Lenweri* or return to Faenwelar?

About half an hour into the forest, they came upon a clearing where the horses were tethered. Those unmounted chose horses, and they continued through the forest. Females with babies strapped them to their chests, and even the heavily pregnant rode with grace and determination. Gwaethe selected a narrow trail little used by humans. If there was pursuit, at least it would be one horse abreast. She set a fair pace, slowed by the injured and pregnant women. Gwaethe ground her teeth at delays brought on by feeding babies or by the need for rest breaks.

She spoke little on the journey, her thoughts occupied with both her plans and with imagining what Jacques was doing at that very moment. The night passed uneventfully, and they stopped to break their fast at dawn, just off the trail. The clearing was carpeted with pine needles, and the women gathered them up and formed beds to lie on. They were soon asleep. Gwaethe posted guards and took her rest as well.

Her dreams were haunted with images of Jacques, first loving her and then disapproving. She awoke after two hours, feeling more tired than when she had laid down. It was as if her body did not know how to feel about Jacques either. She should never have set her sights on him. Then she would not be in this pickle. How would any man ever compare to him?

A fire was set, and they sat and ate their humble fare of nuts and fruit with watered wine to wash it down. Gwaethe longed for a hot tea, but that was a habit that must now be shed. The water of the mountain streams would be good enough. She sighed, thinking how much she had changed in the weeks that had passed since setting out to find Faenwelar.

No matter, she had seen the error of her new habits and desires, and turned her back on Kingdom men and their fickle hearts. From now on, she would concentrate her efforts on her people and bringing them together in peace and prosperity. Even to her own ears, her words rang hollow. She ignored the voice that told her Jacques would not be so easy to push aside in her affections.

Gwaethe lingered over her meal, chatting to the women about their experience at the hands of the Kingdom soldiers. Several openly admitted to killing men to defend their friends. Others turned fearful eyes on Gwaethe when she asked about what had occurred after the riot on the trail to Brightcastle. None wanted to speak of what the future might hold. She wished they seemed more excited about the prospect of joining her *Lenweri*, but most seemed to want to return to Faenwelar's faction.

With the fear of losing these women heavy on her mind, Gwaethe stood and prepared to break camp. Small sounds came to her from down the trail, and she waited for her scouts to report, hoping for news of Isiloe's return, but fearing Kingdom pursuit.

A tall *Lenweri* scout bounded into camp and came to a halt before her. "*Ramar* Isiloe brings the traitor, Princess!" he said, dark eyes glowing with triumph. "From the numbers, they are all present!"

Gwaethe couldn't keep the grin from her face, and when Isiloe dismounted several minutes later, she embraced her cousin before the whole assembly.

"I will see you are handsomely rewarded for your efforts, Isiloe," Gwaethe said. "None have served me so loyally or so well as you."

Isiloe bowed before her and turned the gesture toward Gorin, who sat with head erect, on a black gelding. "I present to you the spoils of battle, Princess. The traitor is yours. No Kingdom justice will rob us of him now."

Gorin kept his head averted, but Gwaethe didn't mind. There would be time to make the prince come to heel. And, in turn, Gorin and his father, Faenwelar, would pay for her father's death.

* * *

Jacques awoke and inhaled a deep breath of fresh, clean air. For the first time in weeks, his chest didn't ache, and the movement didn't incite a coughing fit. He would never take breathing for granted again. He stretched in his gigantic bed in one of the guest chambers and sat up. Finally, he was back in the land of the living. That was another thing he wouldn't take for granted in future: his health. It was time to live every moment to the fullest and accomplish all he had set out to achieve.

He didn't know where to start, but stepping back into his role as captain would be his first task; time to get the lay of the land and decide in which direction his career lay. Was Benae correct when she declared he must leave the army?

He may not have a choice if she was firm in her belief. There had been trouble between them since the death of her husband cast suspicion upon her. He, for one, believed Benae had been more involved in the

Prince's death than she would admit to. And she knew it! It was a wonder she had agreed to tend him at all.

Which reminded him; he must see Gwaethe today and ascertain just how Princess Benae had helped him. If she had used dubious methods to save his life, such as witchcraft, then she should be exposed. No witch should oversee any part of Thorius. He frowned and rubbed his upper chest where the talisman belonging to Vard Anton had rested. Everywhere he looked was stinking black magic. Now it appeared he might be beholden to it for saving his life!

He sat up and swung his legs over the side of the bed then stopped as a wave of dizziness swept over him. It settled soon enough, and Jacques crossed to the wardrobe. His uniform hung there so he dressed and put on his boots. He pulled the bell rope to summon a maid and sat to eat the breakfast that had been laid by the window. As he spooned porridge into his mouth, he observed the activity in the forecourt of the keep. Kingdom soldiers bustled everywhere. They looked like an ant hill that had been poked with a stick.

"You rang, Captain?" A buxom maid stood just inside the door.

"Yes," he said, smiling at her. "Please convey a message to Princess Gwaethe. I would like to see her in my sitting room within the hour."

Her eyes widened. "The Princess is not here, Captain," she said. "The whole place is abuzz with the news. The elves are gone, including some of the prisoners."

Jacques lurched to his feet so quickly his chair smashed over backward, and he almost did too. The maid hurried forward and grabbed his arm. "Steady, sir! You're not long out of your sick bed!"

Jacques pulled his arm from her grip. "Never mind, girl! What you said...you can't be serious!"

She stepped back, hands clasped in front of her. "I wouldn't lie, sir. Princess Gwaethe and Lady Isiloe have vacated their chambers. I was responsible for helping with their care, and their rooms are now being cleaned. Their belongings are gone."

Jacques righted his chair and leaned out the window to view the hustle below. "That's why all the activity in the forecourt? Missing prisoners?"

"I fear so, Captain. You should have seen the General. Fit to burst, he was. I'd hate to be the one who allowed that elven prince to escape."

"Gorin is gone?" Jacques sat on his chair and poured himself a liberal quantity of the wine delivered with breakfast. He drained the goblet and wiped his mouth with the back of his hand. His heart pounded, and his head throbbed as though it might explode any moment. Gwaethe gone, the heavens knew where, and no Gorin either. The two events had to be linked. Gwaethe had to be behind the escape of the prisoners.

"If that is the name of that traitor elven prince, then yes." The maid's eyes were wide, and she appeared close to tears. "Is there anything I can get for you, Captain?"

"The other prisoners; who were they?"

"I think they were the female elves, sir, the ones in the inns. The soldiers on duty were all found asleep at their posts this morning at dawn."

Now he knew it was the female prisoners, Jacques was even more sure Gwaethe was behind the escape. And the General would suspect her, as well. There would be hell to pay. Somehow, he had to fix this before the Kingdom and Gwaethe's *Lenweri* were at war. Already it might be too late. He ignored the voice that told him she had given up on him. Down that road lay too much loss, too much grief. He had made his decision, and so had she.

"Can you find Kain Jazara and have him attend me in my chambers, miss?"

She curtseyed and left.

Kain might have ideas on how they could retrieve Gwaethe and the prisoners from this mess. Jacques forced himself to eat his breakfast and drink a cup of tea. It was almost half an hour before Kain knocked at his door and let himself in.

"I came as soon as I could," he said. "I assume you've heard what has happened."

"I have, but I'd like to hear it from your lips." Jacques stood and shook Kain's hand.

Kain dragged a hand through his dark hair. "I was awoken this morning at dawn to the news Gorin was missing. His guards were asleep at their posts. The lock to the cell had simply been opened with keys from the guards' belts. The other elven prisoners were still in their cells."

"And the women?"

"It's the same story. Guards asleep at their posts, and the women simply missing. I followed tracks from the inns to a clearing in the forest, and from there they headed north. Those who rescued Gorin took the same path but were an hour or so behind."

Jacques strode back and forth across the room as Kain told his story. "Gwaethe must be involved. Where would she go?"

Kain frowned and pursed his lips. "I need to know whose side you're on in this."

"What do you mean?" Jacques snapped. "I want those prisoners back, especially Gorin. I'm a Kingdom man through and through."

"I know that, man! What I wish to know is your feelings for Gwaethe. I can't allow her to be hurt, and yet Formosa will come after her and Gorin. Whose side are you on?"

Jacques huffed out a breath. "She has put us in a difficult position, but I'm not in Formosa's camp. He would have killed Gorin without Benae's intervention, and the Prince is far too valuable alive. I think Gwaethe saw that and didn't trust Formosa to keep the prisoner safe. I think she felt the same about the women."

"Then it's up to you and me to find her and Gorin, and settle this matter before Formosa sticks his nose in." Kain stalked to the window and peered down at the soldiers crisscrossing the forecourt. "They run around like ants when once they were the most disciplined force in Thorius."

"All the better for us, Jazara." Jacques said. "Do you have a small team you can trust?"

Kain glanced at him. "Yes, they're on stand-by. And you?"

"But of course. Any of the Brightcastle men would suffice. However, I have a small trained force, many of which came with me on the last mission."

"Then we take six men each and meet at the tavern. No one will look twice at us as they will think we're looking into the disappearance of the women. From there we can head separately to the rendezvous where Gwaethe took the women before heading north. Formosa will never suspect a thing."

Jacques stepped close to Kain. "We can't allow the General to reach Gwaethe before we do." He stared deep into the other man's dark eyes and saw an answering fear. "It could be the end of any peace between elves and men, not to mention the danger your sister would be in."

Kain nodded. "Whatever happens, we must meet at the rendezvous without Formosa knowing. Now I'll leave you to pack your things. I trust you are recovered enough."

Jacques nodded, knowing he was not. He must depend on the resilience he had always drawn on. And so, less than two days after leaving his sick bed, Jacques would ride north to rescue Gwaethe and Thorius.

Jacques was almost out the castle gate when he was hailed by General Formosa.

"Vorasava! Where are you headed?"

Jacques swore under his breath as he turned to face the General. "I am off to the inns where the elven women were housed, General. I wish to trace their movements, so I can find their trail."

Formosa narrowed his eyes. "Really? Are you sure you don't already know where the elven prisoners are?"

Jacques frowned. "I don't, Sir. I am only just out of my sick bed."

"Irrelevant! You and the elven princess were as thick as thieves; a very apt phrase to use, if you ask me."

"I assure you, Sir, I have no knowledge of where any of the elves have gone, including the ladies. I merely wish to help find them, especially the elven prince Gorin. We cannot allow him to be returned to Faenwelar."

Even though the morning was chilly, sweat popped out on Jacques's brow. If the General spotted his discomfort, he would never leave the keep.

Formosa sighed. "Maybe you are telling the truth and are loyal to the Kingdom. You wouldn't happen to have seen Jazara, would you?"

"No, General. I haven't spoken to him for days. Do you believe he might have colluded with the elves?"

"I have no proof," Formosa said, "but it is just the thing he might do. I don't trust the man, especially since discovering his elven heritage. Blood will always out, and the elven princess is his sister, after all."

"Yes General." *The bastard will not even use Gwaethe's name!*

"You may investigate the inns, then you will bring all information to me directly. Do you understand? Take those men there with you."

"Yes, General." Jacques bowed and rode out immediately, Exmund and his other men following.

Jacques met Kain at the agreed rendezvous without further danger of discovery.

"Well met, Jazara," he said. "Did you face any challenges?"

"Nothing, you?"

"The General wanted to know if I had anything to do with the disappearance of the elves." Jacques said, and blew out a long breath, the first easy one he had taken since meeting Formosa. "I managed to set his mind at rest, and here I am."

"You weren't seen leaving town?"

"We were seen, but only as a scouting party, looking at tracks. No one stopped us or took more than a passing interest." Jacques looked around the clearing. "What have you found?"

Kain pointed to the north. "Two separate small parties left this clearing on horseback about an hour apart. They headed north. I believe Gwaethe is going home."

"Then we must follow and find her."

"The trouble is, Jacques," Kain said, a frown on his tanned face, "what do we do when we find them?"

"That, my friend, is a question I don't have the answer for. Do you?"

Kain shook his head, dismounted, and began erasing all the tracks from the clearing.

CHAPTER EIGHTEEN

Jacques and Kain experienced a world of pain trying to find the path taken by the elves. They had trekked hours up the wrong track before they realized it was a decoy. It would have been death for a larger party but the fourteen of them slowly backtracked while Kain scouted ahead and finally found the small animal trail the elves had taken. Elven trackers were good, but not good enough to completely erase all signs of their passing. Once they found the trail, they pushed on, checking every hour or so to ensure they still followed the correct track.

So far, Gwaethe and the elves had taken no less than five different animal trails, and they had failed to note the change of direction three times. Jacques was becoming increasingly desperate to catch them, but their tracking difficulties had already lost them two days. Kain had worn himself out backtracking and then wiping their trail. To make matters worse, they had ridden until dark the night before to make up time.

Jacques rode almost asleep in the saddle, his drowsy mind reliving the dreams which had prevented him from getting a good night's sleep. Most of them featured Gwaethe: Gwaethe laughing at something, her eyes alight with mischief; Gwaethe leaning over him, searching his eyes for signs of illness; Gwaethe naked on furs, urging him to take her; Gwaethe looking at him over her shoulder, resplendent in Kingdom garb, disappointment in her glorious dark eyes.

He blamed his illness for the dreams and for the way he had treated Gwaethe. She had not deserved to be blamed for caring for him, for seeking help in whatever way she could. Exmund had explained all that had occurred and said he believed Vard Anton's interference had been a turning point in his ailment. Jacques needed to find Gwaethe and apologize to her, explain why he had been so unthinking.

His heart lightened at the thought she might forgive him, and then was plunged into darkness when he realized nothing had changed. She was elven and he human. They had no future together, especially when Gwaethe had such a huge part to play for the *Lenweri*. And he had plans for his future; or did he? Benae would see to it his army commission was resigned. She didn't believe he would be fit enough to carry on as he had. And that would ensure his ambition to be supreme leader of the Kingdom army would never come to pass.

He imagined informing his father of that fact, and his heart fell even further. Father would be devastated his son had failed, would never be able to endure the shame. His father's already crippled body would fail, and it might be the end of him. His mother would certainly understand, as mothers often did, that circumstances had intervened in Jacques's life and changed everything. However, his father had lived through Jacques ever since his mobility was taken away from him by the witch; the woman who had been hired to cure him of an illness but who had left him paralyzed from the waist down.

And now it appeared Jacques had also been assisted by a witch. How could he trust what the woman had done to him? How could he be sure there would be no consequences in the future from the magic that had entered his body? If he ever was able to speak to Vard Anton, he would discover the identity of the sorceress and force her to reveal what she had done.

Jacques shook himself out of his musing. It was taking him nowhere but down a dark hole. He was alive and getting stronger every day. He had Gwaethe, Benae, and Alique to thank for that. Even Exmund had played an important part in his care. He should be grateful to have people who cared for him and were loyal, instead of feeling threatened. It was just difficult to be nonchalant about magic when his family had suffered because of it.

* * *

Five days after fleeing Brightcastle, on a fine, crisp mountain morning, Gwaethe and Isiloe rode between the huge trees that heralded the elven tree city of Selinore, or Greengate as it was known in the Kingdom language. Gwaethe halted Rassar and breathed in the fresh air and scent of her trees.

A rustle swept through the foliage above her, as if the trees knew she was home. Sometimes they did that, and today it meant a lot to her that she was welcome.

"I wish they would acknowledge me like that," Isiloe grumbled. "Uncle Melandrach says the trees select those they will speak to, and I wonder why they ignore me."

Gwaethe understood her cousin's desire to be accepted by the forest they depended upon. "It makes you no less important, Isiloe. In fact, sometimes it is a nuisance the trees respond to me."

"Do they speak to Jazara?" Her cool, blue eyes blazed as she waited for an answer.

Gwaethe frowned. "I think sometimes they do. It is another sign he is destined for greatness; a legacy he can't deny."

"Damn him," Isiloe snapped.

Gwaethe kicked her horse into motion, keen to see her mother after all this time apart. As she rode along the graveled paths between the great trees, she was hailed by many who recognized her. But they fell silent when they saw Gorin, as if they instinctively knew he was trouble. The elven prince rode with his head held high, and his eyes cast across the heads of the crowd as if he was too important to acknowledge them.

They neared Gwaethe's home, and she turned to Isiloe. "Take Gorin to the cage and have him interred there but see every comfort is afforded him. The women will need to be kept under guard. I will leave it to you to decide where. I will speak with them when I have seen mother."

Isiloe nodded and rode on with the bulk of the convoy. Gwaethe waited for them to pass then drew a deep breath and turned her horse in the direction of the great tree at the top of a hill. Four attendants accompanied her, all from those who had escaped the cells in Amitania with her. Chief amongst them were Théoden Leovaris and Ruven Magbalar. They all held their heads high as though daring any to speak against them.

Her mother awaited her before the family tree. Gwaethe took a moment to drink in the sight of Elora Arenil, standing with her staff, dressed in a long robe of forest green, a crown of flowers upon her brow. She hadn't realized just how much she had missed this woman.

Gwaethe approached and kissed Elora lightly on each cheek, but, when she would have stepped back, she found herself enfolded and pulled against her mother's chest. Gwaethe hesitated then hugged her back.

"I have missed you, my daughter," Elora said, still holding Gwaethe against her. "Many a time I feared you would not return. I do not know what I would do without you."

At last, she released her daughter and wiped away tears. Gwaethe dabbed at her own. "I too have missed you, Mother. I would have sent word, but it has been very difficult to do so." She would not tell her mother how close she had come to death; that would be cruel indeed.

"It no longer matters, now you are home." She turned to those with Gwaethe. "I welcome you as honored guests. That you are here with my daughter means she respects you highly and that you have become invaluable to her."

Théoden, Ruven, and the others bowed deeply.

"Lady," Ruven said, "the Princess sits high in my regard. I have pledged my life to her cause."

Elora's brows rose, for it was uncommon for elves to take a pledge of service. Of course, it had occurred because Ruven had needed to confirm his loyalty to Gwaethe, and her mother must know there was more to this than odd behavior.

"Come inside, Mother, and I will tell you all that has occurred since I left you."

They entered the great tree, and Gwaethe feasted, high in its branches, and told her mother all that had passed in the south.

A day later, Gwaethe was no more certain how to proceed. Gorin sat high in a cage, his gaze focused on the forest around him. Gwaethe knew a grudging respect at his regal bearing, but the elven prince had not been beaten as she had. Her fingers twitched with the desire to show him how it felt to be thrashed until his skin bled.

She turned from observing the cage, and Isiloe stood before her, arms crossed below her breasts.

"Good morning, cousin," Gwaethe said.

Isiloe gave a small bow. "Good morning. I came to ask what your next moves would be."

Gwaethe looked around, but no one appeared to be listening to them. "I admit to being uncertain of our next steps."

"We will be followed, despite all our attempts to hide our trail. Your brother will be determined to find you as long as the General has not imprisoned him."

A pang of fear struck Gwaethe. She had deliberately not worn her ring over the past six days so Kain couldn't contact her; however, it meant she had no idea if he was well or not.

"It is a difficulty, indeed," she said. "I had to get Gorin and the women away from the General, but now I may just have brought down the wrath of Thorius on the shoulders of our people."

"They must find us first. Should we flee our home? We will have more chance in the forests."

Gwaethe had considered this, but she must speak to Kain first. He was the common link between the Kingdom and the elves. If he came here, he would see that. He might even agree to rule. Her heart leaped at the possibility. The son of Orionkael might soon sit on the elven throne and avenge the death of his father.

Isiloe narrowed her gaze. "You are trying to lure Kain here, so he will be pressured to take up his rightful place."

Gwaethe glared at her. "I was wholly concerned with keeping Gorin and the women out of the hands of the General. However, if there is a bonus, then I will be grateful."

Isiloe took a deep breath. "I still say we don't need him. You and I are more than capable of taking care of our people."

Gwaethe grasped her cousin by the upper arms. "I know, but don't you sometimes long for a life of your own? I admit over the last few weeks my thoughts have turned to breeding and a home."

Isiloe snorted. "Breeding with the Captain, no doubt. He will never have you. He is more concerned with his military career. Have you so soon forgotten the state I found you in that mornings? Forget him, for he has surely forgotten you."

Gwaethe's hands dropped to her sides. Isiloe was right. Jacques would move on and marry a proper Kingdom noblewoman. Her dream of a life with him was just that; a silly dream.

"But it felt so good to be with him. Sometimes at night I lie and remember…"

"It is permitted to remember, as long as you also recall the harsh words he had for you, and that you were never good enough for him."

"You are wrong. Society dictates he marry one of his own kind. That does not mean Jacques believes I am not good enough for him."

"It is one and the same." Isiloe waited and when Gwaethe remained quiet, she continued. "We must still decide our next moves."

"What do the scouts report?"

"No pursuit yet."

"Send more scouts out, but to differing directions. Also double the watch and have all the fletchers make as many arrows as they can. All swords must be sharpened, and the elderly and children sent to Uncle Melandrach. He will know how to keep them safe."

Isiloe bowed and hurried away to do Gwaethe's bidding, and she went in search of her mother, hoping to convince her to leave the city and seek refuge with the others heading to Melandrach.

The city of Selinore was being prepared for the assault Gwaethe was certain would come. It was only a matter of time before Formosa and his forces arrived. He would use force to take back his prisoner and perhaps the elven women, too. The previous leader of the women in Amitania had been killed in the riots over the rape, and so Gwaethe now had a new person to deal with. She had not had the chance to speak to her until now.

Accompanied by Théoden and Ruven, she arrived at the tree which had been set aside for the newcomers. They were still prisoners, and the tree was surrounded by guards, as well as having guards on the inside. Gwaethe and her companions were ushered into a meeting room at the base of the tree. She tried to maintain her composure as a guard left to fetch the woman she had come to see.

She had no reason to be nervous; she was in charge here, after all. This woman and her clan had killed her father and sided with Faenwelar against the true *Lenweri*. But Gwaethe needed these women if she was to bring the two warring factions of her nation together. If she couldn't broker a peace with them, she may not be able to achieve any of her goals. This was the first step. She refused to worry over how she was going to reinstate peaceful relations with Thorius after stealing Gorin from the General. That was a concern for another day.

An elven woman around her own age entered, and Gwaethe immediately noted her belly swelled as if she was very close to her time. Would her condition be a benefit or a curse? She strode up to Gwaethe and stared her straight in the eye.

"I am Alia Kelsis, and I have been elected to represent the elven prisoners within this tree." She rubbed her hands over her rounded stomach and let them fall by her sides.

Gwaethe swallowed her nerves and smiled. "Welcome, Alia. I am Gwaethe Arenil, current leader of the *Lenweri* until a king can be declared. I am sorry I have not been to speak with you before now."

Alia did not smile. "You seem not to acknowledge the *Sis Lenweri* in your speech."

The smile slipped from Gwaethe's lips. "Your people killed my father and slaughtered my comrades in the most brutal way. I was flogged by your Prince Gorin, who is now my prisoner. I do not acknowledge them. To do so would seal the destruction of the *Lenweri*, and that is something I will not do while there is breath in my chest."

Alia's eyes widened, and her chin lifted a fraction. "Not all my people are as you describe. We struggle to survive just as you have done. But one thing I know. The humans have possession of lands which were once elven. Why should they hold the lowlands and banish us to the forests? Their arms are long while ours are cut from our bodies."

"You must understand, Alia. The history of the *Lenweri* is a peaceful one. We are citizens of the forests. We live in the trees. Why do we need the lowlands? Let the humans have the old territories. We can be happy and safe in our mountain homes."

Alia's eyes narrowed. "Do you really believe the humans will leave us in peace? We must stake our claim, or they will drive us from the mountains and forests as they did when we held the lowlands. I refuse to allow that. I must think of the future and my unborn child."

Gwaethe drew a deep breath and prayed she could convince the woman before her.

"I promise you, if you follow me and place your faith in me, I will not allow us to be marginalized. Together we can defeat Faenwelar and reunite our people in peace. Only then will we have sufficient numbers to ensure our safety from the Kingdom." She turned to Théoden and Ruven. "These are your fellow *Sis Lenweri* who have seen I speak wisely. They believe in me. You and the others can, too. I promise I will always care for you."

"But Highness," Alia said, a hard edge to her voice, "you are a woman and not able to make such promises. Eventually you will step aside for a male. Why should that not be Faenwelar or Gorin? Yes, they are cruel, but they are also strong."

"No! I will never believe Faenwelar has the right of it! Down that path is only conflict. I wish us to return to a life of peace and harmony with the humans, as we were in the past. Tell me, Alia, do you wish for a life of conflict and struggle for your child? Where is the babe's father?"

A shudder ran through Alia's body, and her gaze dropped to the earthen floor. "I know not if he is alive or dead. He fought in the battle of Elvandar, the place humans know as Amitania. I have not seen him since. He may have fled north with Faenwelar or lie dead in the rubble of that once-great city." Tears flowed, and she dashed them away. "My child may never know his father."

"Alia…" Gwaethe grasped the elven woman by the shoulders and forced her to look up. "I will discover what happened to your partner. And I will do all I can to bring him home to you if he still lives. You must believe in me. I wish only the best for the elven race, and I will not allow torture and abuse of them." Gwaethe stepped back, her hands in fists at her sides. This had to work.

Ruven placed a hand on Alia's shoulder. "You can believe in the Princess, Alia. She will do all she says or die trying. I was doubting at first, but I have seen her fight for us. Faenwelar is strong, but he rules with fear. Do you wish to live under the shadow of dread for your leader?"

Théoden joined Ruven. "I know the future is uncertain, but Ruven is correct. You can trust Gwaethe Arenil. Her desire is only for peace and prosperity for our people. And if anyone can stand up for us against the humans, it is she. Faenwelar will be annihilated and we can have the life of peace we crave."

"He appears to be avoiding that so far," Alia said, her arms cradling her abdomen.

Ruven snorted. "And how many human cities has he conquered? He has not even won a single battle. Faenwelar is full of pride and hate. He cares not who he kills as long as he stays leader. He cannot win against the humans, but he does not realize yet." He sighed. "Tell me, Alia, if you were the prisoner of Faenwelar and Gorin, how would you have been treated?"

Alia looked at Gwaethe, a deep frown on her brow. Then she turned back to Ruven and Théoden. "You were both prisoners of Faenwelar and yet here you are, alive and well."

"We were thrown into a dungeon," Ruven snapped. He turned to Gwaethe and pulled her forward by the hand. "This is the leader who rescued us. She freed herself and came looking for others. She found us, freed us, and kept us safe when the Kingdom general chased Faenwelar from Elvandar. I stand with her."

"As do I, for evermore," Théoden said. "What say you?"

Alia looked from one to the other. After long moments, she turned to Gwaethe. "My name is Alia Kelsis, and I speak for the captured women of Elvandar. We will stand with you, even if our husbands do not. It appears to me this is the best course for our children. I hope you will not let us down, Gwaethe Arenil."

Gwaethe smiled. "I will protect you with every breath in my body, every word from my mouth, and each beat of my heart."

Gwaethe left Théoden and Ruven with Alia so they could organize the women's evacuation from Selinore to her uncle Melandrach's forest home. Some of the women were strong enough to fight, the ones who had lost their unborn children, but they were needed to defend the females. She stood in the center of her city and opened her senses to the trees, to the mood of the place.

What she discerned was unrest. It was understandable the trees and her people were troubled. If that unrest was due to the conflict with Faenwelar and the Kingdom, and not due to their uncertainty that she, Gwaethe, could steer them out of their precarious position, it might be managed. However, there were mutterings she had brought trouble down on them by bringing Gorin to Selinore. And lately there was a new feeling, by a small minority, that Faenwelar was male and therefore, he might be the one to unite the elves and save them from the wrath of the Kingdom.

The thought jolted Gwaethe from her communion with the trees and sent her striding toward the tree which held Gorin suspended in a cage. His haughty form greeted her as she gazed up at him. He always looked northeast, across the treetops to his father's forest stronghold. Today he looked down upon her.

"I wondered when you would visit, Princess," he said, his voice more that of a king than a prisoner. "I have an offer for you, one which I believe would be of benefit to both our people."

"I doubt that very much," Gwaethe snapped, folding her arms across her body. Even his voice made her cringe, recalling the beating that almost took her life.

"You are yet to hear my offer. I think it a fair and generous one." He paused, but Gwaethe refused to fill the silence. It was the only defense she had against him.

"My offer is that of a union between our families. I offer myself as your husband. As the daughter of a previous king, you are highly suitable as my wife, and father has agreed. If you consent to the marriage, my father will step down, and I will become leader of the *Sis Lenweri*. You will be my queen, and we shall unite all the *Lenweri*. We shall, of course, live in my mountain home. This…" His hand swept across Selinore. "…is not secure enough to defend."

Gwaethe shuddered. "I see you have it all organized. All I must do is agree, and the *Lenweri* will be one. We will again have a king, and I will be queen. Our children will inherit all elven lands."

Gorin smiled. "What a pretty picture you paint. Do you not long to bring our nation together? Of course, there would be none of your peace talk. The Kingdom of Thorius must be brought to heel. Our lands must be returned to us, as of old. But I think you can see this way would save many lives."

"Indeed." Gwaethe almost wished it were possible. Her people united under a king, the civil war ended, and the responsibility for the safety and prosperity of the elves shared with Gorin. She shuddered again, and he must have seen it.

"Come, Princess," he said. "I am not so ugly that you should shiver like a girl."

"You beat me!" Gwaethe said, desperate to keep her voice under control. "Your father killed mine. You killed my warriors and disrespected their bodies. How can you imagine those atrocities would ever be forgotten or forgiven?"

"Anything can happen if there is enough desire to make it so. You and I will wipe the slate clean and go forward as if none of this happened. Indeed, I am grateful you rescued me from the Kingdom general. He would have ensured I was dead before reaching Wildecoast."

Gwaethe gazed up at him. "I thank you for your proposal, Prince, but I cannot accept." She turned to leave, and his words followed her.

"Know this, Princess. That is the one and only offer I will make. If you choose to walk away, your people are doomed."

Gwaethe kept walking. Eventually she no longer heard the taunts and insults Gorin threw at her retreating form. If she had any doubts about her decision, his behavior banished them. But how many of her *Lenweri* had heard the proposal and believed she should have accepted? Gorin knew a public proposal could make trouble for Gwaethe if she declined. The proposal might even just have been a stunt to cause unrest in her community.

As she made her way to her home, Gwaethe met the stares of her people, and, even though they bowed as she passed, their looks were more assessing than friendly or respectful. *Where is Kain? Will he get here before there is more trouble?* She ground her teeth that she needed rescuing by her brother, a man who didn't even wish for the throne. And she laid this all at the feet of Faenwelar and his killing of her father. She would destroy him if it was the last thing she did!

CHAPTER NINETEEN

All was in readiness. Gwaethe's scouts had warned of a small party of humans approaching Selinore. It sounded like Kain and his men. The puzzling report was of a man in captain's regalia who accompanied them. Surely it could not be Jacques? He was still confined to his sick room.

She dismissed the thought and mentally ticked off her preparations. The women and old folk had left for Melandrach's forest refuge. Archers were stationed in all the large trees with enough arrows for a week of fighting. Fletchers were working around the clock to build supplies for when they were required. All the healers had been moved into the hospital tree which was located on the edge of the city. Her fighting force of swordsmen and women were concealed near the entry into Selinore with more stationed close by. Gwaethe would command the right flank, and Isiloe the left. She met her cousin's eye across the street, and Isiloe nodded. Yes, all was ready.

Besides, this small force would not attack her when Kain was at its head. They would simply be trying to talk to her, gauge her plans, and retrieve the prisoner. She smiled as she imagined Kain's frustration at discovering her disappearance. Finally, she would have him in her elven stronghold where he might be convinced to take up his birthright. *See him wriggle his way out of that!* She suppressed the guilt she felt at forcing his hand.

The first riders appeared and Gwaethe steeled herself, planting her feet and folding her arms across her body. Out of the corner of her eye, she saw Isiloe and her force of twenty move into position. Fourteen

Kingdom soldiers and their horses drew rein in the staging ground of the city entrance. Her gaze was drawn to the captain on his white charger. *Jacques!* Even from a distance, his gaze trapped her, and its blue fire entered her body, searing her heart. But Gwaethe had small chance to absorb the effect as the trees in the surrounding area swayed.

It was as if a huge gale had seized them, ripping the leaves from branches and making them whip back and forth. But there was no wind except that which was caused by the movement of the trees. The swaying of the trees continued, filling the entire area with a mounting wave of noise. Leaves swirled through the air, and dust, carried along with them, stung her eyes.

Gwaethe had not seen anything like it in recent months, but she knew what caused the trees to move. She closed her eyes and spoke to them with her mind.

Be quiet, my friends. Your leader is here! Be at ease.

Slowly, the rustling leaves and dust settled, and the square fell silent. Gwaethe opened her eyes, and her gaze fell upon her brother.

She touched her ring and spoke to him. *They welcome you, brother. You are their king, and they know it.*

He frowned as his hand closed over his bracelet. *We shall see.*

But he was rattled by the uproar, that much was clear. His eyes darted around the closest trees, and his body was stiff. He didn't seem to notice Isiloe and her force had him surrounded.

* * *

Jacques sat, frozen in his saddle, as Gwaethe's dark gaze drew all his attention. It felt like falling into a deep well; one he never wished to escape from. He was about to dismount and go to her when a great wind stirred all the trees in the immediate area. Huge branches tossed leaves through the air and stinging dust pelted him. He sat low in his saddle, his stallion a quivering mess, as leaves whirled around the square. There was black magic at play, there had to be. He sought Gwaethe and found her, eyes closed, lips moving. She must be chanting a spell to make the trees sway. It was a trick to intimidate them. It would not work! He looked sideways at Kain and found him glaring at his sister.

"What the devil is happening?" he snapped.

Just then the trees and leaves seemed to quieten. Jacques looked to his men and found them surrounded by elven archers, each with arrows nocked and drawn. *Perfect!*

"Dismount, men," Jacques said. "Lay your swords on the ground."

He did the same and handed his reins to Exmund. "Keep your wits about you."

He walked forward with Kain and stood before Gwaethe and two elven warriors. Jacques swore he had seen them in Amitania.

"What are you playing at, Princess?" he snapped.

She frowned at him. "The trees are not my doing," she said and looked at her brother. She lowered her voice. "They are welcoming their king to Selinore, as do I." She bowed to Kain, who scowled even deeper.

Jacques couldn't believe his ears. "What is she talking about, man?"

Kain turned to him, his lips close to Jacques's ear. "The trees speak to me sometimes, either by movement or in words in my mind. Apparently, they recognize my elven heritage."

Jacques stared at him and then at Gwaethe. "This is true?"

"It is, Jacques," she said, her gaze softening. "You are looking much better than when we last met."

He still had no words for what he had just witnessed. "You didn't make the trees move?"

She shook her head. "I asked them to quiet. They were upsetting your horses."

He let out a long breath and wiped the sweat off his brow. Kain grasped his shoulder.

"I felt like that once," he said. "I'm somewhat used to it now."

"What are you doing here?" Gwaethe asked Jacques.

He pulled himself together, tried to focus on what was important. "You took our prisoner, and we need him back. Give me one good reason why we shouldn't just take him."

"You are outnumbered," Gwaethe said. "He is mine until I see fit to release him."

Jacques stared into her serious dark eyes. "Look, can we speak somewhere more private? This is too important to be discussed in the open." He turned to Kain for support, but the man appeared to be listening to something. The trees?

"Ah," Kain said. "Yes, I think a parley is just what we need."

"Leave your men and follow me," Gwaethe said, stalking away toward the largest tree Jacques had ever seen.

He followed, wondering what it was about the Princess that had changed. She still possessed the same haughty attitude, as if the whole world should bow down before her. Her body still called to him, encased in its close-fitted elven garb; long legs, slim waist, flaring hips. He pulled his attention away from the sway of those hips. But there was something different about Gwaethe that niggled at him. She had looked upon him with tenderness, but there was an element of... aloofness, remoteness, which hadn't been there last time he was in her company. She appeared wholly consumed with her people, and this moment they found themselves in.

She led them through a door in the tree's huge trunk and climbed the staircase in its center. Jacques and Kain followed with Isiloe bringing up the rear. They emerged onto a large platform in the tree's middle branches which overlooked the square and their soldiers. Jacques walked to the edge and lifted his hand to Exmund.

He turned back to Gwaethe. "It's good to see you again, Princess, though I wish you had spoken to me of your plans."

Her eyebrows lifted. "So you could talk me out of taking Gorin and the women?"

"You have created a problem for us all. I believe we had the matter in hand until you freed the elven prisoners."

"Formosa still has many of his prisoners. I was unwilling to trust Gorin would be safe on the road to Wildecoast. The General cannot be trusted."

"Even so, there were ways to ensure his safety that did not mean wholesale war between elves and men." Jacques felt sweat break out on his brow at the thought. "Even now, Formosa is likely arming to retrieve Gorin and unleash his soldiers on you. You have just become the Kingdom's enemy."

Isiloe snorted. "As if we were not already in the General's eyes."

Jacques appealed to Gwaethe. "What will you do with him?"

Gwaethe frowned. "I will lure Faenwelar to his son and then finish him off."

Jacques stared. "And how many elves will die in the process? What if you fail?"

Gwaethe took two steps toward him. "I cannot fail. Everything I am, everything I have rides on me eradicating Faenwelar from this world."

"The Kingdom would have helped you do that!" Jacques snapped. "But not now. You have diminished all your options. At least before this you had the respect of the King."

Gwaethe's eyes blazed. "Do you think so? I did not feel much respect, only inquisitiveness for the strange beings in his castle seven months ago. We were curiosities and had to be treated with caution until His Majesty learned of our allegiances."

"This will certainly inform him of where your loyalties lie." Jacques walked back and forth across the platform. "But perhaps it isn't too late to mend things." He glanced at Kain.

Kain shook his head. "I don't know. I have little influence where the King is concerned."

"Are you not his advisor?" Jacques said.

"Yes, in a small capacity. He still feels loyalty toward me. I have vouched for Gwaethe in the past, but now she has stolen his prisoners I cannot say where things stand." He frowned at his sister. "I too would have appreciated knowing your intention. I would certainly have tried to talk you out of taking Gorin. At least then you wouldn't be facing the wrath of the King."

Isiloe hissed.

Gwaethe turned to her brother, hands on hips. "We would always have faced Kingdom anger, brother. It was only a matter of time. Your General has nothing but animosity for me and my kind. I saw that, and I also saw I could not depend upon you to stand up for the *Lenweri*. Finally, I came to my senses. I realized if we were to rid ourselves of Faenwelar and reunite, it was up to me."

Kain frowned and crossed his arms. Jacques felt sympathy for his friend, knowing how his world had been turned upside down after learning of his elven father. Hell. He had been the Kingdom army general, and now he was virtually nothing! And Gwaethe had been the one to break the news to Kain, had been trying to convince him to accept his heritage ever since. The man before him should be the next leader of the *Lenweri*.

Kain rubbed a hand down his face, suddenly appearing exhausted. "Gwaethe, I can't be the leader you need. I just can't do it. I must think of Alique."

"Brother," Gwaethe said, her voice soft. "The humans have turned their backs on you. What other choice do you have? Here, you have a throne and a people who need you. You have an enemy to thwart in Faenwelar. I have his son, and you can use him as you see fit. Once Faenwelar is dead, you alone can unite our us. You alone can mend the relationship between *Lenweri* and humans." She stepped closer to him and gazed up into his eyes. "We need you more than anyone ever has. Please take up your rightful place, if not for me than for the cause of peace."

Jacques's chest tightened at her powerful words, made more so by the quiet voice with which they were delivered. How could he deny her?

Kain looked at her, the struggle within obvious. He swallowed and walked over to Jacques.

"What is your council, man?" Kain asked. "Her words ring true, but she is my sister. I need impartial advice."

Jacques heaved a great breath. It was a huge responsibility Kain placed on his shoulders.

"I think this is too large a decision for me to influence you, Jazara. Surely it is one you must seek the answer for deep within you? And there is Alique. What will she say?"

"Truthfully? I can't answer that. She was badly injured by the *Sis Lenweri*, and sometimes I think she doesn't differentiate between the two sides of elven culture. I've been like a tortoise with this decision, drawing my head inside my shell whenever the topic came up. It's so difficult for me to contemplate leading the *Lenweri*, and, yet, I feel a pull to discover that side of myself; the half of me that is elven. I want to know my father."

Jacques grasped Kain's shoulder. "Then it seems to me you owe it to yourself to step into the role your father prepared for you. You've been cast from your position of power within Thorius. Maybe it's time for you to take up your place here?"

Kain turned and stared out across the trees and the elves below. Jacques moved to stand behind him at his shoulder. It was no easy thing Kain was being asked to do, but he believed it might be the best course for his friend to take. Kain was a mighty leader, and his talents were being wasted. He had so much to offer his elven people, and, in time, he would hate himself if he turned his back on them.

Jacques placed his hand on Kain's shoulder. "This decision is yours. However, it might help to imagine yourself two futures: the one where you turn your back on the elves and the one where you step into the shoes of your father. How will people speak of you at your graveside? What will your world look like on the day you die? Which of those futures do you want?"

Kain was silent for long minutes then nodded. "Thank you, Vorasava, that is good advice. I'll give it some thought." He turned to Gwaethe and Isiloe. "This isn't an easy decision. Can I take Isiloe with me now, so she can show me Selinore, and I can meet some of your leaders?"

Gwaethe nodded, and the two left the platform. Her head slumped so her chin almost rested on her upper chest, her eyes closed. Jacques approached, uncertain how he would be received.

"Gwaethe?"

She remained with her back to him, head down and shoulders heaving with her breaths. When she had calmed, she turned to him, tears in her eyes.

"I believe he might be coming to my way of thinking, Jacques. If he does, it will be because of you."

He shook his head. "Don't give me the credit. I don't want or deserve it. There is too much at stake for men to be concerned about themselves. I once thought all I wished for was Formosa's job. But these last weeks have shown me how quickly life can be taken from us. When that happens, what does prestige or a high position mean? I might have died, childless, with few to mourn me."

She stepped toward him. "*I* would have mourned you."

He shook his head. "I have something to say. I was wrong to blame you back in Brightcastle. I'm sorry I hurt you when I found fault with your decision to involve Vard Anton. There was no excuse for my accusations, and I only hope you can forgive me."

She took another step closer. "I forgive you. Can you forgive me for not confiding my plans to you? I was angry at your lack of faith in me. I turned my back on you. Now I see I was foolish. I might have plunged us into war with the Kingdom. I only hope Kain can help dig us out."

Jacques took her hands in his. "While cool heads prevail, there is still hope. But what about us, Gwaethe? Do you think there's hope for us? I made up my mind, after I awoke, that there was no place for you in my life. Then you disappeared, and all I worried about was never seeing you again. It showed me I couldn't so easily turn off my feelings for you."

Her dark gaze looked more fearful than he had ever seen it. "I can't tell you, Jacques. The fact your harsh words wounded me so acutely spoke eloquently to me of my strong love for you. But I too cannot see how our worlds can mesh."

"Strong love?"

She nodded and stepped into his arms. Jacques lowered his mouth to hers, and she sighed as their lips met and fused, breath mingling and tongues tentatively pursuing their own exploration. He lost himself in her lips, her body, and in the small sighs and moans which told him she felt just as strongly as he did.

Gwaethe broke the contact, and he groaned, his body on the verge of explosion. She took his hand and led him back into the trunk, up the staircase, and into a small room at the top of the tree. The door closed, and they were alone. She stripped off her clothes, and, in seconds, Jacques was left breathless by the beauty of her dark skin, the elegance of her long legs, and, the perfection of her breasts.

But she didn't stop there. She approached him and slowly removed his clothes, kissing each inch of bare skin she uncovered, until he was on the verge of disgracing himself. His rod strained against her, and all he wished for was to plunge into her slippery heat and lose himself in her majesty. A pallet lay on the floor in the corner, and she reclined on it, legs apart, her fingers lost in the slick curls between her legs. Her eyes slid closed as she pleasured herself.

"Gwaethe," he groaned and joined her, mind crazed as never before by the temptress before him. He licked her breasts, tugging on the nipples until she gasped and arched into him. She gripped his shoulders and moaned, her hips bucking into his rod as if to drive him insane. Oh, to be within her now and never leave. But his Princess was worth more than a quick roll in the hay. He pulled away and slid his hands under her buttocks then plunged his tongue into her womanly folds. She cried out and started moving, thrusting against his face. Jacques sucked on the hard nub which was the source of her pleasure, and she exploded, her body thrusting higher and higher as she strained for completion.

Jacques knew the moment she reached it and thrust his cock into her, reveling in the way her inner muscles squeezed him senseless. He began to move, slowly at first, burying himself to the hilt and then sliding back. Each movement became more frantic until he lost all sense of where he was and who was within hearing distance. The pressure in his member, in his groin, mounted, and he felt an answering pressure in Gwaethe. She thrust against him, each of her moans sparking more urgency from his body.

Finally, he gave one last glorious thrust and emptied his seed within her, just as she stiffened and gripped him as if she would never let him go.

* * *

Gwaethe came down from the highest high of her life, her arms and legs wrapped around her lover. *My lover.* If only she could be with him like this forever. If only there was nothing that would come between them. She released her hold, and Jacques rolled off her, pulling her with him so they stayed as one. Her heart ached at the thought this might be the last time they coupled. She didn't think she could endure the years ahead without his steady presence by her side. He made her stronger, enabled her to do her job. If that meant she was weak, then so be it.

"My love," he breathed, "how can I turn my back on you when there is such bliss in your arms? You make me a better man."

"I was just thinking the same of you," she said, a tear slipping down her cheek. She dashed it away and caressed his face. "I need you with me if I am to help my people. Without you, I will be incomplete. Isiloe may laugh, but if there is a way, I want to see if we can make it work."

"Plenty will protest. You only have to see how Kain was treated to know they will mock us."

"My mother will be mortified, but perhaps if Kain becomes king, I will be freed to follow my heart."

"Your mother has a suitor for you?"

Gwaethe gave a short laugh. "She has several and has had for many years. I have been too busy to consider them. What of your parents?"

He shook his head. "Any number of ladies would be suitable, but I've always been more concerned about my career. I don't want any of them, Gwaethe. I know there are hurdles to overcome, not the least my distaste of your magic. I have to believe we can be together despite the forces that will try to tear us apart."

Gwaethe kissed him long, and soon their bodies returned to the dance they had come to know. Reluctantly, she pulled back.

"As much as I would give anything to stay here with you, my love," she said, "we must dress and find my brother. They will be looking for us."

She stood and began dressing, admiring Jacques's body as he pulled on his clothes. He was lean after his brush with death, but nothing could hide the powerful shoulders and strong thighs, not to mention his manhood which still stood to attention. *Oh, to have more time with him. Why did the world conspire to make me fall in love with this human, only to tell me it is forbidden?*

When he had finished dressing, they stared at each other. Gwaethe didn't want this precious time to end, and, it seemed, neither did Jacques.

She stepped closer, falling into his deep blue gaze, allowing his love to strengthen her for whatever she must face. He would not abandon her. A knock at the door drew her from her reverie.

"You are needed, Gwaethe." Isiloe's impatient voice sounded from the landing.

Gwaethe sighed. "We must leave this sanctuary, but Jacques…stay with me. Stay close beside me."

"You know I will, love." He kissed her lingeringly and stepped past her to open the door, his hand wrapped around hers.

Isiloe took one look at them and pursed her lips. "I see one thing at least is settled," she snapped. "Kain wishes to speak with you. He has completed his tour of the city."

Gwaethe's heart started pounding again. "Has he made a decision?"

"As if he would tell *me*!"

Jacques squeezed Gwaethe's hand and led her from the room and down the stairs to the parade ground where Kain waited. Her brother appeared calm and more at ease than she had expected.

"Brother," she said. "You wish to speak with me?"

Kain stepped forward and took her hands. "I have spoken with your mother. She is formidable." He smiled. "She gave me more of a welcome than I had a right to expect. She answered many questions I had about my father. It seems she long ago forgave him for loving a human woman. He must have been some man for two such women to have loved him."

Gwaethe struggled to contain the urgency in her body. "He was wonderful. My heart grieves that you will never know him." *But by leading his subjects, perhaps you can come to understand him somewhat.* Gwaethe couldn't say those words until she had Kain's commitment. "Have you made a decision?"

She hated to put the question into words, but everything depended on her brother.

He straightened his shoulders and looked her in the eye. "I have." He took a deep breath. "You understand I must speak with Alique and secure her approval of this?"

Gwaethe could hardly contain her excitement. He was going to agree to lead the *Lenweri*! Mother had given him her blessing! She nodded, lost for words, hardly believing her fondest dreams were all coming true this day.

"Then I wish to advise I intend to step into the role left vacant by my father Orionkael Arenil. If the *Lenweri* will have me, I will lead them faithfully according to the rule of elven law." He turned to those assembled, including his own Kingdom men. "I tell you this day, I am the son of Orionkael Arenil. I declare my father was killed by High Prince Faenwelar, and I will do everything in my power to bring the killer to justice. As such, I will be known as High Prince Kain Arenil until such time that I get the approval of the entire elven court, *Lenweri* and *Sis Lenweri*."

A cheer went up from those standing within hearing and then rippled through the city as it was passed from mouth to mouth. Gwaethe's heart filled to bursting, and she turned to Jacques. His arms went around her, and he crushed her to him, his lips finding hers in a moment of union she would never forget. She did not know if the huge cheer that went up was for her or for Kain, but she chose to believe the love she and Jacques had found would see them through all their challenges.

Epilogue

The meeting between elves and man had been arranged by Kain and Jacques. For the second time in her life, Gwaethe's gut clenched with shame. Her precipitous actions had brought about its necessity. The purpose of the gathering was to hand back the *Sis Lenweri* Prince Gorin to General Formosa. Preliminary talks with the army leader had ensured Gwaethe and her people would suffer no serious repercussions from the abduction of the elven prince.

Still, things might turn nasty if Formosa went back on his word. Gwaethe would be a lot happier if King Beniel was present. At least Ramón Zorba was in attendance. He was the King's hand in this region, so Gwaethe had chosen to put her faith in him. If only Princess Benae could have traveled here, but she was due to give birth any day. She looked up at Jacques, and he smiled, settling her nerves as he always did. After the successful exchange, Gwaethe and Jacques would say their vows and become husband and wife.

The venue for the prisoner exchange was the ruined city of Amitania. Vard Anton had suggested the location when he arrived in Selinore soon after Kain had accepted his birthright. The secretive man had retrieved his amber talisman from Gwaethe and left soon after, declaring he would seek out Melandrach. She hoped her uncle could help Anton, who seemed to be important to Princess Alecia. And now that Jacques had placed his hope in Alecia, it was critical that she return whole and happy.

Gwaethe held hope in her heart that this region would again be a thriving center of elven and human endeavor, as it had in days of old.

But there was much to accomplish before Amitania, or *Elvandang* as the elves named it, was restored to its former glory.

They had set up a hall in one of the palaces in the center of the city. The rubble had been cleaned away and two thrones found amongst the ruins. A dais was constructed, and now Steward Ramón Zorba sat on one of the thrones, appearing very regal in his crimson robe. Kain sat on the second throne. He had chosen all black tunic and leggings with silver trim, and Gwaethe thought he had never looked so handsome. Since accepting his inheritance two weeks ago, her brother had grown into his role. It had been the right choice for him, even though his wife, Lady Alique Zorba, seemed unconvinced.

Lady Alique sat in the first row of the hall, a heavy shawl drawn around her shoulders, with Isiloe beside her. Gwaethe couldn't accustom herself to the two being friends, so stormy was their beginning. However, Alique seemed glad of the support, today of all days. It must be difficult for one of the nobility to be wrenched away from all she knew and thrown into the midst of elven culture. Gwaethe met her eyes, and she smiled, but sadness lay like a cloak upon her. Maybe in time she would grow used to the new order of things.

Gwaethe had no wish to see others unhappy when her heart was bursting with joy and love for her husband to be. However, there were first important events to take place.

Steward Zorba stood, and the assembled nobles and army and elven leaders stood with her.

"I welcome you to Amitania and this momentous event," he said, his arm sweeping across the hall. "The elven people have agreed to return Prince Gorin of the *Sis Lenweri*. We shall waste no more time in recriminations, for I do not wish to open old wounds. The King has declared that the common enemy is Faenwelar, and there is to be no open war with the *Lenweri*. As such, he has declared that if Gorin is returned, the female elven prisoners taken can remain with the *Lenweri*. We shall keep those elven fighters seized after the battle of Amitania and, over time, they may be allowed to be returned to the *Lenweri* if they show they are a friend of the Kingdom."

The Steward stepped forward. "Please bring in the prisoner."

Théoden Leovaris and Ruven Magbalar entered with Prince Gorin between them. He had his hands tied behind his back but held his head high. He was brought before the Steward and General Formosa stepped forward from his seat in the front row.

"Please be seated," the Steward said.

Kain moved forward to stand beside Ramón Zorba.

Once the company was seated, Ramón turned to General Formosa.

"Here is the prisoner who was taken from you in our city. He is yours by right of conquest. Today we return Prince Gorin, so he may be used in diplomatic channels to affect an end to the civil war amongst the elves, and to end the aggression which the *Sis Lenweri* have directed toward us."

Kain stepped closer to the General. "We appreciate your understanding in this matter, General."

Gwaethe held her breath, sure Formosa would say something to anger Kain.

Formosa signaled to his sergeants who moved forward to take the place of Théoden and Ruven, and Gorin was led from the hall. He then cleared his throat.

"Thank you, Steward, and Prince Arenil. May I extend my congratulations on your new position, Your Highness. I look forward to a peaceful future with you at the helm. However, there is still much to be accomplished. That is why it is vital that the Kingdom holds Gorin. He will be quite safe in Wildecoast. I trust we have the same goal and that is peace in the Kingdom."

Kain extended his hand. "To peace in Thorius, and between man and elves."

Formosa hesitated, and Gwaethe gripped Jacques's hand, certain the General had no interest in peace between elves and man.

Then Formosa gripped Kain's hand, and a cheer arose in the hall. The first hurdle had been jumped. Now both leaders could turn their attention to the *Sis Lenweri*. She closed her eyes and gave thanks for all the gifts she had been given so recently, not the least being Jacques and Kain.

The soldiers left the hall and soon only the wedding party remained. Ramón called Gwaethe and Jacques to him. Kain stood up for Jacques, and Isiloe for Gwaethe. She couldn't help the tears that streamed down her face at the proximity of all those dear to her. Her mother wasn't here, but they planned an elven ceremony as soon as they returned to Selinore.

The Steward stepped aside, and a priestess of the Goddess joined their hands.

"Welcome, Gwaethe Arenil and Jacques Vorasava," the priestess said. "Today is a special day, for we have seen the beginning of peace in the Kingdom. We now witness the commitment of two people from different races who wish to become one. As such, they have chosen to bring back an ancient ceremony, being the exchange of their blood."

An attendant handed the priestess a knife, and she turned both their hands over, palms upward. She cut a small wound in each of their palms then bound them together, so their blood could mix. Gwaethe looked up into Jacques's eyes and saw awe at what they were doing, at the enormity of their commitment. It was how she felt too. This was a melding of their races that could herald a future of peace. At least that was what she hoped the outcome would be.

Jacques smiled at her and squared his shoulders as the priestess blessed their union.

"With this mixing of blood and the commitment of their lives to one another, Gwaethe and Jacques have shown they can overcome obstacles that would be fatal to the love of most couples. This indicates a strength they will require in the future, as they navigate both personal and political impediments. May they always remember this day and the hope they have for the future, not only for themselves but for their families and their nations."

The priestess turned to those assembled and ushered them closer. "Family and friends, I charge you with the duty of supporting Jacques and Gwaethe as they go forward. Always remember what brought them together, and that is love and respect. Hold in your hearts the peace and hope of this great day and always stay true to its remembrance.

May the Holy Goddess bless you and all who attend this day." She looked at Gwaethe and Jacques.

"I declare you are husband and wife, forever, even after death parts you, as deemed by the sharing of your blood." She smiled. "Jacques, you may kiss your wife."

Gwaethe looked up at the man who had once seemed so aloof, and her heart swelled with more love than she had ever imagined. He drew her close and captured her lips in a sweet yet possessive kiss.

"Congratulations, wife," he said. "I promise I will always love and protect you."

"I love you more than any words can ever express, husband." Gwaethe whispered. "I will always honor and obey."

His eyes widened. "You will?"

Gwaethe smiled. "I know you will never ask anything of me I cannot accept, so that is my pledge. We are now one, and it is all I ever wished for."

Jacques tugged her close, and Gwaethe relaxed against him as her companions gathered to wish them well. There would be troubles aplenty, but for now she was content to bask in the love of her husband and the good wishes of her family and friends.

THE END

GLOSSARY

Places

Kingdom of Thorius - the kingdom of men which encompasses the King's seat of Wildecoast and the prince's seat of Brightcastle, along with many smaller towns

Wildecoast - city perched on the top of a cliff overlooking the sea on the east coast of Thorius; climate is mild but windy

Brightcastle - large inland town surrounded by forests, around four days ride west of Wildecoast

Amitania - or *Elvandang* in elvish - the deserted city north of the Usetar Mountain Range in northern Thorius; once a thriving city

Usetar Range - the mountain range running across the northern parts of Thorius

Selinore - the forest home of the peaceful *Lenweri*, in the mountains north of Brightcastle

People

Lenweri - the elven people who are tall and elegant with black skin and pointed ears; live in mountainous forests north and west of Thorius, in places encroaching onto Kingdom lands; also known as dark elves

Sis Lenweri - the faction of dark elves that wishes to take the kingdom of Thorius back from men

Defender - a race of shapeshifters who are created to defend those in danger; they sense those in need of their help; a Defender can shift into animal form and the ability is inherited through family lines

Characters

Gwaethe (Gway-eth-a) *Arenil* - Lenweri princess, daughter of King Orionkael Arenil, who was murdered by High Prince Faenwelar of the *Sis Lenweri*. She has a golden stallion with silver mane and tail called *Rassar* which means Sunbeam

Jacques Vorasava - Captain in the Brightcastle army. Jacques is tall with dark hair, beard and moustache; he has an olive complexion

Isiloe (Iz-il-oe) - Gwaethe's cousin by Orionkael's sister- unlike most of her race, Isiloe is short with white hair and pale blue eyes. She is a captain (*Ramar*) in the elven army

Exmund - Jacques's aide and corporal in the Brightcastle army; youngest brother of James Tomel, hero of **The Master and the Sorceress.**

Benae (Ben-nay) *Zorba* - Princess of Brightcastle and joint Steward with her husband Ramón Zorba; she was once married to Prince Jiseve Zialni (now deceased) and is expecting his child; Benae can heal with her mind and has a close relationship with her stallion, Flaire. Benae's story was told in **The Lady's Choice**

Ramón Zorba - Lord of Wildecoast and once squire to Prince Jiseve Zialni; now joint Steward of Brightcastle with his wife Benae; brother to Lady Alique Zorba

Princess Alecia Zialni - the King's niece and daughter of Prince Jiseve Zialni who once ruled in Brightcastle and was next in line to the throne. Alecia's story began in **Princess Avenger** and continued in **Princess in Exile.**

Vard Anton - the love of Princess Alecia's life and a shapeshifting Defender; once army captain of Brightcastle in **Princess Avenger**

Alique (Ah-leek) *Jazara* nee *Zorba* - beautiful blonde healer, married to Kain and brother to Ramón; cousin to General Josef Formosa. Her story was told in **The Elf King's Lady**

Kain Jazara – once general of the Thorian army, now part time advisor to the King; married to Alique and half-brother to Gwaethe Arenil; son of Orionkael Arenil, the murdered elven king; has a black horse called Snow

King Beniel - the King; lives in Wildecoast; Alecia's uncle

Queen Adriana - wife of the King; lives in Wildecoast; Alecia's aunt

Elvor Faenwelar - High Prince of the *Sis Lenweri*; enemy of Gwaethe and the humans

Gorin Faenwelar- of the Sis Lenweri; Elvor's son

Rasalar (Raz-a-lar) - Isiloe's mother- is sister to Orionkael and Melandrach- once a soldier and still trains recruits

Melandrach (Mel-on-drac) Arenil - brother to King Orionkael and uncle to Gwaethe and Isiloe; a hermit who lives in isolation in the remote mountains above Selinore

Sergeant Dodlan - second in command to Jacques in his trek north

Sergeant Jer Blas - helps Kain rescue Gwaethe from the *Sis Lenweri*

Tyra - Benae's maid- stocky, blonde; helps with healing

Julli (Ju-lee) - Alique's maid; gifted helper and healer; not a great horsewoman; gentle and caring

Alia Kelsis - the elven woman who leads the female *Sis Lenweri* in Selinore

Ruven Magbalar - *Sis Lenweri* soldier rescued by Gwaethe and became a loyal supporter

Théoden Leovaris - *Sis Lenweri* soldier rescued by Gwaethe who became a loyal supporter

About The Author

Bernadette Rowley is a lover of epic fantasy who is a veterinarian by day and an author by night. She is currently published in the genre of fantasy/paranormal romance with eight books, all set in her fantasy world of Thorius.

When she was a young teenager, an aunt gave her a copy of The Sword of Shannara by Terry Brooks and Bernadette has lived in various fantasy worlds ever since. So, it's no surprise that her chosen genre when writing romance is fantasy.

"I can see these settings so vibrantly in my mind and hope my readers can too."

But Bernadette has no desire to spoon-feed her readers by laboriously describing her fantasy settings. She would rather the reader use their own imagination a little.

Along with sword and sorcery, dashing heroes and strong heroines, this author includes healing themes in many of her books- an element which is central to her everyday job.

"When I started writing this series, I never imagined my day job would force its way into my stories as it has."

And of course, there are animals, especially Bernadette's beloved horses.

Bernadette lives in Brisbane, Australia, with the four heroes in her life - her husband Michael and three grown sons.

CONNECT WITH THE AUTHOR

Website: www.bernadetterowley.com
Subscribe to the Bernadette Rowley newsletter and
get a free map of the world of Thorius

Facebook: www.facebook.com/bernadetterowleyfantasy
Twitter: www.twitter.com/bt_rowley